Inner Workings

Also from Metaphorosis

Metaphorosis Magazine

Metaphorosis: Best of 20xx
Metaphorosis 20xx: The Complete Stories
annual issues, from 2016
Monthly / Quarterly issues
Library Collection series

Plant Based Press

Best Vegan Science Fiction & Fantasy
annual issues, 2016-2020

from B. Morris Allen:
Chambers of the Heart: speculative stories
Susurrus
Allenthology: Volume I
Tocsin: and other stories
Start with Stones: collected stories
Metaphorosis: a collection of stories

Verdage

Reading 5X5 x3: Changes
Reading 5X5 x2: Duets
Score — an SFF symphony
Reading 5X5: Readers' Edition
Reading 5X5: Writers' Edition

Vestige

The Nocturnals, by Mariah Montoya

Joyful Heave

Museum Piece: an unusual collection

Inner Workings

*mental fragility
and resilience in the
outer spaces*

METAPHOROSIS LIBRARY COLLECTION

edited by
B. Morris Allen

ISSN: 2573-136X (online)
ISBN: 978-1-64076-304-3 (e-book)
ISBN: 978-1-64076-305-0 (paperback)
ISBN: 978-1-64076-306-7 (hardcover)

Metaphorosis
a magazine of speculative fiction
from
Metaphorosis Publishing

Neskowin

Contents

From the Editor

The *Metaphorosis Library Collection* arose from a conversation with a Metaphorosis author who is also a librarian, and is initially intended to suit library needs. When a reader comes in and says, "Hey, do you have any SFF stories by this type of author?" here they are! But of course, the books are available to any reader.

Happily, over the past decades, we've come to accept more openly that, just as we all need to care for our physical health, our mental health is equally vital — in all senses of 'vital'. Just as important, we're slowly moving toward a point of accepting that there's a broader range of experience and presentation than the narrow and rigid 'normal' that used to box us in.

There's still a long way to go. Life is stressful for most of us, and even more so for those that experience things in ways outside the average. This volume collects stories by authors either **coping with mental health challenges or just seeing the world in neurodivergent or atypical ways** — or all those at once. Regardless of definition, we all benefit from stories and people who see life differently than we do. Enjoy these!

B. Morris Allen
1 July 2024

Communication Breakdown

Andrew Knighton

"No." I pushed my chair back from the conference table. I could see myself in the window opposite, Herrje's deep night sky turning the glass wall into a giant mirror. Beyond that window was one of the most amazing cities in the universe, a melting pot in which dozens of races and cultures mixed, their mingled architectural styles creating a cityscape like no other. But all I could see was myself, looking angry and in need of a shave. "No sodding way."

Thea Canning peered at me across her glasses. The British ambassador in Herrje was used to arguing with alien species, not her own staff. She nearly managed to hide her surprise behind her inexpressive face and sharply tailored suit.

"This is going to happen, Julian." She was still using my first name. I wasn't in trouble yet. "Britain needs this peace. Earth needs this peace."

"Earth doesn't need me for it." I stared at the jar on the table, which everyone else seemed so blasé about. An inch-long black parasite writhed inside it like an excitable slug. The sight was stomach-churning. "Let someone else play host to the Veng."

It was easy for me to say that. I hadn't lost anyone I cared about in the war, because there were so few people I even halfway liked. But Canning had lost a brother fighting for the outer colonies; Warren, our security officer, had been a marine in the lunar landings; even Hannah, my placid assistant, got nervous when messages came in from her sister in the RAF. As the three of them stared at me, I could feel the pressure of their collective need.

Of everyone in this room, I was the one with least at stake, and I was the one being asked to pay the price.

"You are our communications officer," Canning said.

"That means I do public relations, not body swaps."

"Mister Atticus, you speak thirteen languages and have spent time with a score of different races. You are the ideal choice for this task."

"But this task is a terrible choice for me." I pressed a hand against my chest. "I love my body. I don't want to have it violated by that thing."

"Don't try that "my body is a temple" nonsense with me." Canning tapped a finger against the table. "You eat like a horse and you haven't been to the gym in months."

"I have a job to do, briefings to deliver, press releases to write."

"You work for me, and as of right now this is part of your job. Given the PR blackout around the negotiations, there's nothing on your plate that Hannah can't handle. Isn't that right, Hannah?"

"I'd be honoured to do it," Hannah said brightly.

I glared at her. "Kiss arse."

Her face fell.

"I'm only trying to help," she said, staring at her hands.

Of course she was. Hannah was far too sweet to be stuck as my emotional punchbag, but PR was too harsh a world to start pulling my blows.

I looked at the jar again. On the inside of my contact lenses, a readout provided facts about Veng biology, such as how they laid their eggs and how much mucus they secreted in a week. The thought of swallowing all that slime and tentacles made me shudder.

"This must be a violation of my human rights," I said.

Canning sighed. "Are you really going to try that one on?"

"No." I slumped in my seat.

"Good. Now open wide and swallow the Veng emissary."

"This isn't fair!" Even I was embarrassed by my petulance.

"Life is not fair, Mister Atticus. We make of it what we can."

She took the lid off the jar and pushed it towards me. The Veng representative raised the part of itself that came closest to a head — a cluster of tiny, writhing limbs. It wasn't even a conscious being in its own right, just an appendage of a portion of a vast collective intelligence, one of many that shared Veng space. I reached in and picked it up, my skin crawling as it pulsed beneath my fingertips.

I gave Canning one last pleading look, then tipped my head back and dropped the Veng into my mouth. It squirmed for a moment and then writhed at alarming speed back along my tongue. I gagged, then choked, then almost vomited as it wriggled down my throat and into my belly.

I couldn't feel it anchoring itself within me, or the tendrils that reached out to tap into my nervous system. What I felt was a coldness spreading through my guts, and tangled, nonsensical thoughts spilling across my brain, images that were not my own. Far away creatures and places that made me sigh wistfully even though I had never been there. I slumped in my seat as a sudden lethargy overtook me.

"Good man," Canning said. "And remember, caffeine disrupts the mental bond, so no coffee until this is done."

●

I was still half present for the initial negotiations the next day, listening numbly as the Veng consciousness used the parasite to control my body, my mouth conveying its message, my eyes and ears taking in the response. There was talk of reparations, border demarcations, and future trade relations, setting out the crude picture which the next few days would refine.

I had hundreds of questions about what was happening to me and no chance to ask any of them. Instead, I sat like a passenger in my own body, brooding on how I could avoid having to do this again — a career change, a better assistant, perhaps some sort of drug problem that would make my body unusable. It wasn't exactly productive, but what else was I going to do?

I watched events around me as if they were happening on a distant screen. The longer the talks went on, the further I drifted, greyness descending like the gentle touch of sleep. I was aware of Hannah giving my shoulder a reassuring squeeze and of Canning's look of approval. After that, it was someone else's life.

I had known in advance that there were going to be blackouts. You don't play host to another consciousness and always get to be yourself.

What I didn't expect was to be left hungover.

The first time was fine. I lost two days, then found myself sitting back in the conference room, mouth dry and head fuzzy, Canning giving me an uncertain look.

"That is you, isn't it, Julian?" she said.

I nodded, blinked, and looked around, assessing my environment as I pulled my consciousness back together.

"I thought so. There's a different look to those eyes when they belong to the Veng."

"Belong," I said with a frown. "Huh."

I didn't like the idea of belonging to anyone. Even my loyalty is my own, not the property of His Majesty's Government.

"The talks seem to be going well," Canning said. "How does it look from the other side?"

"No idea." My thoughts came slowly, as if I had had just one too many drinks the previous night. It seemed that downing a Veng was not so different from downing tequila shots — there was the same memory loss and the same aftermath of distant and unaccountable sadness, but with less of a headache.

I reached for the coffee pot in the middle of the table, then remembered the sacrifices I was making and slammed the pot back down.

"As I said when you first fielded this plan, the talk of "shared consciousness" is a mistranslation," I said. "That idiot Hemming can barely get French right, never mind Veng. This isn't a team-up. The brain slug replaces me."

"That's a shame," Canning said, her brow crumpling. "I had hoped to gain some insider insight, but at least you get to feel vindicated."

"What a huge comfort."

"It's better than nothing." She smiled slightly. "Alright, you go rest. And you might want to check in with Hannah — she's been worried about you."

"All the more reason not to see her." I didn't want to encourage my assistant's personal interest in me. In less senior company I would have said as much, and not politely. But Canning, as well as my boss, was a smart lady who could read between the lines.

"Go," she said. "Sleep."

I went back to my room, had a shower and a meal — carefully avoiding any trace of caffeine — and waited for the thing to take over again. Normally when I was that tense I would have put on a porn movie and given myself some biological relaxation, but the thought of someone else turning up in my body mid-wank was just too embarrassing.

The second time around was different. I woke up in my usual slacks and black shirt, but this time I was in bed. The damned slug hadn't bothered getting undressed.

"What is this bullshit?" I shouted, leaping to my feet. The room spun around me and I collapsed back in a heap.

I smelt like a nightclub toilet, all stale booze, week-old sweat and dead cigarettes. My head was pounding — part pain, part the sound of knocking on my door. According to the digits on the inside of my contact lens, a week had passed.

Strangely, I didn't feel like I'd had a lot of fun. The Veng was somewhere in the back of my brain, looking out through my eyes, but there was no joy in it, just a sense of distance, even disappointment, as if it had turned up to a much-anticipated party and found that it didn't like the rest of the guests. And for some reason, my arm was aching.

I crawled out of bed, moving more carefully this time, and pulled myself upright using the bookcase in the corner of the room. Someone had emptied all the bottles from the top shelf, leaving only the dregs of something sickly in the bottom of the cocktail shaker. I staggered to the door and swung it open.

Hannah looked up at me with big, concerned eyes. I sighed. I did not want to be doing this.

"Are you alright, Mister Atticus?" She gestured towards a stain on the carpet. "Warren said you were bleeding when you came in."

I rolled up the sleeve of my aching arm and looked down at a thick, ugly scab.

"What the...?"

My pulse quickened as I stared at the wound. That bastard Veng had done this, and not even bothered to get it treated.

"The ambassador wants to see you," Hannah said.

"The ambassador can sod off," I snapped.

Hannah took a step back, lip trembling, and some of my fury turned inward. This wasn't her fault, it was the Veng's.

"Can I shower first?" I asked.

"The ambassador called you Mister Atticus."

"You call me Mister Atticus."

"But I think it's a nice name."

I sighed and followed Hannah out of the room. The door closed behind me, its click like a dagger in my skull. In the back of my mind, the Veng was feeling sorry for itself, but I didn't think that was about how it had messed with me. The bastard was in a sulk and I was on the receiving end.

When I got to Canning's office, with its empty desk and plain walls, the ambassador was stood by the window, looking out across the skyline of Herrje. It was a spectacularly eclectic sight, human skyscrapers standing amidst the vaulted arches of the shoji sector, low groundling domes running up against the battered blocks of the k'kiri markets. I might get frustrated at this place, angry even, but I never got bored.

"Close the door," Canning said.

I turned to obey. Warren, the head of security, was there ahead of me. Gone was his usual affectation of a twentieth century tie. At least he still wore the smugness he showed whenever I was in trouble.

I sank into a chair. My stomach sank with me.

"Where have you been?" Canning turned to face me. She held a cup of coffee, the most delicious thing I had ever smelled. Between the hangover and a fortnight without caffeine, I would have killed for a cup, but just thinking that set the Veng writhing angrily inside me.

"Where have you been?" she repeated as I stared slack-jawed at her cup.

"I don't know," I said, snapping back to reality. "Isn't it Warren's job to keep track of me and my passenger?"

"You lost him three days ago," she said. "After a particularly fruitless day of negotiations. It's almost as if the Veng don't want peace."

It was a chilling thought. The war hadn't been lost, but there was no doubting that we had suffered the most. If the Veng decided to push on, thousands more soldiers would be joining Canning's brother in floating mausoleums far from home.

She sipped at the coffee and narrowed her gaze as she watched my reaction. Was she still hoping that I would remember something the alien had thought?

"Maybe they don't want peace." It was a dark idea, but I was in a dark place, full of the hollowness that follows an epic night out. I'd put my body through some hellish hangovers, but none that left me as despondent as I felt now, with the tendrils of Veng thought trailing through my brain.

"They put too much effort into making this happen," Canning said. "Even choosing a fragment of a Veng consciousness to send took weeks. Something else is going on."

"I pity the poor Veng that got stuck with this job," I said. "When you're used to sharing in a collective consciousness, it's got to be lonely only having a single human's thoughts for company."

"Especially when that human's you," Warren said.

I ignored the taunt, closed my eyes, and tried to feel the Veng's presence in my mind. It did seem a little sad, though that could just have been home sickness or a hangover. I wondered what was getting to it and whether there was anything I could do to help. With a little effort, maybe I could bridge the gap between us and be a better host.

"Shit!" I jumped as Warren stuck a needle in my arm, pulled it out and read the syringe's electronic display.

"How sexually active are you, Atticus?" He looked up from the readout with a grin.

"Far less than I'd like." I stared despondently at the syringe. Was my parasite getting lucky behind my back? "Tell me the worst."

"K'kiri vein crabs." Warren passed the syringe to Canning. "A couple of psychotropic drugs too. Your body's been living the high life."

"I didn't think you could catch vein crabs off humans." The ambassador put down her coffee and examined the syringe.

"You can't," I said, frozen in my seat. Now I was glad for the mercy of full blackout. Inter-alien fun-times might be a turn-on for some people, but I was a one species man. I felt violated in the worst possible way.

"Increase the guards," Canning said to Warren. "We need to get these negotiations on track."

"Whoah whoah whoah!" I staggered red-faced to my feet. "I've been turned into a pervert by the damn Veng brain slug. You're getting it out of me, right?"

"Once we're done."

"Screw that." I had to do something to avoid another takeover. Still befuddled, I snatched the coffee cup and downed its lukewarm contents.

The scab on my arm cracked, blood dripping on the carpet. Canning looked at me with cold, dead eyes.

"Pray that does not cause a problem, Mister Atticus," she said. "Warren, lock down the east wing apartments. He won't be going out."

●

I woke to the strangest sensation. I'd been dreaming about having sex with Hannah, her pasty little body wobbling around beneath me. As consciousness took hold, I could feel myself moving on her still, and then I realised that my eyes were open.

Oh sweet horror, it was real.

I tried to jerk away but my body wouldn't respond. I could feel someone else in there with me, grinding away in a desperate hunt for a pleasure it barely felt. A half-empty bottle of whiskey lay beside the bed and the room smelled of pot. Someone was having a wild time, and they were using my body to do it.

"Oh, yes," Hannah gasped. "Oh Julian, you don't know how long I've wanted this."

This was bad. This was very, very bad.

Not the sex itself. What I felt through the dreamlike haze was surprisingly good. Not the weed and the booze either, though I wished I'd been around to enjoy the high.

No, doing this with Hannah was bad. The admin pool had bets on when I'd give in and hook up with her. Warren had sworn to break my legs if I broke her heart. I didn't want to be with my soppy, soft-hearted assistant, and yet some treacherous part of me was enjoying this.

Screw Canning's failed negotiations, this was my diplomatic hell.

I tried again to take control of my body, but the Veng sensed me now. It paused in its activities and I could feel its attention bearing down on me. Its thoughts whirled through the same space as my own. I struggled to make sense of the words and images, too wild and disjointed to have meaning for me, and I could sense a similar frustration on its part.

Frustration. I might not recognise its thoughts, but I recognised its feelings.

I probed deeper. There was loneliness, disappointment, a grey fog of loss all revolving around this time with me. The highs it had sought were nothing compared with the lows of being here. The poor bastard.

As I stared into the alien's feelings its gaze was drawn there too, sucking it deeper into its own depression. I let it ride that desolation, let it wallow, and took the moment to take control.

"Julian?" Hannah looked up at me uncertainly, raised a hand to stroke my face. "Julian, is something the matter?"

I got to my feet, stumbled naked and woozy towards the kitchen. The damn thing had been fighting deep sorrow, cut off from the rest of its hive mind just as I had been from my body. But how much whiskey had it drunk trying to cheer itself up?

Enough was enough. I needed this thing out.

I moved for the kettle, but there wasn't time. The Veng mind was stirring in me again, trying to take control. Tentacles of desperation battled with my own determination to be free.

"Julian?" Hannah rose. "Julian, what's the matter?"

No time. I yanked the fridge open, grabbed a bag of coffee beans and tipped them into my mouth. I chewed those acrid brown seeds like they were candy. They popped and crunched, and I swallowed the jagged, caffeinated shards. Chewed and swallowed, chewed and swallowed, the caffeine buzz breaking the Veng's hold.

In the last moment of connection, it seemed to be pleading with me, reaching out for something I didn't understand. Tears ran down my face and I sobbed at the terrible loneliness of it all.

My stomach lurched. I fell to my knees, vomiting up coffee grounds and the black, slug-like blob of the Veng.

Hannah crouched beside me, rubbing my back.

"It'll be OK," she murmured. "Whatever it is, it'll be OK."

I leaned in towards her, and it felt surprisingly good.

●

"That's it?" Canning asked.

I nodded and sipped at my tea.

"Separation from the hive took away all its pleasure," I said, peering at the slug-like blob in its jar on the desk. I felt sorry for it now, having felt what it did during those final shared moments in my room. But unlike the Veng, I was glad not to have anyone else in my thoughts. "Must be something to do with human bodies, or a lifetime of dousing myself with coffee. Once it realised, it spent the whole time seeking other thrills. Send it back. It'll be so relieved we'll have peace within days."

"Without a host, we can't talk with them." Canning frowned and tapped a finger on her desk.

"We don't need to," I said with confidence. "After that experience, they won't want anything we've got."

Canning turned toward Warren. For all his petty failings — and there were many of them — even I acknowledged that he knew security issues.

"Makes sense, given their other priorities," he growled, giving me the filthiest look I've ever received. "It's not like the talks were working."

"Very well." Canning turned from us back to her computer. "Thank you, gentlemen."

We rose to leave.

"I warned you, Atticus," Warren said as he followed to the door. "You hurt Hannah and now I'm going to break both your legs."

As we stepped out of the office, Hannah appeared and took my arm. Warren glared. I smiled and kissed the top of Hannah's head.

"We're off out for dinner," I said. "Don't wait up."

I didn't turn to see his expression, just enjoyed the feeling of having my thoughts to myself and of having Hannah beside me. Alone in my head, but not in the world.

Andrew Knighton's story "Communication Breakdown" was originally published in Metaphorosis on Friday, 19 July 2019. See magazine.metaphorosis.com

About the author

Andrew is a British ghostwriter, who pays his way by writing books and articles in other people's names. He lives in Yorkshire with his cat, his computer, and a huge pile of unread books. When he's not writing, he enjoys board games, bouldering, and trying to get through that pile of books.

andrewknighton.com, @gibbondemon

The Waves in Which We Drown

Rubella Dithers

June 8th, 2189

I'm afraid of space.

That's why you're up there and I'm down here, sitting on a dune with a broken nose and a split lip, stabbing a shuttle into my hand while I try to repair the net I dropped on a reef last week. We don't even have any spare rope; I have to scavenge what I can off of even worse nets. The fibers are all rotting and falling apart on me. It would be easier to get through this if you were here. Stupid of me to think 'friends forever' implied being together in some capacity.

It's easy to ignore the pain in my hand. I feel like giving up and just sewing the loose edges of this net together, but I know what your dad would say. *You half-assed it, as usual. This is your last chance. You should be grateful. What else do you have? You failed the first time, dropped out the second time. This is your only chance. Be grateful.*

The worst thing is you don't even write.

It's like you want to forget this place, like you want to forget us. Like when you swore that as soon as you left this town you'd never eat fish again, as if that amalgamated goop they pump into you isn't pasted together with carrageenan and anchovies and bonito.

I don't blame you. I want to leave too. It didn't work out as well for me, did it? Because now I'm stuck here with a bunch of old people and kids and everyone in between is dead or gone.

Can you believe your parents still buy into the line that we're doing something vital with our duct-taped trawlers and broken nets? Like we can't see the state's big commercial ships sitting on the horizon, picking up every fish that so much as waves a fin in their direction? Half the town works on them as it is. And our own catches keep getting smaller. Listening to your parents' cheering when another supply shuttle is launched makes my skin crawl.

While I'm on forced shore leave, I also get to watch over Nila. Did you forget about your real sister too? We don't have a shovel for her, so she's digging with her hands. We've been out here since before dawn and she's barely got half a bucket of clams. After this I'm supposed to tutor her, since the school server went down again.

I'm going to give up on fixing the net for today and help Nila with the clams. I don't have anything else to say, so I'll sign off. I miss you and I hate you and I really, really wish you'd get back to me.

●

June 10th, 2189

I'm at the bar reviewing Nila's curriculum, trying to understand why a 9-year-old needs to learn set theory. Instead of times tables, she's doing Cayley tables, because knowing $ab = ba$ is more important than knowing 7×6. Right.

A bar is the worst possible place for me to be studying, but it's the only building that's still on the power grid. If that goes down, they've got fish oil lamps, and everyone's too drunk to care about the smell. I miss studying together, it was easier to focus. For me, at least. I have no idea what you got out of it. I look at a proof and I'm like, sure, it makes sense, it's obvious to me. But I say that about anything, even if it's wrong. You were always so formal, so meticulous.

The only possible way this experience could be worse is if what's-his-face showed up. So of course he has. He's with some rich girl. I can tell she has money because she's wearing shoes, how fucked up is that? I have to scrub my feet with sand for half an hour to get all the dried wine and ash off. But that's how bad things have gotten since you left. It sounds like I'm connecting the two events, but I'm not. OK, maybe.

I never liked him. And no, it's not because dating him meant that you spent less time with me. It's because he's a creep. I mean, when you told him you were studying for the navigator exam, he dropped off. Then, when I failed and you didn't, he came up to me talking about how 'selfish' you were. As if I'd want to commiserate with him, of all people. I didn't just lose you, I lost the chance to leave.

Now he's got this new girl, like you never existed. This one looks like she's pregnant. I mean the dangerous, beyond the point of no return kind of pregnant. Why anyone would risk having kids now is beyond me, but people keep doing it. Do they think they'll get on a generation ship? Do they think there's still room? Who needs fishers in space?

I fixed the rope situation. Once I figured out what to do it was pretty easy. I sold some of your stuff. Nothing important, just your old computer. The one I bought parts for, when I worked between two ships all year and didn't see land once while you stayed in school.

I sold it to the scrap yard.

●

June 16th, 2189

The ping timed out for the last few messages I sent. Either the sat relay is down or you're still ignoring me. We both know which is more likely.

Your dad took the crew out and left me behind. Took the new net with him, though.

Since there is nothing else for me to do, I was thinking about taking the entrance exam again. I'm not past the cut-off age. Yet.

Nila wants to take it, after she finishes the standard curriculum in a few years. I think she'll do fine, she's a lot like you. The problem is, your parents can't afford the textbooks. I could try to teach her myself, but it's not like

I'm doing a great job now. I don't even know if I'll be around long enough.

I could pirate the books if I hadn't scrapped your old computer for a net. And if we had internet access. I might turn into a real pirate if I can't figure out what to do with myself. I'd be robbing other poor people, though, so probably not.

If you pass by one of those nonresponsive satellites, do me a solid and hack it so we get free access in town.

●

June 30th, 2189

I got the bends.

I know we used to joke about it when we were diving, but this seriously sucks. I've been in bed for a week.

Nila is the one who spotted me. I don't remember being pulled out of the water. They think... Well, I'm sure you know what they think. If someone else went out alone on a banged-up fiberglass dinghy, without the sense to even tie a line to herself, I'd think the same thing.

I just wanted to try diving again. Remember how we used to freedive every day after school, jumping off that big sea stack in the cove? I haven't gone since you've left, and I pushed myself too far, that's all. And I'm paying for it. Everything hurts. There's this deep, frightening ache throughout my arms and legs. When I told the nurse about it, she just upped the oxygen intake.

Nila keeps checking on me. It's sweet, but kind of annoying. I hate that she saw me like that. Like this. I think she thinks it's her fault, that she should have been watching me closer. I'm supposed to be the one looking out for her. She treats me like your replacement. I'm not. I can't be the kind of big sister you were. I'm glad I'm an only child. What a shitty role model I would have been.

When I was down there, in the water, I could pretend I was with you. I could pretend that I wasn't afraid to drift through space just above Earth, from where you look down on the rest of us through the hazy veil of atmosphere. Falling weightless through that ambivalent medium, the vast and unknowable water that siphons heat and deadens sound, sustained the illusion. I felt terribly alone. My chest seized. I wanted to claw my way back to the surface, but I forced myself down. I needed to be deeper.

I didn't notice the regulator's pressure dropping until I was struggling to breathe. There was a leak in the line. I was fucked. I ditched the useless gear and struggled towards the surface, growing weaker with each stroke. I could feel the sun's warmth and I pushed through the current. The closer I got, the more blackness invaded the edges of my vision. I was tired, Sarah. I'm always fucking tired.

That's where my memory ends, as abruptly as a dream. It was beautiful, for a moment.

●

July 10th, 2189

I caught Nila going through a massive copy of Dummit and Foote. Kids these days. She's claiming it 'just showed up', but she probably stole it from the university library. At her age she shouldn't be skipping school to go all the way to the city for that, especially not alone. I would've done it if she asked me. Still, I don't think she's wrong for doing it, and we were worse at her age. She's mad I don't believe her, though, because when I asked if I could look at it she flipped me off. I didn't teach her that. Did you?

●

August 22nd, 2189

Your dad still won't let me on the boat. In fact, he's told everyone else in town not to give me work, period. I spent a few days walking up the coast to see if anyone would hire me. It was a bad idea.

At the first group of shacks I approached, an old auntie came out to shoo me away. Her hands were splotchy pink and shaking. I could see through the door she came out of. Inside there was another thin woman, holding a twisted child who screamed like a pig being slaughtered. Someone saw me looking and slammed the door shut, but I could still hear the kid. I walked down to the little cove they fished in. The waves were lethargic, lapping fetid red foam onto the shore.

The farther north I went, the worse it got.

I went home, thinking about clam digging. The problem is everyone's got their kids doing it these days. Even old folks are out there. They're pulling clams out of the sand faster than they can breed.

It took me a while to figure out, but I finally realized what I could do to make money. Salt. I'm a salt woman now. I can't say I came up with the idea on my own. I heard the packing house was having trouble getting shipments. It's only a matter of time before other people in town get the same idea. It's not exactly novel.

I borrowed a few sheets from your room. I hope you don't mind. I can't afford to keep a fire burning all day, so after I boil off most of the water I spread the salt over the sheets to dry the rest of the way.

Your mom talked to me about paying rent. Your dad must have asked her to; I don't think she cares. The original deal was I would work for your dad while staying there, which I did. For years. Of course he'd make me work, not pay me, and then charge me room and board. Honestly? I don't blame them.

Nila says she wants to accelerate her curriculum. I told her not to overwork herself and she rolled her eyes. I think she's sick of fish.

●

September 6th, 2189

I was at the bar again last night. It's kind of a regular thing now, a weekly ritual. Remember how much I used to hate drinking? The veil has been lifted.

I was sitting at the bar, nursing my watered-down seaweed wine. Normally I'd be studying at one of the tables, where the lighting is better and the surfaces less sticky, but the lights were out. That's been happening a lot more lately.

The counter is also farther from the pool table and its endless clacking. A few weeks ago the bartender dug this wind-up radio out of somewhere. I didn't know what it was at first, and now I'm obsessed with the thing. We take turns cranking it. It's the only way to get regular news. That's how I learned they're doing a mass launch next month.

The remaining cohort in orbit, your cohort, will start their flybys, siphoning gravitational force off planets and comets and whatever's convenient so they can be flung deeper into space. You'll break and scatter like billiard balls, each mapped trajectory a new path for humanity to follow towards some possibly viable world. Even if it takes us millennia, even if we never find a new planet to latch onto like a leech, at least you'll be out there, an eternal reminder of what we were.

Since trying to contact you directly isn't working, I'm relaying future messages. The navigation base enabled permissions for me to use their ground proxy, and confirmed your signal is extant. When are you going to respond?

When you finally get what you want, when you finally leave this place for good, how will I be able to reach you?

●

September 15th, 2189

This is a rude question. You're probably not in any shape to answer it.

What's it like to lose your autonomy? I know they say that isn't what happens, but that's not true. If something else, some executable set of instructions, controls your decision making you cannot be autonomous. By definition.

Is that why you aren't writing back? Am I sending this to an empty shell?

The idea of losing who I am. That is what I'm afraid of, more than being in space. What happens during that discontinuity? I think about it when I fall asleep. How easily I trust that I will wake up as the same person.

What happens in that space of time? Where do *you* go? Are you still the old *you*, or is this a new *you* that merely shares the same memories?

How would you even know?

●

October 24th, 2189

I have achieved a new low. Some people in town got together and set up a bigger salt operation. They've got an entire field for evaporating the water, huge piles of salt raked up. The packing house isn't buying from me anymore.

Since I can't pay him, your dad kicked me out of the house. I'm sleeping on the beach, living off of ice plants, kelp, and whatever else washes up. Like that dead sea nettle I've been eyeing all day.

I still carry a lighter, though you're not around to borrow it, and if you were there's no fuel for it anyway. I'm trying to start a fire with some driftwood but most of the pieces I find are still wet. I've spun the flint wheel so many times my thumb's starting to bleed.

I did, finally, get a couple of sticks to light up. It's not very warm, but at least the flames are pretty.

●

November 20th, 2189

Nila turned 10. When that was us, we thought it was a big deal. Double digits and all that. It was significant. Nila wasn't that excited.

The bar radio's been less reliable lately. Some of the usual bands we pick up are garbled. I took Nila with me for her birthday, figuring she'd enjoy the novelty of it. Not that a bar is the best place for a kid, but it's not like we've got anything else around here. We were able to hear a few pieces of news, nothing interesting to a child, but she seemed happy enough. Whenever the sound cut out, or was jumbled, I pretended it was an encrypted message from you. I told her that you said how much you miss her, how grown up she is now. It made her day.

●

December 15th, 2189

I always hated it when you called me negative. I think you were trying to turn it into a joke, or maybe you wanted it to be true so we could be opposite. Magnetic poles.

Negative, positive. You know, the designations are completely arbitrary.

This morning your mom said something that reminded me of that. She lets me in the house when your dad's out. We were in the kitchen, threshing foxtails, bitching about how hard it was getting to find *weeds*, of all things. She told me to shut up, that I never have anything good to say. But I do. I'll prove it.

On the first of the month, that big factory purser went dark. Dead in the water. At the bar, people were talking about some satellites being knocked out of orbit. The reports we got over the radio just said 'systems malfunction'. I don't care what happened, I'm just glad it did. It took a week for tugboats to get out to the purser. Its crew had to abandon their net.

As soon as the purser limped out of sight, the town fishers moved in. I've never seen your dad move so fast in my life. Together, they got the abandoned net up. The town's still arguing about what to do with it, like anyone can actually use it.

Ever since, your dad has been able to go out farther than usual, and he got a big catch of quality herring, not the chewed-on stragglers he normally pulls up. The packing house needed extra workers and they hired me on the spot. So I've been gutting, filleting, pickling, and packing fish for the past three weeks. I know we said we would never work there, but what choice do I have?

It'd be better if they had enough gloves to go around.

●

December 16th, 2189

I forgot to mention that I watched the new cohort launch last month. Those improbably perfect orbs always creep me out. I know you're in one too. It's still weird. Plus, the speed, those maneuvers, aren't things a living person could withstand.

●

January 1st, 2190

Happy New Year. Can you tell I'm excited?

Nila got a tablet for her New Year's gift. She said I can use it when she's at school. I don't know where your parents got the money for it. Or high-speed sat access, for that matter. They seemed as surprised as I was when Nila opened the box. Maybe someone upstairs is looking out for us.

Through a combination of Nila whining and bribery, my 'gift' was your parents letting me stay in your room again. It's a bit infantilizing to have to follow their rules, but at least I have a bed. It beats fighting seagulls for half-eaten crabs any day.

More commercial ships showed up, effectively trapping us in the bay again. The fish rush is over, which means I got laid off from the factory. I'm back to harvesting salt, but I've got a new idea for it. I thought of it when I had to make lye water for the lutefisk. Who eats that stuff? Me, me eats it. Anyway, after my shifts I raided the dumpsters for the offal. I've been boiling it and skimming oil off the top to resell to the factory. I make less than I would if I were hired by them to do it. It's bullshit.

I put some aside for myself, and your family. Do you know how many kilos of fish guts it takes to make a bar of soap? I do. I have to render it a couple of times to get the fishiness out. I don't have anything to make it smell good, so the best I can do is make it smell like nothing.

In six months you'll be passing Jupiter in your space orb. At the rate I'm going, I'll be tanning fish skins in their own offal. Once I am clad entirely in fish leather, you will know I have accepted my lot in life.

●

February 13th, 2190

Every time I see a matrix, I think my brain dies a little. I'm on Jordan decomposition, it's a nightmare. There is no practical use for it; a computer can crunch linear equations faster than I could put them in normal form. A computer doesn't need to change the base first. Programming exists. Why should we have to learn something that a calculator can do? Whoever decides what material goes on the math exam is forever on my shit list.

I know what you'd say. You'd say it helps create convenient neural pathways to implement said programs, if one so chooses. A place where a memory can be stored. To exploit what we have that a computer lacks: consciousness, agency. Choice.

I don't care how many organic parts they replace, the human brain is not a computer. It shouldn't be treated like one. You're still a person. You're still in there, somewhere. Right?

I have money saved up for the exam. The way it ended for me last time was embarrassing. I freaked out during the first round of injections. I only got half the shots and felt like shit for weeks after, like I was going through withdrawal. Next time, they'll probably sedate me and keep going. If I get in.

I don't know. I mean, there aren't that many able-bodied adults anymore. I'm a bigger help than your parents want to admit. And what about Nila? It's not all about me.

I've been making the same excuse for years. We both know the truth.

I'm not as brave as you.

●

March 22nd, 2190

I saw him again at the bar. He actually came up to me, asking about you. I asked him about that pregnant woman. I haven't seen her for months. No baby, either. It was a shitty thing to do. I knew as soon as I saw the look on his face that she was dead.

If you had wanted kids, would you have stayed? Is it worth dying for?

●

April 21st, 2190

Your dad got it in his head that he wants to be a shrimper. I mean, if you've seen one eyeless cod with its scales slipping off and an oozing hole in its side, you've seen them all. No need to change careers over it. I'm pretty sure shrimp are bottom feeders and are at the top of the list for 'things in the ocean horribly deformed by pollution'.

His crew is very literally falling apart. Mercury poisoning is leaving more of the older folks too fucked-up to work. They're all shaky and confused. So, he's got me out on the boat again, picking crabs out of the traps and tossing them back in the water. They pinch me every time. You'd think they'd be happy for the chance to grow up before being killed. That's more than you can say for the rest of us.

The way these white shrimps' little legs flail around is too relatable. I'm close to throwing them all overboard. I mean, most of them are under the size limit. Not like anyone gives a shit about that.

Your dad has hinted, i.e., outright stated, that he wants me to take the shrimp up to the city's farmers' market this week with your mom and sister. He says he's already paid for a spot, assuming we can even get past the tent cities.

We'll have to borrow a truck to get there, and the toll fees, and I'll probably be up all night working the generator, charging the battery.

I think his usual clients aren't buying from him anymore. And if they aren't buying from him, they aren't buying from anyone else in town.

I don't know what to do. I suggested to your dad that we, as a town, could consolidate our resources, find a better distributor, and split the profits. You know, like a co-op.

He told me I'm the reason he has high blood pressure, but really, it's the mercury.

●

June 3rd, 2190

Well, Sarah, a funny thing happened. The commercial fishing ships went down again last month. Three at once. We were packing up for another drive to the market when it happened. Feds came through town a few days later, interrogating anyone who might have a motive. So, like, everyone. I'm surprised they didn't leave as soon as they took a look at how run down we all are.

Coincidentally, it was just in time for halibut season. There's a two-fish bag limit, so I'm out trolling on the boat again. We pulled up a six footer, took us nearly an hour. Imagine existing for that long just to end up on a hook. I prefer salmon. When we catch the run headed for the delta, at least I know they're going to die either way.

●

July 16th, 2190

I'm reviewing complex analysis, which is a relief. I found your copy of Ahlfors. I'm surprised your parents didn't sell it. The cover's faded to grey, and the pages are all soft along the edges. After this, it's all modular forms and L-functions.

I'm doing fine, I guess. At least with respect to the exam. Pretty confident. I got a copy of the official review material. The core content hasn't changed, so I'm not worried. About the exam, at least.

Your cohort's final flyby of Earth is coming up. Then you'll be swinging past Jupiter, Neptune, hurtling back to the Sun, glancing off it and getting the hell out of here. A human couldn't stand the acceleration. And you will reach a point when and where time stands still. You'll leave the galaxy in the time it takes to translate thought to action.

What I'm saying is, if you are planning to get back to me, do it soon. In a few months you'll be 20,000 years too late.

●

September 2nd, 2190

The exams are next week. I paid the fee in advance so I'll have some incentive to go through with it again. I hate finishing early, then reviewing my answers, then reviewing it again, then just sitting there doing nothing until time is out. I just want to get it over with.

Your sister's excited for me.

Does she know what happens to us? Not that 'ambassador to the universe, next stage of humanity' bullshit, but what they actually, physically, do to navigators?

Maybe she doesn't. She was only 6 when you left.

I don't know if I should tell her. People like us don't have many choices. That's how they reel us in. Give us the opportunity to become 'more than what we are'. If I tell her the truth, she might not go through with it. Maybe that's the best life for her. Maybe she will be too afraid of that choice, like me. And look at me, what kind of life is this? I have no dreams, no goals. My only friend isn't capable of verbal communication and is on the other side of the solar system. Is this the kind of future Nila would want for herself?

I keep sending these, hoping you'll actually say something. Instead I get these enticing little hints that I'm half convinced are just in my head. Just talk to me, please. I have no one else.

●

September 16th, 2190

I went swimming tonight. It's been hotter than usual, clinging to the upper 80s even this late into summer. They've been shutting down the power grid an hour after sundown. For the entire coast. We're all using fish-oil lamps. The beach is the only place I can get fresh air. The wind picks up in the evening, blowing away the lingering haze, exposing the stars cluttering the sky.

They say that when you get to space you'll be among the stars. But, really, you are surrounded by emptiness, caught in the vast distances between bright spots. That perfectly encapsulates how I feel about my life. Maybe I do belong up there.

So, I'm swimming. It isn't quite high tide, but it's getting there. I swim past the few summer algal blooms still clinging to what's left of the pilings. I'm out far enough that I won't get pushed back to shore right away. When the dunes blend into the murky sky, I stop. I float on my back, looking up at all those stars. Too many, if you ask me. The waves are gentle, as you might remember, and they pass under me. There are a few boats out, not many, too far away for me to care. I'm trying not to think about the exam tomorrow. This time it feels inevitable. Irrevocable.

Me. Ocean. Stars. Obsessive thinking. Have I set the scene yet? Good, because next thing I know, my pity party gets crashed. I hear something big slam the water, and it sends a huge wave over me. I flip over and swim under it, coming up to face the direction of the sound. I push wet hair out of my eyes, but I still can't see it. What I do see is a wave coming, and a shape bobbing on top of it. I swim for it fast, muscles burning, spitting out salt water. After a few minutes, when my arm comes down for another stroke, it hits something firm. I hit it again, and with a dull thud, it yields under my fist. It's enticingly warm. Somehow its surface is bending light, reflecting, refracting, I don't know, and I suddenly hope the physics portion doesn't include optics. I swim around the object and start pushing it towards shore. It is disturbingly light. I attribute this to the relative density of the salt water.

I get to shore and roll it through the sand, above the tide line. Since it rolls, I know it is spherical, and I feel a heavy sense of dread with that realization. I still can't see it that well, amid the confusion of sand and stars, but my hands tell me it's there. Two meters in diameter. I don't want to touch it again; it terrifies and disgusts me. But what if?

I keep my hands on it. I feel its warmth, the way the surface feels like skin, and nausea swells over me. I think about how humans are homeomorphic to the sphere. You would say a torus, to be pedantic. I'd counter with n-torus, to be worse. It depends on how many holes there are.

I think of more stupid, old arguments we had, trying to detach myself from the hands exploring this thing. I trigger something, or it reacts to me in some way, because light flashes across its surface like an asterisk, leaking some clear fluid, defining the shape. It abruptly splits along these lines with a wet, sucking sound, opening like a lotus, and the liquid oozes thickly over my bare feet. I squint against the light, but it only continues for a moment, then it dulls. Dies. My eyes start to readjust to starlight. I move in close, any caution I had erased.

I always thought it would smell bad inside these things, but there is no smell at all and that's worse.

Vision restored, I see long hair, a rounded face, lips slightly parted, an upturned nose, swaddled in dusk. And then I see all these things together and my heart cracks because it isn't you.

It's some other girl, naked and curled like a fetus in her womb, asleep. Her spine has been replaced with a bundle of impossibly thin strands of glass that shimmer with rainbows, even in this distant light. Her body is prosthetic. Mind and body are fundamentally the same; when they tried to entirely eliminate the latter, integration simply did not work. I know this much. And though human brains are not constructed to last forever, this silicone will last hundreds of years. You can synthesize it. These new parts of you can be replaced.

My next thought is to cover her. I believe there is no true her to mind, but if it were you, I would want you covered, against the cold wind coming off the water, against invasive eyes. Maybe it's a stupid thing to care about. My shirt is drenched with salt water, but it's the best I can do, so I peel it off. I step closer, between the petals of her ship, and lay my shirt across her. And then I go for help.

Within the hour, a team arrives, cordons off the entire beach. One of the helmeted workers in dark, rippling layers of complex polymers looks for a moment at the shirt I have left on her. They leave and return with a silvery safety blanket to replace it.

The questions they ask leave me unsettled, and they grow disturbed with my answers. If this were some simple error, an accident, they wouldn't need to ask anything at all. They ultimately decide I have nothing to do with this. I did the right thing by bringing her to shore. I climb up the dunes to go home, to your home. I take one last look as they guide the petals gently back into place. It's for her own good.

Now I'm home, failing to sleep. My thoughts keep jumping to her face, looking as if she were about to cry, forever locked in that expression. The exam is in a few short hours.

It was a violation. Touching that sphere, that ship. Touching her.

●

November 1st, 2190

I passed. Top ten. I'd be impressed if I weren't a decade older than everyone else.

Nila was thrilled. I acted like I was too, though I know she will follow me, like I'm following you. Your parents looked relieved. I leave in two months.

I wish I had something to make this headache go away.

●

December 31st, 2190

This is the last New Year I will celebrate. No gifts this time. Just food, the things we never have. Gritty bread, a few withered tangerines. Desalinated water without the aftertaste of iodine. Your mom managed to find chicken somewhere, or at least something that tastes enough like it for us.

There is nothing left for me here. There's no reason for me to feel so sad.

●

January 1st, 2191

I'm standing in front of the house. I didn't bother waking anyone up to say goodbye. The small pile of battered textbooks I've left for Nila says it all.

The power's still off, this early in the morning, so it's pitch black. I barely notice the white van pulling up. The headlights make it stand out, make it more obvious how the mist clings to everything. Someone comes out wearing a white hazard suit, white helmet, and an impenetrable silver visor. They don't dare breathe the same toxic air as us poors. I take a deep breath, testing the air. Brine, ammonia, decay. The ubiquitous, scentless, heavy metal particulate.

They open up the back, revealing a shadowed interior, then turn their mercurial expression on me. Inside there are two benches loaded with teenagers. I stand out as the only adult. I'm at least twice as old as the youngest. I look at these children and think *neuroplasticity*. I take the end of the bench closest to the driver, who is distorted by a thick pane of fluted plastic. The air has an odd, metallic tang to it.

The girl sitting across from me bounces minutely in her seat. She keeps leaning forward, stealing glances at everyone else in the faint light. The van starts, and we're all clutching the benches so we don't go flying.

After half an hour, I can't take the loaded silence, so I tap on the plastic. No one responds, so I knock it a little harder.

"Hey, is it okay if we talk back here?"

The kids look shocked that I have the balls to ask. Still, no one responds.

"I think it's fine. Go ahead, talk to each other."

As if they'd been waiting for my permission, they all start babbling. After a few hours, as the conversation rises and falls, things quiet as the van slows, stops, and lets on another kid. We bump along, increasingly nauseated. No one talks to me, though they keep looking at me. I cross my arms over my chest and pretend I'm comfortable.

Indeterminable hours later, the van slows, and we hear the rattle of a gate being pulled back. We rumble forward, tilting down, into a tunnel. The van brightens intermittently, the air becomes dry and stale. There is no talking now.

The van shudders to its final halt. The back opens to two more people in haz suits. Behind them the cement tunnel curves up into darkness. We are quickly escorted into an empty room bathed in a cold, clinical light. They take us into an adjacent room, one by one. No one returns. I go last.

●

January 15th, 2191

My stomach hurts. My upper arm is a knot of pain.

I don't remember this from last time. I don't trust my memories. Remembering is such a feeble thing, it seems strange to have tested us based on it. How can it compare to simultaneous access and near instant recall? I see the appeal. What I have now feels fragmented and lossy. Still, what is a person if not their memories?

It's hard to think when I feel this bad. I don't know how I managed it before. I think the injections are meant to break us down in more than one way.

●

February 2191

I don't mind the acrid taste of the nutritional fish paste anymore. Soon, I won't be able to taste it at all. Or need it.

My relationship with time has changed. As endless billions of neural proteins crystallize into invisible silicate lattices, new connections are forming in me and with the others. The others linger on the fringes, but they are there. We have formed a local network for our cohort. It's strange, to be present both with them and within myself, and yet remain undivided. This new unity helps us forget the people we've left behind.

They have access to all of this, these things we share with each other, that we keep to ourselves. We are not our own creatures. I know, now, that to respond to me would have been to reveal yourself. I comfort myself with this.

It is almost perverse to compose these missives. I feel closer to you, as if I could drift across this electromagnetic field that spans between us and find you floating behind the crest of an oncoming wave.

●

November 2191

We who are left are now fully encased in our sacs, our albumen, and I note with disinterest the titanium mesh beginning to coalesce about me. It creates a shimmering, fibrous network that will be my interface for external stimuli. A second skin, a third eyelid. It scrapes against the delicacy of my consciousness.

I look outside of myself, while I still can, at what remains of some other girl. She is curled and suspended in her own electrolyte bath. A sleeve has been fitted over her spinal bundle, and code streams across the surface of her tank. An external cue, a flicker of her otherwise vacant eyes, and I know *she* is still in there.

●

2192

I thought the question I asked you was one I'd be able to answer myself at some point. Are you the same? Am I? How much control over myself could I have, when all these pieces of me have been co-opted? The *me now* and the *me then* seem as different as the *me* at 29 and the *me* at 19. The changes were imperceptible. I feel like I'm the same person, but I suspect I'm not. I don't think I'll ever know. The Fleet of Theseus, one of the girls calls us. It's supposed to be funny, but none of us can laugh.

They've got us rolled out on the beach this morning, like some massive carton of filigree eggs. Boosters and fins abrade our shells. We don't have an audience, just our own silent and discrete company.

There is no preamble, no ceremony. The launch is abrupt. We huddle close as the ice-white flames propel us through the atmosphere, leaving cutouts in the clouds we pass through. I feel the temperature like a breath, a blush, a fever. Our flight accoutrements, depleted and useless as they are, melt and adsorb into our hulls. I feel the first wave of unabated radiation splash across me, converted into electricity that courses through me.

I expect the fear to come, choking me back down to Earth, but it doesn't.

They said I would feel starlight on my skin. All I feel is sick.

●

????

I measure time in tedious revolutions about Jupiter and Neptune.

They have me on a course $\left(\cos(\frac{\pi}{24}), .17\sin(\frac{\pi}{6}), -.28\sin(\frac{\pi}{6}), 1.63\sin(\frac{\pi}{6})\right)$ rotated from your initial trajectory.

I adjusted it to $\theta = \frac{\pi}{4}$.

Asteroid 5772156 Aglaonoe will aid in correcting this to your vector in 13,268 lightyears.

I guess those fucking matrices were useful after all.

One more pass of Jupiter, then the Sun. I'll greedily store her gamma rays and x-rays. Then I'll be riding your wake, deeper into space.

I'll be there soon. I'm right behind you.

Rubella Dithers' story "The Waves In Which We Drown" was originally published in Metaphorosis on Friday, 13 August 2021. See magazine.metaphorosis.com

About the author

During a family trip to Coos Bay, a pair of pirates wandered up from the beach and asked Rubella if "the lass 'ad a bit o' seaweed in 'er 'air". Alas, the lass did not.

The Memory Dresser

Nicholas M. Stillman

Our parlor is small — tucked in a corner of Helm, folded between an empty Gassa stall and the home of a half-deaf mystic. For this reason, discretion numbers as one of our services. Not even the moon bears full witness, as Illsea, the largest Tower on the hill, shades us from the first few hours of evening light. Under our lamps, we shape the memories of the people of Helm, our people. Unlike the royals in Illsea, they are not looking for beauty. No shine-oil treatments or the newest configuration of knots and trellises. Our client's memories are coated in the dirt that lines our streets and our teeth. They sit in my grandmother's chair and weep at their reflections. Each length tracks the harrowing years of their lives in the dim lamps or beady sun: yesterday's shame growing from their scalp, their unfortunate births dragged through the streets. My grandmother's job is to make them feel well — to clean and wrap, braid and twist them into people who can walk back into their lives without shame dragging them down.

My own memories are unremarkable. Ordinary, frizzed, limp. My childhood must have been something to forget, because I all but have. There are a few years, though, that are different. Four finger lengths that hold the light like river rocks after rain. Memories that burst forth like the sweet juices of thin-fleshed berries, eclipsing all other flavor. My mother excited, touching my shoulder, pointing at the marigolds and the poppies not yet in bloom around the village pond. Fresh bread and cool paya juice as the fireworks erupt above the Towers during the New Sun dance. Then, below the shore rocks we clambered onto, the rich Oversea folk filing in and out of their boats — their strange memories gleaming in impenetrable designs, fractals upon fractals. Mother's breath curling warmly in the cold night onto my scalp and tips of my ears, running her thin fingers through my memories while we watched the beautiful people glisten. *One day,* her voice sounds as if she were still beside me, *you'll have memories like that.*

Whenever I felt the dull ache of boredom begin to blossom throughout my body, I would twine these strands between my fingers, feeling their health against my skin, or else tie the lengths around my forehead so that everyone who met me met the finest version.

"If your chin were any higher you'd break your neck," said Grandmother, tugging at the steeple knot holding my best memories in view. "You want the world to think you're better than them? Who are you to do that?" She would make me fold them beneath less pleasant memories. Dull evenings in the parlor. Sweaty days jostling through the market's center. Father's long trips dragging a net into salty water for exotic hues of sea life to be shipped and filleted and served to the people he despised most. My mother's last year, bed-bound and shivering.

Grandmother was disdainful of the extravagant. She despised my secret yearnings for things I had seen: marigolds and poppies and beautiful memories rippling like the sea as the Oversea folk slipped onto boats. She preferred a meek life of quiet dignity, a healthy distrust of laughter.

One morning, before the clients lined out her door, she cut a sheet into strips with my father's old gutting knife and, leaving one end intact and tied to the Dressing chair, she pressed the strips into my sweating palms. Grandmother turned the strands one by one — revealing the sheet's bloodstain, oil spot, jagged edges, holes from ash. I nodded. I folded strips into one another, braided them, looped them, curled them with brass rollers. My fingers were small but eager as I worked a loose approximation of the Sargusoa style — limp and casual, with two elaborate loops. I made sure to hide each imperfection beneath the cleaner lengths. My memory Dressing would impress upon others the wearer's connection to a rich childhood, as the brightest ends of sheet I bent at angles that would catch the sunlight. When I finished, I dabbed sweat from my forehead and smiled.

Grandmother slapped my cheek.

"Look what you've done." She flipped over my knots, pointed to the blood, oil, jagged edges I'd disguised.

"It looks better this way," I said, my voice faltering.

"So like your mother." She said it as a curse. She pulled at my release thread and the Sargosa collapsed back into a tattered sheet. When she saw my eyes filling with anger, my fists balling, she cocked her head. "What, you want a village of pretenders? Whoever hides the best is the winner? You want your people to think they have to compete with each other, compete with the Towers? All they do is try to survive. Don't take that from them."

I bit back tears. I could not imagine letting a client walk out with their poverty, their abuses and vices and regrets plain in the sun for all to see. Surely there was a way to cover them? "Why should there always be something to hide? Not everyone is so miserable."

"There will always be stains," she said, cutting down the sheet and twisting the strands to be dipped in oil and used as lantern wicks. "These people are decent, Helm people. They don't want to be glamorized like an oiled Tower empress. They want to be understood. That is why we do not hide pasts, but weave the hurt and joy together so that both catch the light. Our job is to frame their lives in such a way that others can see dignity, not glamor, not suffering. We cannot afford to play games with our memories Not here." I followed her eyes to the dust whistling through the empty street, the sun already baking the walking boards stretched between the gutters. Illsea loomed over us, its shadow not yet cast.

●

Days in the parlor turned like the trapped figurine of a music box while my memories grew stale. The same clients to seat, well buckets to drag, lavender to pick, stones to heat, cloth to wash, rice to cook. I waited. I cut my sheets into strips. Practiced in the moonlight before the tower eclipsed the light. I snuck pamphlets of the latest Dressing styles from the market and slid them under my mattress. I exercised my fingers and wrists. I trained myself for a life I was better suited to.

Then, one night, after I had closed the doors and drawn the sunshade over the window, a confident knock rapped at the door. Then another.

"Oh, go on," Grandmother sighed, no doubt preparing her speech — *Your memories will still be there in the morning.*

At the door, however, was not Ginja the mystic who wanted to sell us another memory-reading, but a stranger. She was tall and lean, her neck long and seamless. A dark cloak was draped over her shoulders and a dust wrap pleated neatly over her face so that her dark eyes and long lashes poked through like hermit crab antenna. She stepped through me as if I occupied no space at all.

Before Grandmother could speak, the woman flipped the cloak off of her shoulders, revealing a white silk tunic and her loose-wrapped memories shining like polished ore in the lamplight. A medallion of Illsea hung from her neck. I lost the ability to move.

She glided to the dressing chair in silence and seated herself. A chair that had, only minutes before, held Malik, who bathed once a week in the camel water trough. She crossed her legs and examined the shelves cluttered with abandoned dressing equipment — rusted iron clips and outdated bows. My cheeks burned.

Grandmother wiped her hands on her tunic. Wiped them again. She did not speak. Only stood like a low-cast shadow, clearing her throat to no avail.

The woman spoke without turning her head. "Girl, what's your name?"

Grandmother opened her mouth to respond, but realized too late that she was not the girl.

"Mina," I managed in a hoarse whisper.

"Do you live here?"

"My room is upstairs."

"Mina, this is my daughter, Tengi."

I turned, startled to find a small, dark girl standing just inside the door. She seemed to be everything her mother was not — short, wide-hipped with small eyes and a flat face. She was pretty in her own way, and prettier still than anyone I'd seen in the parlor besides her mother.

"Please take Tengi up to your room to play while I speak with the Dresser."

Tengi made a face that indicated she would rather run with street dogs than climb the thin wooden staircase to my room. I searched Grandmother's eyes for guidance, but found none. Her body was rigid, as if a wild animal had entered the room.

Tengi was already marching petulantly to the staircase. I followed. Her memories bounced before my eyes as we climbed. Her head was covered in a silken maroon cloth and a thick braid fell down and wrapped around her waist. The braid was deeper and richer than the silk covering, making the latter look cheap; the kind of cloth we would sell unfaithful spouses attempting to disguise their guilt. I marveled. It was as if Tengi's entire life had been fireworks and fresh bread. With a start I realized Grandmother was wrong — not everyone had stains.

●

That first evening, and several after, Tengi refused to speak to me. We would sit in silence, Tengi's hands clasped in her lap, face turned up to Illsea, as we waited for my grandmother to finish her secret work. Later, Tengi brought a book and read it when there was enough light. Finally, one night when Tengi's eyes were wild with anger, her memory scattered about her shoulders, she spoke:

"You should apply a Barosa nut oil twice a day if you don't want your memories to collect all that dust."

I nodded. I felt that a critical gap had been bridged. I let loose all of my caged questions. About her purpose in my room, her mother in our shop, her bedroom in the Tower, her thick, syrupy memories. But my questions were like throwing stones at a circling hawk. Tengi watched them with interest before diving: *Tell me, what's it like being so poor?*

Our words began to search out our differences, curiously prodding each other's edges. Each revelation was like a flash river after a rain as we encouraged more questions. I surprised her with my knowledge of the latest Dressing styles, my love of the Oveasea fractal knots, my awareness of the various uses of poppies and marigolds. And she both surprised me and didn't surprise me; every detail a revelation I could not have anticipated. The Tower competitions for memory shine, the strong-necked men tying their memories together and pulling like reluctant lovers until one buckled, the heartbreak of the smallest memory imperfections, the scandal of memory painting. "There are some who refuse to do anything but fuck and eat and travel before a dance," she'd said, her language embarrassing me. "There are servants who shield them from crumbs. Some refuse to see their children in case the child cries or falls or misspeaks, and so taints their memories. The competition is shit. And yet if you don't do those things, you stand alone at the dance and your memories get even weaker. There's no way out."

"And here you will be ridiculed for trying too hard," I said, breathless. "If I try to clean Malik's tangle or hide his embarrassment with a clip or cloth, Grandmother would call me a pretender. Nothing I do is allowed to be beautiful."

Tengi and I spent our nights comparing our lives while the two women worked and the constellations did slow battle through the slats of my roof. Sometimes we would climb out my window and wander to the spice fields and rub Tougo into our teeth, sometimes we would chance a trip to the market when the sun was still up and hold hands and call each other *beloved* to watch the old men bend incline their heads at our parting. I knew that every week Tengi would arrive at my doorstep, and she did without fail. I had never met anyone like her and she, she confided one night, had never met anyone like me. Her presence textured my days and gave a shape to my daily life.

As the weeks wore on, there were more Dressings, which meant more Tengi in my life. Tengi did not tell me why her mother came so much often than other clients, but I knew the New Sun dance was approaching and I guessed there was some secret vanity, or problem that needed mending before the start. When I did glimpse her mother, mostly from my window as I watched Tengi leave, I saw that she looked vacant, her steps unnecessarily cautious. Tengi would guide her by the hand away from the shop to wherever the escorts had hidden the carriage.

One night, while the moths threw their bodies at my window, we touched memories. It was late — the women below us were working long, as usual. It was Tengi's idea. To have me practice working with healthy memory, to prepare for the day she would bring me to the Towers as her personal Dresser. I asked her to show me what they did in Illsea, how the Dressers prepared. She swallowed as she loosened her tunic and dropped it down below her bare shoulders, shook her memories out of its braid. I listened to the tapping of moths trying to hurl themselves at my lamp.

We sat on our knees, facing each other, the flesh of our thighs touching.

Tengi's memories were like ripples in water. So bright they felt like liquid glass, or something else I could not describe. My breath came in small gasps as her fingers danced along the hollow strands of my boredom and routine, clicking her tongue lightly. My eyes fluttered and the floor groaned as we delved deeper into each other's lives. I felt something shift beneath my breastbone. A stirring.

I worked my fingers up her memory, then allowed my fingers to explore the hidden days and weeks beneath the maroon silk covering. Tengi screamed. Scrambled away from me, gathering spare bits of herself and pinning them behind her. I didn't know what I'd done wrong.

Tengi reluctantly untied the maroon cloth, and I saw it. Falling just above the tip of her ear, was a section of memory that was white and hollow as a feather's heart. The kind of loss I thought only those in Helm had experienced. I tracked the growth with practiced eyes. She had been carrying it silently since the week we'd met.

"Tengi, I — what happened?"

She smoothed the memory behind her, clipping them back. "I forgot. I'm sorry. I should have warned you."

I stood, angry and frightened and still drunk off her touch. "What happened? Who did this?"

She shook her head.

"Why is your mother here? Why are you here? Please. You need to tell me."

Tengi opened her mouth, closed it. She stood and went to the window, to look up at the Tower. Her Tower. "These memories are the same ones my mother has. The ones my mother is paying your grandmother to cut."

"What?"

Tengi slid open the window and the moths went in search of their flame. "They would kill her if anyone knew."

"I — cut?" The thought churned in my stomach; a mutilation I had not considered. To cut memories was a heinous act, punishable by execution. Killing a person ended their life, but cutting them ended who they were. Who would choose to lose themselves?

"She wants to forget." Tengi turned to look at me, her mouth clenched in a smile. "And now I am the only one who will remember." She passed her face through the window, closed her eyes.

I didn't know what to do, what to say. I had so many questions, knew so little. Silent, I walked behind her, closed my eyes, and joined her, our faces waiting for a breeze.

●

My grandmother and I took to standing like hungry cats by the door on the days we knew they would come. We turned away clients, as neither of us could focus until they arrived. They were our great secrets. Grandmother spoke less about my attraction to dreaminess, my selfishness, even as I lingered in front of the Dressing mirror turning my head to admire how my new memories seemed to brighten my eyes, add color to my cheeks. In my reflection I saw an open, bright person. Someone brimming with possibility.

Tengi snuck me Tower oil and ribbons and when Grandmother was not around I would walk into the market with my most recent memories oiled. I shimmered in the heat. In return, I said nothing to Grandmother about the cutting. She would stop her work if she thought I knew, and I could not risk losing Tengi.

Tengi was changing, too. Her memories were growing crooked. She took to hiding them with bows and expensive ribbon. She shrank from touch if I approached her too quickly, moved too quietly. Wind from the streets would cause her to spasm in fear and it would take me minutes of careful teasing to distract her. I never touched her recent growth and it pained me that we had becomes so different. I would try to find gaps in conversation to ask her about the white growth, what had happened to her, and how I could help. All I wanted to do was help. Tengi told me not to worry, nothing was my fault, it wasn't me.

●

One evening, after Tengi and her mother had gone, father arrived. He greeted us without his right foot — a result of a rationing mistake on board his ship and several short straws drawn in a life of short straws. It had been years since he'd been home, and I barely recognized the man from my childhood. His memory was thick and clotted and smelled of fish viscera and left an oily trail like a slug.

After an awkward and stilted embrace, he sniffed my memories, and I became aware of the thick, nutty oil still seated there. His eyes wandered to Grandmother, who hid behind her the old gutting knife she used for cutting. At her feet lay the strands of two dead memories she had yet to sweep from the floor.

I felt his hand tighten around my shoulder. "This is what happens when I leave?" he spat. "I ought to turn you in for risking my wife's parlor. *My* rightful parlor."

"It's not like that," I said, unable to release myself from his grip. "They came from Illsea, they're not like you think."

He rounded on me. For a moment, while he had me pinched in his grip, I thought he would flay me like a fish, his muscles having formed the habit.

Seeing the terror in my eyes seemed to shift something in him.

He released me. Searched me for what felt like signs of someone else. Someone who was not me.

"I'm home now. For good," he said as if reminding himself. "Illsea took my foot and then dropped me on the shore. So if either of you think you still want to play your Tower games, then maybe I'll have to cut those memories from you myself." His face crinkled in pain, his eyes darted to the memories of my childhood. "Your mother would never have wanted this. Never this."

●

In the months that followed, I would often lie in bed, tracking the sun's progress across my floor. Grandmother stopped promising to train me, and I stopped collecting pamphlets from market, stopped practicing on my sheets. I watched my father's memories grow out white. Grandmother tried to clean them, to dress them lightly, but he refused her, preferring to wallow.

The few decent memories I had made with Tengi began to fade as dull, frizzed ones pushed them down my neck. I could no longer face the market, watch their eyes take in how far I had fallen. I became angry with Tengi for her ability to continue on with her life while I sat in the same room she'd found me in, waiting for her to return. I felt our lives together slipping further into my past and wondered if she felt that distance, too. If she even noticed.

The rains came. I grew hollow, forgetful. Grandmother covered my memories with a dashini so that I would have enough courage to leave the room. I refused to remove it, even at my grandmother's pleading for memories to have light and air. In her mind, a little damage was better than hiding completely. But I knew she was wrong. The more you show the damage, the more of you it becomes, until it is all you are.

●

And then, on the eve of the New Sun dance, Tengi climbed through my window. She smelled of the red dirt from the back roads below the Towers. She must have ridden all day.

"Tengi?" I stood perfectly still, just as I had the day her mother first entered our parlor. "What...Why are you here?"

Tengi's face was stretched tight, her memories frizzed and loose, dragging behind her. She pulled it through the window.

"Because I need help," she said.

"Where have you been?" I felt my surprise leaking into bitterness. "Why didn't you come back for me?"

Tengi shrugged past me. She cradled something heavy in her coat. "I am watched, my mother and me. When your grandmother sent word that she would no longer..." she lifted her head, thinking. "The message was discovered. Now I can't piss without someone holding my hand."

I did not know what to say, how to respond, what to do with the anger I had been holding for her — anger for abandoning me here, stranding me in a desert with my father.

"What do you want?"

Tengi placed a silken maroon bundle from her coat onto my bed. I recognized the cloth as the one that once covered her damage. "I want you to help me," she said, staring at the cloth. "I am not going to the dance. There is not a skilled enough Dresser in the world to hide all of this." She found my eyes with hers.

"You came to tell me that?"

"I am going on a boat. Oversea."

I approached her as if she might, at any moment, collapse into nothing. I was still unsure of her, but my mind filled with new possibilities. Boats. Dances. I absently recalled those years with my mother, as I often did, the memories still burning brightly in my mind. "And how do you want me to help you?" I said coolly.

Tengi looked at me with what might have been hurt at my tone. Or sadness. "Oh," she said. "I want you to come with me."

My mouth dried. The room shifted slightly. "But I thought you wanted my help."

"That's part of it. I... I'm leaving whether or not you come. But I want you too."

"Oh." I could not think of what to say. I touched my dashini, recalling how much I'd changed. I felt weak at my inability to move on without her. I resented her for it.

"I need to show you something," Tengi said as she kneeled and unwrapped the bundle. Beneath the maroon silk lay a dagger. A thin blade wide as my finger and long as my hand, with a handle of pearl. I stepped back, knocking a book from my shelf. It thudded to the floor, and I heard my father shifting in his bed beneath us. He rarely slept, and his temper was deep and treacherous in the middle of the night. I held my breath.

"I need you," Tengi said, picking the blade up off of the bed and carrying it like a child to where I stood. "I need you to cut me. To let me start over."

I took the blade, if only to stop her speaking. "I can't do that, Tengi," I whispered. "I couldn't. Not to anyone."

Tengi nodded but did not move. "I know how it sounds, but look at me. Look at what has become of me, Mina." For the first time she looked at me closely, her eyes on my hidden memories. "Look what's happened to you!" Her voice bounced around my room and I held my finger to her lips.

"My father," I whispered.

She batted my hand like a fly. "We have been destroyed by the acts of others. Two people locked my door and held me down and made me remember something I want to forget. Why should *I* have to remember what *they* did? Why should you have to hide yourself when you're alone?"

"But your mother!" I said, losing grip on my voice. "You always said she would regret this, that she was a pretender."

Tengi nodded. "She was. She didn't do it for herself. She did it so that others wouldn't think less of her. She was a coward. I'm not afraid to let go."

I stared at Tengi, her nostrils flaring, her eyes wide as a street cat. My heart swam in my ears. My grandmother would say it was cowardice, not bravery. "You aren't serious," I said. "You can't be."

Her fingers wrapped around my shoulders. Ropes of tendon sprung out on her neck. "We deserve something new. The dance is coming tomorrow. There will be so many boats lining the dock that slipping in to one will be easy. While everyone stares at the sky, their eyes filled with fireworks, we will move beneath them and climb onto the boat unseen. We'll start our new lives without *these*," Tengi shook her memories in her fists like they were chains, "weighing us down. It's the New Sun. It's the time of new beginnings."

"Not for people like me," I said. Memories of my mother flooded me. Fireworks above new-budded flowers, her breath on my scalp, her voice in my ear. Watching the lives of other people.

Tengi reached behind me, undid my knots, and I felt my memories crash around my shoulders. She found those four finger lengths, held them. They were the most precious things I possessed. Yet they were also nothing. They were not real. Not like Tengi. Not like the dagger in my hand. Not like the moon filtering through the cracks of my ceiling. Not like the cold air seeping through the floor. Not like my father dragging himself from the mattress, where I could hear him hobbling now beneath us.

Tengi placed her memory in my hand and closed her eyes. I held her and wondered which memories she would miss most. Her comfortable childhood, or the sweaty nights cramped in a room above a Helm parlor? Would she long for what she'd lost, even if she couldn't remember? Be like my father, still reaching down to scratch his missing foot? Would she lose herself? Lose her interest in me?

And who would I be without my mother's breath on my scalp, my grandmother's slap against my cheek? I thought of the fireworks, the fractals, the poppies. *One day you will have memories like that.*

"Take all but right now," said Tengi, her breath hot against my face. "I don't want to remember anything but us and our plan for the boats. I've written down all we need to remember."

I felt my body vibrate. I did not move.

"We can meet again. That will be our first memory." And then Tengi pressed her lips against my scalp, my damage, so that they came to me like a memory and a moment all at once.

We are silent as we listen to my father's halting steps beneath, hear his hoarse voice calling: "Mina?" It will take him some time to climb to my room. To find our spirits entwined. It will take him only moments to understand when he opens my door. To step his way into my room in the eclipsed moonlight, to find my past dead on the ground. Find my life spread out in tight curls at his feet. Find me taken up by a longed-for breeze, flying around the room. He will pass the moths heading for the flames through my open window, intent on breaking through the glass of the lamp to experience the moment they have lived for, that they will die for. He will hear familiar nervous laughter and confused footsteps pattering on the walking boards outside. He will peer out into the inky dark, the moon now lost behind the Tower, and will try to find me. He will see instead two strangers, their hands clasped, bouncing as if unmoored and drifting from a dock. Watch them feeling in the black for the way forward.

Nicholas M. Stillman's story "The Memory Dresser" was originally published in Metaphorosis on Friday, 24 May 2019. See magazine.metaphorosis.com

About the author

Nicholas M. Stillman is a writer, teacher, and reluctant service worker living in the east bay in California. He received his MFA from Saint Mary's College of California in 2018, where he currently teaches English. He desperately wants to live in the woods, raise crops, write eight hours a day, and play an unhealthy amount of PS4. He shares this impossible dream with his girlfriend, Sabrina, and their cats, Gnocchi and Fusilli, who all insisted on being part of this bio.

@nick_at_day

Rooks on Sundays

Jack Neel Waddell

"You never liked to play chess with me," she says.

The board lies on a tray across her bed. Pillows prop her up slightly, just enough to see the pieces.

She reaches out a wrinkled hand, skin both pale and blotched brown, like the flesh of an apple left out too long. She grabs a rook that she carved, perhaps twenty-five years ago, from purpleheart wood. Today she remembers how it moves.

"I know how much you love it, Mom," I say, the word still feeling awkward in my mouth. It took me weeks to even say it.

We play until the end of visiting hours. She frowns as a nurse comes in. She weakly tries to push him away as he hooks her oxygen mask back over her face, clasping the straps behind her head within the milkweed-seed wisps of her hair.

I walk out of her room and toward the door of St. Agatha's hospice.

"You have to sign out, ma'am," calls the registration nurse after me.

The log book is open, with the heading, "Patient: Ella Reilly."

I sign Katherine Reilly, the only name on the list going back every Sunday for pages.

I've hidden the case in a park a few blocks away. A few cherries are blooming, but a chilling drizzle drives away any strolling couples.

I press the button on the front of the case to return.

I tuck the case back under the bench in my garage shop. Then I get inside my Corolla and drive.

There's one other place I go on Sundays.

It isn't raining here, now. The sun shines with vernal tenderness through the willows onto a pair of monument stones, dated only months apart. I place butter-yellow mums on my dearest James's grave, the one on the right. Kay, our daughter, buried in the other, never cared for flowers.

She injured her back when a Land Rover drove her into a ditch on her way to the coffee shop. She was taking an extra shift to pay us rent, which I imposed when she refused to sign up for classes at the community college.

The doctor gave her pills, which ran out. She found more, then she took too many.

James always blamed me for the gulf between us and our daughter. He left me after Kay's funeral, but his heart gave out before the divorce was final, whether from grief or stress or coincidence.

I wish I could take my case back to one or any moment during that time, to pull them back to me. Or, if not that, just to have them again as I push them from me — an arm's length away is closer than six feet deep. But the past is Hermetically sealed, even to my machine.

I've already purchased the bare plot to the right of James, but I won't need it for twenty-eight years. Now I'm saving up for the Catholic rest home in town, the best in the county, since I will have no one to tend to me but myself, and only on Sundays.

I drive back to my shop. Small blocks of exotic wood lie scattered on the workbench. I reach for a piece of purpleheart I rounded on the lathe, then hesitate. Instead, I select ebony. I pick up a gouge and carve.

Slivers of the past fall away with each splinter. Soon I think of nothing but the piece hidden in the grain and, after a while, I finish the crenellated parapet of a rook.

●

"What's this?" she asks as I hand her the box. It's wide, long, and thin, like a box of chocolates.

"A gift, Mom," I say. "Open it."

She pulls the ribbon and lifts the top. Laid out in four rows is the chess set I've made over the past month, of ebony and olivewood. She picks up the kings of each color.

"They're beautiful, Kay," she says.

She smiles, eyes beaming, and it warms my heart.

"You made these?" she asks.

I nod, with a strangely proud smile spreading across my face. But her eyebrows draw together in suspicion. She turns her eyes up and left, as if she's trying to call something elusive to mind.

"Mom?"

She looks at me, and I see something change in her.

She puts the pieces back in the box and places it aside, then leans out and places a pale hand on my own. She looks into my eyes, and I into hers. I see the peanut-brown of her irises, not the forest-floor hue of Kay's, and I know she sees the same because within her eyes shines a spark of recognition. A spark that fades into sorrow.

"You're so good to visit me," she says, voice breaking. "All we've got is each other."

Jack Neel Waddell's story "Rooks on Sundays" was originally published in Metaphorosis on Friday, 1 November 2019. See magazine.metaphorosis.com

About the author

Jack Neel Waddell is a Southern writer, physicist, and educator who lives with his wife and daughters in an old, white house nestled among the bones of the Ouachita Mountains. Threads of his bipolar type 2 and generalized anxiety disorders weave through much of his work. He has been a semi-finalist in the Writers of the Future contest and his fiction appears in the *Strange Economics* anthology published by David Shultz, the *SQ Mag Best of the Year* anthology, and an upcoming issue of *Fantasy and Science Fiction*.

Forever and a Life

Daniel Roy

Transcripts of Mayfly interviews by Dr. Leanne Jansen.
Sarah al-Awqati (childhood friend): "Fuck forever."
Yup, I was right in front of the stage when she first said
that. I can say "she," right?
Interviewer: Sure, if you like.
Al-Awqati: She was smoking a cig on stage when she
said it. Ever seen those? Little paper sticks that smelled like
burnt grass. Anyway: [Al-Awqati inhales an imaginary cig,
then exhales invisible smoke as she speaks.] "Fuck forever."
Like that.
Esra Agnarsson (Mayfly survivor): You asked if
Sylvia Castro believed it. Look, there's no denying that a few
of us thought it was an act, but me... Castro was so much
larger than life, y'know? I could tell she meant it. She
wanted to punch immortality in the balls.
Interviewer: Do you think she acted out of anger
against the Autocracy?
Agnarsson: What? Oh, no no no. Of course not.

●

*Recorded at the Olivia Castro Center of the Arts on the fiftieth
anniversary of Sylvia Castro's death.*
[Polite applause.]
Olivia Castro: Freedom. That's what my grandson
wanted, not just for himself but for each and every one of

us. The freedom to *choose* to be immortal, to embrace this great gift that the Autocracy, praise be, has made possible.

Now, you might wonder who in their right mind would choose *not* to live forever. That's okay, I do too, sometimes. [Laughter.] It's tempting to look down on those poor souls who would rather live short, brutish lives than shine like a beacon through the ages with us. Some historians look back on the life of Sylvain Castro and find all sorts of pathologies and mental defects that led him down this path.

But I know my grandson. I bounced him on my lap when he was just a little boy. Whatever mental state led him to reject immortality, it doesn't diminish the importance of his grand idea. It doesn't negate the significance of his contribution.

Each of us here is alive because we *want* it. The Autocracy is our *choice*. This is our freedom, and we have Sylvain Castro to thank for reminding us. Thank you, Sylvain. And praise the Autocracy for keeping us safe through the centuries to come!

[Sustained applause.]

●

[Wang Xian-zhi frowns as he listens to the recording of Olivia Castro's speech.]

Wang Xian-zhi (Mayfly survivor, *Rotting Corpse* drummer): Yeah, Olivia's full of shit. [Laughter.]

Interviewer: Why do you say that?

Wang: Sylvain — *Sylvia*. Sylvia didn't do all this to give us a choice, man. She hated immortality, plain and simple. She hated that we all gave up on our freedom because we were afraid of what might happen three hundred years down the line. What Olivia talks about isn't a choice at all. "Be young and healthy forever barring traumatic injury, or die a slow, agonizing death as your body breaks down." Who in hell would choose the latter?

Olivia's notion of freedom is like setting a cage on the edge of a cliff and opening the door. No one in their right mind would step out.

Now back before Sylvia, that door wasn't even open. Then came the attacks in '89 —

Interviewer: The London Underground gas attacks that claimed the immortality of three hundred and fifty-seven victims.

Wang: Right, right. Back then, Sylvia and I were getting the band started on the Montreal music scene, and we'd play these songs that were critical of the Autocracy, right? So even though we had nothing to do with '89, the Secret Police had their eye on us. And the Secret Police had developed, like, this vaccine that could switch off your immortality. The Mayfly Shot, you know about it! They used it to threaten us.

Interviewer: Threaten you how?

Wang: Like, they'd rough us up pretty bad, then while a nurse tends to you, bam! They'd stab you with a syringe and let you think you just got the Mayfly Shot. Rattle our nerves. Shit, it worked.

Interviewer: Did you believe it at the time? That they had an immortality vaccine?

Wang: We didn't know for sure, but we were scared. I begged Sylvia to take it down a notch with the anti-Autocracy lyrics and speeches, but, man, she just didn't care. "Relax, Wangie!" she'd say, and she'd laugh that deep laugh of hers, like life was just a big joke. Then one day she showed up at practice and she had the syringe.

●

Video footage seized from Wang's personal collection, on lease from Montreal's Self-Enforcement Agency.

[The grainy, amateur video is shot in a loft in Downtown Montreal. It focuses on Sylvia Castro, unaware she's being filmed, as she bounces a small syringe on her knuckles, staring into the distance. At the back of the shot, someone is tuning an electric guitar.]

Wang Xian-zhi (offscreen, filming): What you got there, Syl?

[Sylvia looks up. Her long hair and painted face make her look unmistakably feminine. She twirls the syringe like a drumstick, and grins at the camera.]

Sylvia Castro: Mayfly Shot. Want a go?

Wang: Bullshit, man, that's totally mouthwash.

Sylvia: You think? Let's find out!

[Sylvia places the syringe against her arm, smiling wide.]

Wang: Hey. Hey! Sylvia! Take it easy, man!

[Sylvia pockets the syringe, seemingly pleased with Wang's reaction.]

Sylvia: Don't worry, I'm not gonna waste this for a documentary that no one's ever gonna watch.

Wang: Anything else you wanna say to the camera, since nobody's watching this?

Sylvia: [Cheerfully.] Fuck the Autocracy!

Esra Agnarsson (off-screen): Hey! Not cool.

Sylvia: See, Wangie? That's what I'm talking about. Eternal life has turned us all into wimps, man. We used to know better! "Better to burn out than to fade away."

Wang: Here we go —

Sylvia: You know I'm right. We've given up our freedoms because we're scared of what might happen a thousand years from now! It's fucked up.

Esra (off-screen): Living beats dying.

Sylvia: Does it? Maybe dying is the only way to live.

Wang: Okay. I'm turning this off.

[The video ends.]

●

Interviewer: State your name and occupation, please.

Doctor Gerald Stone: Doctor Gerald Stone, Mayfly Program Director.

Interviewer: What was your position at the time Castro was admitted?

Stone: I was the director of the Melody Dementia Care Center in Stark, New Hampshire. It wasn't devoted to Mayflies back then.

Interviewer: So Castro was considered mentally unsound when he —

Stone: She.

Interviewer: Yes, of course. I'm just careful around officials when it comes to Castro's... That is...

Stone: I'm a medical practitioner, Miss, not a politician.

Interviewer: Is this why you allowed Sylvia and the others freedom around the facilities?

Stone: It was a sound medical practice. By taking the vaccine, they had inflicted grievous self-harm. They condemned themselves to a slow, life-long death.

I just did what was right by them, as my patients. I gave them an environment where they could be themselves. Who cared about the Autocracy's official party line if these people were gonna die sixty, eighty years later? It was the humane thing to do. That's all.

Interviewer: Why do you think Sylvia Castro took the Mayfly Shot? Was it an act of suicide or rebellion?

Stone: Yes.

●

Attached: picture of Rotting Corpse *in concert in the Melody community hall in January '91.*

Description: Sylvia Castro, wearing a white tank top and frilly camouflage skirt over ripped fishnets, holds her fist up at a crowd of patients. The crowd, excited by the performance, hold up their fists in response. Behind Sylvia, to the right of the frame, is Wang Xian-zhi.

●

Esra Agnarsson (Mayfly survivor): Word got around. The way the rumors put it, Sylvia was running the asylum, like, literally. They put on punk performances almost every night. *Rotting Corpse*, but also a few others that had followed Sylvia's example and taken the shot, like *Short Flight* and *Kick the System*. There were rumors of drugs and sex, y'know. And other stuff.

Nabila Safar (Mayfly survivor): We couldn't believe it. Sylvia had spoken against the Autocracy, and now she was in some sort of utopian center where she played music and got to be a girl and shit! Like Esra said... Word got around.

Agnarsson: Some of us got hold of the Mayfly Shot. I asked Sylvia's friends, and someone put me in touch. Friend of a friend kinda deal. They didn't even charge me for it… They were just thrilled to give them out. All you had to do was take it, and you'd get sent to Melody.

Interviewer: Did you realize you were gonna die if you took the vaccine?

Agnarsson: Well, yeah. But not right away, know what I mean? It just didn't feel real. Eighty years isn't a long time, but it's long enough that you don't have to think about it too much. Of course, I hadn't realized I'd get progressively older, y'know? I thought I'd stay twenty until I turned ninety, then bam, old woman.

Safar: I didn't really think about it at the time, to be honest. I thought someone would find a way to reverse the vaccine.

Agnarsson: Well, they did, but not before… [Agnarsson motions to her wrinkled face.]

Safar: Yeah.

Interviewer: What were you told when you got to the center?

Agnarsson: The medical staff called us "Mayflies." They said they wanted us happy in the time we had left, that this was a safe space. I remember one nurse — Jenny, I think her name was. She did my check-in, and near the end she took my hand and just… teared up. She couldn't speak for a while.

Interviewer: What about you, Sarah? Why didn't you take the shot?

Sarah al-Awqadi (childhood friend): Me? [Nervous laughter.] I was scared, what do you think? I mean, I thought about it. I even got my own shot. I sat in my room one night and put the tip of the syringe to my arm… I must have spent an hour just poking at my skin with it. But I… I couldn't go through with it. I just couldn't.

Interviewer: Do you regret not doing it?

Al-Awqadi: Well, no, I… [Long pause.] No.

●

Jenny Preston (Melody nurse): I didn't like their music. To call it "music" is charitable, to be honest. It was mostly yelling and mindless strumming on antique instruments. I got one of those old music files the Mayflies passed around, stuff like *Sex Pistols* and *Dead Kennedys*. First time I heard them, I thought the file was corrupted.

Interviewer: Were you aware that recordings were being smuggled out?

Preston: Not at first. When the Mayfly Riots started, though, there was no doubt where the rioters out there were getting their inspiration. Doctor Stone put security measures in place, but it didn't do any good. I'm pretty sure it was one of the orderlies smuggling out the recordings. We never found out who.

Interviewer: Stone didn't put a stop to the shows even then?

Preston: Well, the damage was already done. Besides, Doctor Stone would never let politics influence his medical practice. The only thing he cared about was the well-being of his patients, and it was clear they were happier this way.

Interviewer: One of the Mayflies has testified under oath that you were the one smuggling the tapes out.

Preston: Hmm.

Interviewer: You don't dispute it?

Preston: Probably someone out to get me. Like I said, the music was garbage.

●

James Maarten (rioter): Everybody in the movement saw the recordings. Sylvia and the others, they looked so damn *free*! No disciplinary circles, no loyalty broadcasts, no Secret Police. It made us question whether immortality was really worth it. We all understood you can't have a society of immortals without absolute rule of law, of course, but still, the question itself bugged the hell out of us.

Castro's choice meant that things could be different. None of us wanted to die, not really. I mean, the Mayfly Shot was outlawed at this point, but it was still available if you knew the right people. And sure, some in the movement ended up in Melody, but for most of us, it wasn't immortality that was the problem.

Interviewer: What was the problem, then?

Maarten: I, uh... [Nervous laugh.]

Interviewer: Can I show you a video?

[Maarten shrugs.]

Video attached: Maarten speech in September '82. He is standing in front of a small crowd in Central Park, holding up his fist and speaking in a megaphone being held by a woman with her face out of frame.

Maarten (in video): *We offered them peace, and they answered with crowd control drones! We held out our hand and they slapped it with nightsticks! You know why, right?* [Incoherent whooping.] *Yeah, I'll tell you why! Because violence is the only language the Autocracy understands.* [Boos.] *Violence is the only way they know!*

Maarten: Ah... [Pause.] Look, we weren't thinking straight... I never meant for the riots to happen. Those were fringe elements of the movement. Extremists.

Interviewer: You didn't mean what you said about the Autocracy?

Maarten: [Agitated.] No. No, of course not!

●

Interviewer: Tell me about your grandson.

Olivia Castro (grandmother of Sylvia Castro): He is a hero to us all. His thirst for freedom has inspired a new generation to not only embrace immortality and its infinite rewards, but also appreciate what it means by giving us a vision of the alternative. It helped a new generation understand the need for the Autocracy.

Interviewer: And as a person? Tell me how he was growing up.

Castro: Oh, well, what is there to tell? He was a happy little boy. Full of life and energy, always laughing and running around. That's what surprised me when I heard he took the Mayfly Shot... He always seemed to love life so much.

Interviewer: Were there early signs of his madness?

Castro: Yeah. Yeah, sure.

Interviewer: Can you talk about those?

Castro: Well, for one he liked girl clothes. And playing with dolls. Once his mom tried to convince him to play with trucks and took his dolls away, but he just put the trucks to bed and told them bedtime stories. [Laughter.]

Interviewer: Do you think this has something to do with his decision to take the shot?

Castro: No.

Interviewer: Perhaps his gender dysphoria caused him a great deal of stress... Do you think it's possible that —

Castro: I thought you were writing a history of the Mayflies? Is this line of questioning sanctioned by your university's monitors?

Interviewer: I mean no dis —

Castro: Well, I resent your implication that Sylvain's parents and I failed him as caretakers.

Interviewer: That's not what I'm saying at all.

[Long pause.]

Castro: Oh my, look at the time. My apologies, but I have to prepare for a meeting.

●

Interviewer: Describe Sylvia Castro in the last days.

Wang Xian-zhi: In public or in private? In public she was her old self, like, boisterous, didn't give a shit about authority. She'd say things just to rile you up, then laugh with her mouth open and her head thrown back, like she just heard the funniest joke. She'd party harder than any of us, even when she was stuck in bed. One time she had us pour vodka directly into her saline bag!

Interviewer: And in private?

Wang: Well, she was... quieter. She'd watch us from her bed with that big grin of hers, like she wanted to make sure everyone had a good time. But when she figured no one was looking, she'd get that look in her eyes.

Interviewer: That look?

Wang: You know, man. Like she couldn't wait for this shit to be over.

●

Interviewer: You were one of the first rioters to enter Melody, correct?

Herbert Gilmore (rioter): I was an activist, not a rioter. But yeah.

Interviewer: Why were you and other activists trying to enter the center?

Gilmore: The movement was losing steam. The media was portraying us as looters and madmen, so we knew we had to do something big. And the Mayflies, well, they had started all of this, right? We figured they could help. Especially Sylvia.

Interviewer: Were the Mayflies what you expected?

Gilmore: Not at all. I mean, I've seen pictures of old people from ancient times, I know what they're like. They don't feel real, though, know what I mean? You see all those wrinkles... You don't realize they're actual *grooves*. And some of the Mayflies didn't seem entirely lucid, either. And they moved so slow, like frozen bugs...

Interviewer: Tell me what it was like seeing the Mayflies for the first time in sixty years.

Gilmore: The Melody staff had moved them to the community hall because the Autocracy had warned them we were coming. We, well... We convinced the staff to let us talk to them. When I opened the door... It's the smell I noticed first. It was an *animal* smell, like when you get a whiff of a carcass by the side of the road, right? Except... It came from living human beings.

Interviewer: How did the Mayflies react?

Gilmore: They were... Honestly, they were relieved to see us. A bunch of them were crying. They thought we had come to save them.

Interviewer: Save them from what?

Gilmore: Yeah, well. That's the question that keeps me up at night.

●

Video footage seized from Wang's personal collection, on lease from Montreal's Self-Enforcement Agency.

[The video is shot at the Mayfly Center during the break-in, and shows Sylvia, in bed, surrounded by monitors and hooked up to a dialysis machine. Her cheekbones jut through the parchment-like skin of her face.]

Wang Xian-zhi (offscreen, filming): Sylvia! We gotta go! The protestors have broken in. They're here for us!

[Sylvia half-opens her eyes.]

Sylvia: Tell them they're too late.

Wang: C'mon, Syl. They say they can reverse the Mayfly Shot. We don't have to die anymore, man!

[Sylvia, her eyes now fully open, stares in silent anger at Wang.]

Wang: You're a legend out there, Sylvia! They need a leader.

Sylvia: [Tired chuckle.] Please. I can't even piss by myself anymore. [Long silence.] No... Better they think I went out rocking with my tits out and a cig in my mouth.

Wang: [Choking back tears.] C'mon, Syl. You can't die. Not you.

[Sylvia attempts to laugh, but all she manages is a wheeze. Still, in that moment, she looks something like her old self.]

Sylvia: Of course I can. I've been dying my whole life.

Daniel Roy's story "Forever and a Life" was originally published in Metaphorosis on Friday, 12 April 2019. See magazine.metaphorosis.com

About the author

Daniel Roy is a Canadian video game narrative writer, slow traveler, and backpack foodie. Originally from Montreal, he has also lived in China, South Korea, India, Mexico, and Bulgaria.

Country Whispers

Matthew Amundsen

Seeing the bodies of them girls hanging outside the town's gates made me think coming here was a bad idea, but it was too late to go back now. The driver, Finnas, didn't seem the type to turn these horses around no matter what I said, and Maw would send me right back even if he did. The kitties dangling alongside the girls made me feel worse. I didn't know if the girls did anything bad to anybody, but I knew for sure those kitties never hurt anyone. Witches, that told me, but who knew if it was true. Town folk tend to blame natural things they don't understand on witches.

Finnas shoved my head back between the haystacks and told me to keep my mouth shut. Just as well. I didn't want to see any more.

Snapping the reins, he drove the cart through the gates. Since it was almost nighttime, the town was quiet. All I heard was the rumble of the wheels until we came to a stop. He hopped down quick, and I heard him heave and grunt as some big doors groaned open. He jumped back up and drove the cart a little ways more before stopping for good. Somebody said something and he got down again.

I stuck out my head and saw a tall, fancy-dressed lady standing in a dusty courtyard surrounded by a fence taller than two men. Just beyond was a wide house, bigger than any I'd ever seen. Finnas tried to give her a hug and a kiss, but she pushed him off and cocked her head at me. I sucked in air and ducked down, but it was too late. The woman had spotted me.

"You girl, come down here."

My face burning like a kid caught stealing a pie, I climbed down from the cart to show myself.

"Are you Leusa Wrothburn?"

"Yes'm." I ducked my head down like Maw said I should, but I couldn't bring myself to curtsy. Just ain't something I'm much good at. I didn't see what the big deal was anyway. This woman had no reason to make me feel bad for being who I was. From the look of her, she was a tough bird, but I hadn't done anything to be ashamed of.

"Do you know where you are?"

"Yes'm. I reckon we're in the town of Stonefeld."

"Correct. And do you know who I am?"

I gave her another look without trying to be nosy. "No, ma'am, but I reckon you're somebody important by your fancy dress and the size of this here house."

"Good. Maybe you're not as simple as they said you were. I'm Ulna Fustable. The Magistrate of Stonefeld is my husband. I don't know if you've heard way out in the woods where your folk are from, but he's been having some problems with witches." She said the word like it was something too nasty to say out loud but she had to anyway. All I could think about when she said it was those poor kitties strung up with the girls at the town's gate. "We need another serving girl around here after the last one was found to be lacking, and my husband doesn't trust any of the girls from town. The birth register said you have a sister. That true?"

"Yes'm. Tessa's working for a family over in Brasston now." Daft cow got herself seeded by one of the lord's manservants, but the Magistrate's wife didn't need to know that.

"Your mama all alone now?"

I nodded. This lady was sharp.

"I'll make sure she gets your pay then. Nothing you can spend it on around here anyway."

I wanted to say that Maw didn't deserve anything from me on account of the way she treats me, but just this once I kept my mouth shut. I wasn't happy about it but complaining never solved anything.

"You'll do anything you're asked — laundry, sweep, help prepare food. I expect you to be the first one up in the morning and the last one to sleep. Don't talk to any of the other serving girls unless spoken to, and stay out of my husband's way. Understand that you are not allowed beyond these walls. The last thing my husband needs is gossiping townsfolk." She looked me up and down to make sure I'd been listening. "All that sit okay with you?"

"Yes'm."

"Good. You can stay in the room next to the stable for now. Supper's in the kitchen but it's cold. Finnas will show you."

"Thank you, ma'am," I said. Seemed the right thing to say.

"And get that straw out of your hair, girl. Try to look proper."

Finnas unhitched the horses from the cart, and I followed him.

"Over there," he said, pointing at a door.

"Aye."

The room was nothing but a closet under the stairs that led to Finnas' loft. Maw told me I had to sleep inside if the Fustables told me to. Town folk look down on them who sleep outside, like we were some kind of animal. Maybe I was an animal. Didn't bother me none. Animals never did wrong to nobody who didn't deserve it.

Through the wall, I heard them horses hassling Finnas because he didn't understand them. He thought sugar cubes and a switch was the answer to everything. When they finally gave up and quieted, he trudged up the stairs to his room. His boots boomed when they hit the floor. He never did show me where they kept the leftovers. Didn't matter. I wasn't hungry.

I tried to sleep, but couldn't. Rooms and I never got along, and this one felt like as much of a jail as any other. The stillness and the quiet suffocated me. At least I could smell the horses through the walls. That was some comfort, anyway.

In the middle of the night, a door from the house sighed open, feet scuffed the courtyard and then someone stalked the stairs above my room. Finnas' bed creaked for a while overhead, and then that someone came back down. Wasn't my business who, though I had a guess.

I waited another hour or two before getting up to take a look around the courtyard and see what I could do to stay busy. First thing I noticed was a measly stack of logs next to the kitchen. Place this size always needs firewood. Problem was, I didn't see an ax anywhere and I wasn't about to go rattling the stable doors and get Finnas after me at this hour.

Since no one else was around, I wandered around the back of the stables, out of sight of the main house. The property went only a little farther before the fence hemmed it in. Clusters of hospras grew here, stiff and unhappy. I felt bad for them trees, trapped here while others grew free on the other side of the fence, where there weren't no folks to tame them into lesser versions of themselves.

I dropped a seed and sprouted a taccab leaf from it with a few quiet words. I dried it with a hush and rolled it into a smoke, which helped me think about what to do with what I been dealt. Something itched my scalp as I stood there sucking that taccab, telling me I found what I forgot I was looking for. I pinched the cherry off the taccab and kicked around in the scrub until I felt that unsettled thing. There.

Trapped under a bush thick with long grass and vines, a dull throbbing ax head stuck atop a shriveled handle. Rusted and forgotten, I knew how to make it feel better. Metal was dangerous to whisper, but I could see this poor tool needed my help. I reminded the blade of when it was properly seasoned and sharp and full o' glory, and it responded in kind. I told the shrunken handle how it used to be stout and firm, fit to be swinging. At first ashamed at its fallen state, it soon remembered its bold peak and found its shape again. Now I could do my job.

A bunch of the hospras weren't tended proper, and leaned over as if all their life had dripped out already. I listened for the right ones calling for mercy. Taking care since people was sleeping, I asked the sound to turn inside-out so no one would hear. Half a dozen hospras came down that way. I chopped and split and stacked them next to the logs outside the kitchen and then continued the pile around the corner when I ran out of room. That should last them a few weeks or a month if they were frugal. The tightness in Miss Ulna's mouth made me think squandering resources was not something she tolerated.

I didn't know where the ax should rightly go, so I stuck it back under the same bush and thanked it for letting me borrow it. I asked the bush to hold the ax in its branches tight like a babe, to blanket it with leaves. Any stranger who stumbled upon it would have a hard time convincing the bush to let go.

Figuring I'd done enough for now, I climbed a thick hospra to watch the sun rise. I must have fallen asleep because the next thing I knew, the cock jumped up and told everybody what was on his mind.

I heard scuffling from the kitchen and jumped down to wait outside the door. With a mop of grey curls and a long-faded apron, the cook looked like she'd been sampling her own creations for years. Which was a good sign, since nobody trusted skinny cooks anyway. Yawning, she grabbed a couple of logs for morningfire, saw the new stacks I'd made and stood in shock. She jumped like she saw a ghost when she noticed me hovering.

"You must be the new girl. Miss Ulna told me to look out for you." She followed the stack of wood around the corner. "You see who did this?"

"I chopped the wood, ma'am."

She looked me up and down, suspicious. "You? In one night? In the dark?"

"Yes, ma'am. The moon was plenty bright."

She narrowed her eyes like she didn't believe me. "How come nobody woke up?"

Maw told me not to do my whispers in town 'cause people will think I'm a witch or such. I been called worse by Maw herself in one of her moods, but I seen how this town treated girls they didn't like, and their cats, so I figured Maw's advice made as much sense as any.

I shrugged. "I did it quiet."

She looked at me like I was trying to be smart with her, but I didn't smile or nothing and she let it go. Looking again at the woodpile, she stepped close to me, wide-eyed and whispering so no one would overhear. "Did you use an ax?"

I chuckled at this. "How else do you chop wood?"

Her voice grew stern. "This ain't a laughing matter, country girl. Didn't you see what the menfolk did to those poor girls when you came here?"

I started to worry a little. "Hard to miss."

"No woman in town is allowed to use a metal blade or anything with a sharp edge."

Stonefeld was even worse than I imagined. "That's crazy talk."

The cook huffed. "You don't know the half of it. But things are gonna change real soon."

Didn't seem likely, but no point arguing.

She took another look at me and must have noticed the simple way I dressed in clothes I'd sown myself, with hair I cut without so much as looking in a river for a reflection. "I don't suppose you get much news about Stonefeld where you're from."

"Nothing that happened in this town was any of my business before today."

"Well, you best make it your business now. Yet I can't lie, we needed that wood. So, thanks for that. Play dumb around Finnas and Miss Ulna if they ask you about it. I get the feeling you're smarter than they think."

"I don't know about that, ma'am." I smiled despite myself.

"Save that 'ma'am' business for Miss Ulna. Call me Makzeet."

She stuck out her hand, and I gave it the customary one-shake like men do. "Leusa."

"Don't wander too far in case I need you later, but steer clear of the menfolk. They're no good. Us women got to stick together."

I found a broom and swept up the courtyard some until Makzeet had me fetch eggs from the coop. I felt a little bad telling them hens I was gonna treat their eggs nice, but they had to believe that so they wouldn't peck me when I swiped their unborn babies. The eggs were pretty blues and browns, sometimes a swirl of both, and I gathered them in the dopey apron Maw insisted I wear when Finnas drove me off from her place. Funny that the thing was useful after all.

I brought my bounty into the kitchen and felt someone's eyes sticking to me. I didn't dare peek who until Makzeet took the last egg from the bundle and shooed me back outside. When I ducked out the door, I looked back and saw a serving girl around my age, wearing clothes no better than mine. Her eyes said she didn't know what kind of creature I was; not scared or disgusted, only curious.

After lunch, I spied the Magistrate for the first time when Finnas helped him lurch into the wagon. Bloated and crabby, fella like that gave me the shivers just thinking about him. He and Finnas left the compound in a cloud of dust, flapping like a couple of pompous geese kicked out of a pond. I almost felt bad for the horses pulling them, though really they were happy just to get out of the stables. Being stuck in small places ain't good for nobody.

The whole place grew real quiet once their cart rumbled away. Even Makzeet knocked off somewhere, her big copper pot drying outside. Nobody was coming or going or asking for me, so I slipped around the back of the stables and found me a wide hospra I could lean against and watch the sky over the fence, dreaming of the forest where I wished I was.

Bored and homesick, I dropped another taccab seed and encouraged a tendril from it, one I sweet-talked into sprouting and bursting enough for me to pull off a few leaves. With a word, they shriveled in my hand and rolled themselves tight. I dared one to ignite and spent its length basking in the smoke of home. The home I made, not the one I came from. A couple of footsteps behind me made me pinch the roll dead, tuck it and the fresh ones under my skirt.

"Don't stop on my account." The serving girl from before sat across from me, both of us hidden from anyone who might be looking our way from the back of the house. "I was hoping you'd share."

I smiled at that and handed her a fresh one while plucking out my leftover for myself. She looked around then back at me, wondering how to light it. I'd forgotten town folk don't know the name of the flame or the proper way to talk to it.

"Is that the best you can do?" I asked. Nothing motivates fire like antagonism.

The serving girl looked at me funny, thinking I was talking to her and almost scared about it, until her roll started smoldering on its own.

"Oh," she said, nodding like she understood all along. She took a greedy drag and yakked like a badger. She smiled once she caught her breath and shook her head. "Been so long, I forgot how it was. I'm Trixa."

"Leusa."

"Nice to meet you."

She took a more practiced drag this time and grimaced only a little. "I don't know what it's like where you're from, but women are forbidden to smoke in Stonefeld."

"Between all the things women ain't supposed to do and those hangings, I got to wonder why any women live here at all."

Trixa scrunched her eyes and looked upset. Maybe I shouldn't have said anything. "Where are we supposed to go?"

She had a point. Not everyone is cut out to live by themselves in the woods like me or Maw. Just ask my sister. And even Maw insisted on a proper home with four walls and a roof. I was different than most, I guess.

"What did those dead girls do?"

Trixa scowled at me until she realized I really didn't know. Looking over my shoulder back toward the house, she whispered that the girls were found together in the woods, naked, their cats nearby. She leaned back, drifting away like the smoke from her dwindling roll.

I rolled my eyes. If these people could only see me on a warm day with nobody but the bugs, birds, and beasts watching me, they'd think me just as wicked. I couldn't say that to Trixa, though.

"Before they were hung, they said Miss Sangela put them up to it."

"Who's that?"

Trixa's jaw dropped though her smile was genuine. "You really are from the middle of nowhere, aren't you?"

I never told her that, but it was true. I'd still be there but for having to do my daughterly duty so as not to dishonor our family name or our progeny. Maw and I both knew I'd never have progeny, so I figured she meant my sister's bastard.

"Miss Sangela was our schoolteacher, but now she's going to be tried as a witch day after tomorrow. We won't let the same thing happen to her."

In a place where a girl couldn't smoke or hold a knife and had to wear clothes like a dress-up dolly, a place where being natural got you killed, I didn't see any way out of it. People who would hang cats would hang anybody for anything. No point saying that to Trixa, though. Let her have hope, if only for another day.

A door slapped against a frame, and we both jumped to our feet.

"Stay away from the Magistrate and Finnas," Trixa whispered. She ran to the kitchen before Makzeet could call her name.

I hung back, because I didn't like the way the wind stirred in the courtyard. Not much later, Finnas ran his horses through the gate, trotting them to a halt outside the Magistrate's residence. Part of me wanted to disappear among the hospras, but curiosity got the better of me. I wanted another look at the man who ran a town like this.

Heaving, corpulent, the Magistrate needed Finnas to help him down from the carriage. To his credit, Finnas spared his boss the curses he used to guide his stable. The Magistrate waddled toward his home without looking backward until he stiffened like a hound catching the stink of a fox. Me, had to be. But Finnas led him on inside, and the Magistrate never saw me. Next time I had to stay out of sight.

That night, Makzeet let me finish what was left in the pot after everyone had their fill. I didn't mind going last. The bits at the bottom had the most taste anyhow, soaking in all them flavors all day long. I even used a spoon, which woulda made Maw proud. Felt good not to have to make my own fire, cook my own food. Had to admit it tasted better than mine too.

I washed the dish I messed and went to my room. Any fresh bed I could make myself in the forest would be softer and cleaner than the lifeless flop they gave me here. I made do, though, as Maw said I had to, and fell asleep after wondering how that would ever happen in this dank box. I don't think I'd been sleeping long when the soft thump of bare feet padding up the stairs over my head woke me. The door to Finnas' quarters creaked in the stillness, and pretty soon the sound of two people trying to be quiet kept me from falling back asleep. I used their escalating rutting to hide the creak of my own door, and slipped out back. I lay tucked away between a pair of bushes I softened with flattery and flowers, and dozed off before I knew it.

Something soft and ticklish ran under my nose, waking me while the swollen moon reigned over everything. I started awake, suddenly alert, and saw a cat. The creature came back for another pass, and I reached out a hand, welcoming, accepting. I knew she was a she as soon as I touched her. She leaned into my touch, receptive, and we were friends. She swiped past me one more time and then sauntered away. Curious, I watched her go. She sensed I wasn't following her and swiveled her head over her shoulder, looking for my eyes. Smirking at the boldness of this creature I stood up and shadowed her.

This cat didn't know any better and headed for the house, which made me nervous. I knew cats were mysterious to the point of sacred, but I was pretty sure these town folk didn't feel the same way. The closer she got to the building, the faster I chased after her, until it became some kind of game. She stopped at the kitchen door and skirted aside when I caught up to her. Rubbing up against my leg and looking up at me, her mouth stretched as if mewing, but made no sound. I didn't know what she wanted until she clawed the bottom of the door and attempted to pull it open. By the marks on the wood, this wasn't the first time. This cat obviously lived here, and I was the only one who didn't know it. Should have expected the Magistrate to be a hypocrite.

"Here, girl," I said, guiding a stick through a gap in the door to unlatch it and holding the door open long enough for her to disappear inside. I couldn't latch it back, but didn't expect anyone would know the difference. Too tired to go back where I'd been, I gave my room another try. That might have been the thing that spared my life.

Some time later, I heard a muffled scream from within the house. Someone wailed at some offence, and everything stilled that heard it. Even Finnas startled in his bed above me, his snorts stifled unexpectedly aware, waiting for another shout from the dark. An erratic wail keened from the house in stops and stutters until concerned murmuring blanketed it into silence. Whatever happened in there, best I didn't know. After that, it was quiet so long that I figured the worst was over. Even Finnas fell back asleep, by the sawing breath above me.

Yells from the house cut that short. The Magistrate opened a second floor window and shouted for us to present ourselves in the courtyard immediately. He sniffed and slammed the window shut.

Finnas came down the steps faster than I could get out of the closet underneath. Makzeet, Trixa, and half a dozen other servants filed from the house, everybody but me in their sleeping clothes. Groggy, disheveled, and confused, we lined up as asked. I looked toward the two I knew, but couldn't read their faces. We waited, nervous, but nothing happened for a long time. I wanted to go back to bed, even the pathetic one that was mine, rather than stand here.

The Magistrate finally hobbled into the courtyard to confront us. With his wife at his side, he resumed yelling for us to present ourselves as if we were the tardy ones and not his sorry self. He stabbed the air with his cane as he accosted us with a bizarre tantrum about his importance to Stonefeld and the sanctity of his lineage. He referred a couple of times to scratches and stitches and the demonic nature of felines, and I slowly pieced together what made him rave. That cat had gouged him deep and true, and he knew someone had let it in.

"That sort of vermin isn't allowed in town, let alone these premises! Do any of you understand how serious this is? I could have you all flogged — or worse!"

None of us looked him in the eye. Whenever I tried to sneak a peek, Miss Ulna stared me down. She knew. Maybe she didn't know exactly what she knew, but she knew it had something to do with me. I knew all along it wasn't right for me to live in town. I tried telling Maw and Finnas too, but no one listened, and here I was stuck where I didn't belong.

"Maybe one of you is a witch," the Magistrate spewed at last, as if confirming to himself aloud his gut instinct.

Miss Ulna reacted sharp and cross to that. "You think I'd let a witch slip past me, Harmon? I'm the one who runs this place while you're besotting yourself at the public house."

The Magistrate glowered but had no answer, looking embarrassed. His grip on his cane wobbled like he wasn't sure what to do next. He looked me up and down, seeing me for the first time. "What about that one?"

"She's nothing but a shivering little field mouse. Look at her."

I didn't agree, but played along. What her game was, I didn't know. But it worked.

"If it happens again, I'll blame you," her husband finally gruffed at her, limping away without looking back.

Miss Ulna spared us the dramatics, but not the sparks. She seethed like she was about to jump right out of her skull. "I expect you all know that felines are not welcome here. Any exceptions to this will be dealt with next time by the town council, and they will not be so forgiving as me. Is that understood?"

We said yes, almost under our breaths, but audible enough to qualify as a response.

"Good. Now leave my sight."

The moon fell before I ventured outside of my closet again. I wanted a taccab roll real bad, but couldn't risk Miss Ulna's anger if she caught a whiff. With the fear of witches in the air, now wasn't the time to take chances on little things. After last night's fiasco, I could tell the Magistrate was the type of man who looked for excuses to make people feel lesser than him. But damnation did I want a smoke.

I hid among the hospras when I heard Finnas come down for morning meal. The Magistrate's bellowing chased him from the kitchen before long. Finnas scrambled into the stables and returned with the horses and carriage. After grunts, groaning, and complaints from both him and the horses, he helped the Magistrate clamber aboard. Only when I heard the clopping hooves and strike of reins fading away did I dare venture out. Shy, I peered into the kitchen without a word until Makzeet noticed me poking around. She wiped her hands on her apron, looked over her shoulder, and waved me in.

"Quick, eat before she comes down."

Makzeet pushed a bowl of grain meal at me before I could object and sat across from me, watching me pitch it in. The look in her eye worried me some, and I swallowed without hardly chewing.

"She's in a fit this morning. You'd best make yourself scarce."

I nodded, gulping down my last mouthful. I stood and went toward the wash bucket, but Makzeet took the bowl from me and shooed me out the door.

Apologizing to a hospra for my rudeness, I climbed its low branches and asked nicely if it would turn its coarse bark smooth for a little while. Now soft, its branches snugged together to cradle me like a babe. In return, I promised it would grow tall and strong and with a few words made it safe from blade and fire. Anything less would be rude.

I was almost asleep when the back door clapped shut with a bang. From my perch, I saw Trixa carrying a basket of laundry piled as high as her head. I climbed down to help. Trixa acted like she didn't want to see me. She changed direction when she saw me coming and tried to again when I grabbed the basket. She wouldn't look me in the eyes, and I didn't know why until I remembered about the cat. Why anyone hated cats still made no sense to me, but I guess I did get everybody yelled at.

"He could have hung us all because of you," she growled at last.

"Let me help," I said. "I can do that much."

Trixa acted like she hadn't heard, but she couldn't get away if I didn't let go. She looked over her shoulder to make sure no one watched us before dropping the basket. She said nothing more while we hung the clothes and linens to dry. After a while I got tired of her silence and tried acting silly to make her laugh so she'd remember we were friends, but she didn't budge. After we hung the last sheets, I noticed we had corridors of cloth hiding us from the house. I spun around to spark a roll and turned back to Trixa with it lit only to find Miss Ulna instead. Her anger still boiled with a fury that could end me right quick.

"Did you scratch my husband?" The sheets whipped behind her like a curse.

I yelped and dropped the roll. "I never hurt nothing or nobody."

By the cooling of her face, she believed me. She nodded as if knowing my mind, acknowledging the truth of it. "You're not a shapeshifter, are you? You prefer the company of animals to people, but most of your powers lie with plants. The chopped wood, the extra flowers, the taccab. I get it." She waved her hand as if it were beneath her.

I shook my head, denying everything.

"Really, Leusa Wrothburn. Do you really think I would have hired you without knowing who you were and what you could do? That would have been irresponsible."

"How did — ?"

"None of your business. But you don't have to worry about me. What you do isn't like that witch stuff. Your talent is natural."

The sheets stopped flapping behind her, my heart slowed to normal, and I calmed my breathing.

"Those girls hanging —"

"Those girls hanging are lucky. The forces they were fooling with were about to tear them apart. They are none of your concern."

The kitties were what really concerned me, but she didn't need to know that.

Miss Ulna bent toward me to speak quietly even though the drying laundry sheltered us plenty. "Trixa told you there's a trial tomorrow. Between you and me, my husband fears for his life, and wants every man in town to carry a freshly sharpened blade to the trial. Problem is, the smith can't handle it all by himself and could use some help. What do you think?"

I shook my head. "I've never done anything like that."

"That ax doesn't count?"

"It's not the same. I can't do something that might hurt somebody."

Miss Ulna leaned closer and whispered mean. "How do you think my husband will react when I tell him you were the one who put that cat in our house? Does he seem like a forgiving man to you?"

Thinking of Maw, I bowed my head. She probably wouldn't approve even if she knew I had no choice. "I don't know if I can do it, but I'll try."

Miss Ulna picked up the empty laundry basket and straightened. "Wonderful. Finnas will bring the blades to your room. Finish what you can, and he'll get them in the morning. Don't speak of this to anyone."

She left without looking back, and I climbed a tree.

Sure enough, later that afternoon, Finnas clattered into the courtyard with a loaded wagon. I didn't have to guess where he was gonna drop his cargo. No point in watching. I didn't have time to get down before he rode off and returned with another load. I wondered if there'd be a third one, but heard him putting the horses to bed. Not until he clomped up the stairs after dinner did I dare peek inside what they called my room.

I caught them preening when I walked in, their squeaks like hungry chicks. They rattled in their boxes, following me with their glittery crescent smiles topped with motley handles of different makes, different ages, and different life experiences. Maw always said never to walk with metal, said it so much I couldn't tell if it was her powers of insistence or a motherly warning. But I saw them now and understood how easy it was to fall in love.

I didn't know how I knew their language until I heard it. Stepping inside and closing the door behind me, I knelt to be near them. Yearning so close to their true selves, wanting to be their best versions — that I understood. But they weren't like the ax, which was a necessary tool for survival. These blades wanted death and power. This was wrong, profane, but I couldn't help myself.

The proper way to sharpen metal is to tell it stories. They have to be the kind metal likes, stories about bravery and love and sacrifice. As I whispered some faerie tales I knew, they grew, matured, sparkled. Their glass promises became crystalline realities. The closer I realized their vision, they less they needed me until they didn't need me at all. I'd shown them the way, and now I was spent. Helpless, I watched them swell and glisten, elongate and narrow to the finest edge forever, fulfilling their destiny of harm. Their screeches grew so loud it hurt my ears, terrified me.

I ran from the room to the farthest hospra on the Magistrate's property, ripping up that foolish apron Maw made me wear, leaving it in shreds on the ground. How that false sense of purpose had filled me and drained me just as quick left me sick. I never wanted to come here, to live among town folk, to sharpen knives for a bunch of men to make themselves feel stronger in a world they already controlled. I was half-tempted to climb the fence and disappear into the woods, but thought them town folk would brand me a witch for sure if I did. I fell asleep in the hospra pondering what to do next about those blades I had made my children.

●

The faded sweet perfume of a parfenia blossom clung to the air when I woke up. That surprised me, since it wasn't spring. Nor did I see any petals, but they usually withered when the sun come up anyhow. The dumb cock had long since spoken. Groggy from parfenia-induced sleep, I climbed down from my hospra bed resolved. The knives had to listen to reason. They had to go back to what they had been. Then I'd tell Miss Ulna that it was beyond my powers to do what she wanted.

Finnas and his horses were already gone, and the rest of the estate was silent as an eclipse. Nor were there any sounds from my room. The knives were gone.

There would be no peace with my children loose like this. The compound gates were open, and I ran outside. The distant roar of a crowd told me why the streets were empty and where everybody was. Huffing, I made it to the edge of the crowd. The square was packed, and the Magistrate's cart was nowhere to be found. Slipping between people who never knew I existed, I could only get so far before people congealed around me. I heard the tiny chattering of the overeager knives, but couldn't figure where they were coming from.

On a platform in the middle of the square stood a tall, dark-haired woman with a rope draped around her neck and hands tied behind her back. Underneath the platform was a pile of firewood, as if hanging weren't permanent enough. Whatever she was accused of doing, it must have been so bad they wanted to kill her twice.

The crowd shushed, and I pushed forward looking for my unnatural creations. I didn't want my whispers to hurt anybody. Some folks were put off by my boldness and put up enough of a grumble that it caught Miss Ulna's attention from where she stood at the front of the mob. Rather than get mad, she gave me half a smile and put a finger to her lips. Makzeet and Trixa stood on either side of her, nodding when they saw me. In Trixa's hair was a pink parfenia blossom, impossibly preserved.

The Magistrate gimped the short distance to the front of the platform. Townsmen crowded around him, shouting their support while hoisting axes and wheat scythes, bows and spears. None of their weapons talked to me, though I still heard the knives' faint voices.

Clearing his throat, the Magistrate puffed liked a bullfrog. "Sangela Terns of Stonefeld, you stand accused of foulness against the Maker. You have brought animality, wanton sensuality, and unnatural congress to our town. How do you plead before your fellow townsfolk?"

"I don't have to answer to anybody here."

The Magistrate harrumphed like this sort of outrageous response was beneath him. "Then I have no choice but to pronounce you guilty."

Sangela spit at the Magistrate, though she was too far away to reach him. She laughed when his puss soured and even more at the crowd's gasps and curses. Her hair collected itself into a ponytail, slunk across her shoulder and twitched like a cat's tail. Not just any cat, I saw now. Black and silky like it would glow in the moonlight, like it would waltz through the courtyard, like it would rub up against you and make you its friend.

"By official decree of the township of Stonefeld, I condemn you to death by hanging and burning." He made it sound more like a condition than a judgment.

Sangela only laughed louder. "Hanging and burning? Is that all?"

Some in the crowd guffed despite themselves. The Magistrate stumbled backward as if the words had been physical blows. He called his supporters to him. The knives hushed completely, like they were preparing to strike, and that scared me most.

"Enough. Men, ignite the pyre and drop the ropes by the common decree of Stonefeld and the Maker we serve."

As the men of Stonefeld came forward with their weapons and torches, I heard the voices of my children begin to sing as, one by one, the women of Stonefeld withdrew blades from under their aprons, the folds of their skirts, the hems of their gowns.

Miss Ulna unveiled one of largest and most violent of my pupils as she approached her husband, speaking so everyone could hear. "Harmon Fustable, your authority means no more to us than the fortunes told in the smatterings of pigeon droppings."

Before he could close his gaping mouth, she stabbed her husband in the belly. Overwhelmed and dumbstruck, his men had no immediate reaction. The other women didn't hesitate, and soon all I could hear was the screams of men, the shrieking laughter of women and the harmonic voices of my babies in their bloody glory. The Magistrate climbed the scaffolding behind the platform but was hunted by both Miss Ulna and Sangela. I couldn't watch them carve him up.

Some of the men put up their hands in surrender, and they were spared. Those who fought back didn't last long. There were too many women and too many knives. Whether or not anybody deserved this, I didn't know anymore. I hated bloodshed, killing, death, and felt sick that I had helped this happen. Miss Ulna, Makzeet, and Trixa had made me their fool. Maybe even Maw. None of them cared about me any more than the knives had at the end.

I hated tears but they came anyway as I ran from the massacre toward the town's gates. Howls followed me like accusations, pushing me forward through the panicking masses. Wiping my eyes, I headed toward those morbid city gates. They burst open as I approached, and I didn't dare look up.

Beyond a small gulley lay the forest, wild and lush. Maybe there I could find a way to forgive myself. I left the road as fast as my legs would take me, disappearing into the woods. The air chased me like a zephyr, batting me like a toy, lashing my back like a hiss.

Matthew Amundsen's story "Country Whispers" was originally published in Metaphorosis on Friday, 7 June 2019. See magazine.metaphorosis.com

About the author

Matthew has lived in seven states and has worked in advertising, film and commercial production, and information management. He has been publishing fiction since 1990. When not writing, he is a musician and sound engineer in Minneapolis, where he lives with his daughter.

@gallopingfoxley

The Hissing Trees

Ian Donnell Arbuckle

The biovin Charis heard the rumors about the messenger long before he arrived at her laboratory. The watergirls whispered that he had come from the Calomlands, further east than their maps could show with any accuracy. He bore an important text for the yurchief, said one of the boiler technicians, though nobody had heard even a hint of the contents. One of the guard faithful let slip that the messenger had personally angered the yurchief and had been restrained almost immediately upon his arrival.

All took care to mention that he appeared to be on his last legs, having collapsed just on their borders, and that his hideous body bore the bloat of illness.

The yurchief's orders came to Charis through the precise, bored imperiousness of one of the younger faithful, his voice struggling to hold up the import of the words without cracking beneath the strain. "The biovin Charis is to extract from the messenger the content of the message. There will be no tolerance for fault, no allowance for failure."

Charis accepted the order with a calm nod, reserving her questions for the voice inside her. Why was she, a biovin, being tasked with this? Charis had none of the skills of the cryptonos, and she knew her political acumen was inadequate for the delicate job of interrogation. It had, in fact, been the cause of her effective banishment to this lab in the canyons, deep in Sound territory and far from the yurchief's gatherings.

She hadn't minded the isolation, and instead considered it something of a blessing. A place had been found for her where she could contribute the bread of her skills to the feast of her people. For the last few years, she had been reviewing the pharmaceutical work of her predecessor in the role, improving some compounds and helping to fabricate tabs for the yurchief and those in his pull. Most of the changes were incremental, glacial things that nevertheless gave her a continuing satisfaction that each small, stable adjustment maintained the whole.

Rarely did she see the results of her efforts, but she knew they were successful, if for no other reason than because the yurchief permitted her to continue her work undisturbed and untroubled. For the most part. She liked her work, and her work accepted her in silence. Days could pass between opportunities for her to speak with another living creature. She liked that just fine.

"What am I to do with this foreign messenger?" She only asked it aloud after the young guard faithful had left to deliver her note of obedience back to the yurchief. She kept asking it, mostly to the quiet spaces in her head, until she got her first look at the messenger himself the next day.

Two more of the guard faithful escorted him into her lab. The rumors had been inadequate. He was repulsive to behold, his body a battlefield of open sores, wild lumps of tumors, and ulcerous cavities. He hunched beneath rags that scraped over uneven shoulders, blood and pus staining the stinking fabric. His face could hardly bear an expression, given how the flesh had mottled and bulged with disease. Growths settling from his brow and rising up from his cheeks trapped his eyes in a deep valley, but within all that they shone a clear blue and his gaze was direct. He seemed to study Charis with at least as much intensity as she did him.

He wore shackles on his wrists which, though loose, had nevertheless left deep red welts where they touched his skin.

"Am I to cure him?" asked Charis, taken aback.

"You are to extract from the messenger the content of his message." It was the same instruction, repeated. Though it came from a different pair of lips, the tone was the same as the first time she had heard it: a committed, tremulous tenor.

"By means of...?" Charis prompted.

"There will be no tolerance for fault —"

"I understand," interrupted Charis, who could not abide time wasted on repetition.

"I may be able to illuminate somewhat," said the messenger. "If I may?" His voice was pitched low and each word carried a polite deference. There was a gentle if unpleasant rumble beneath them. Charis recognized the sound as betraying the presence of some fluid or phlegm in the lungs.

"I would appreciate that," she said.

"Of course." The messenger glanced to either side before continuing. Neither of the faithful made a move to stop him. "You see, I carry the message inside my cells." He raised limp hands to indicate the deformities about his body. The obvious effort of doing so was not solely due to the weight of the shackles, Charis guessed.

"Spun into the helices?" she asked, after running the messenger's words through the sieve of her mind.

The messenger's lips twisted into what may have been a smile or a grimace. "Essentially, yes," he said. "The text of the message is encoded among the information there, intended to be read only be those able to retrieve it. Do you think you can?"

Charis nodded faintly, the motion diminishing like the vibration of a loose cord. "Doing so will not relieve you of the cancer, you understand."

"I defer to your expertise," replied the messenger. His lungs convulsed and a wet coughing fit overcame him.

Charis frowned sharply at the faithful. "You may leave him with me. Tell the yurchief I will begin work immediately." With gratitude they were unable to conceal, the two young men backed away, then turned and left the laboratory. The messenger, unable to convey much with expression, cleared his throat and raised his arms a second time, this time in supplication. The chains on the shackles clanked heavily.

"May these be removed, my friend?"

Charis gave him a long look, calculating, and then shook her head. "I would be uncomfortable doing so at this time, though I do have some gauze I will insert as a buffer."

"I would appreciate that, thank you," said the messenger, echoing her tone from earlier. The mimicry didn't escape Charis' notice, but she was unsure of what to do with the information and set it aside for the time being.

"Please have a seat," she said, indicating the only chair in the room. It had five metal spokes at its base, each ending in a black caster. It rolled slightly as the messenger sank onto it.

"Thank you," he repeated.

Charis turned away to retrieve the roll of gauze from her supplies. The laboratory was a single, large space, lit in part by fluorescent tubes that hung low over a repurposed dining table, the sort one might expect to find in a chieftain's meeting hall. The table bore the wreckage of old electronics and automators, salvaged and scavenged and in various states of repair. A workstation idled at the center of one side, three wide monitors standing as bulwark against the junk. A dozen fans hummed away.

Beyond the sharp radius of the artificial lights, gray filtered sun sifted down from two high windows, one set to the north and the other to the south. Tree branches tapped against panes which had never been cleaned.

The walls were lined with mismatched shelves. The only thing each shared in common was how deeply they bowed under the weight of the materials Charis and her predecessors had collected. As much as was possible, the shelves had been kept tidy. Boxes and containers were arranged with clear separations and angles, as if snapped to an invisible grid.

Charis returned with the gauze. She cut two lengths and taped them around the messenger's wrists. She stood back as he adjusted the fall of the metal bracelets. He nodded once to her.

"Thank you again, my friend," he said.

"My name is Charis." She forestalled the smile that appeared to be growing on his lips with one raised finger. "I'm telling you this so you can call me something other than your friend."

"I understand," said the messenger.

"May I examine you?"

"Of course, Charis. I am an open book. Would you like me to move over toward the light?"

"Yes, if you would."

The messenger rolled the chair over toward the pool of fluorescent light with a series of kicks. He almost looked as if he were having fun. The joints of the chair squeaked with each movement.

Charis sat on a bench next to him and held him steady, spinning the chair slowly like a potter with a fresh lump of clay. "Which is the original tumor?" she asked, letting her eyes travel up and down his body.

"Ah, an interesting question. You're worried the message may not have been copied faithfully during metastasis, yes?"

Charis' first answer was a distracted half-nod. The messenger's back was to her now and she noted the dampness of blood across his shoulders. "Yes," she said, upon realizing she had turned him so that he could no longer see her.

"The message was originally encoded in my liver cells," the messenger said. "The tumors came after, I'm afraid."

"Hmm. I think I might biopsy some of these ones that are more easily accessible first."

"Whatever you think best, Charis, my friend."

●

It took some hours for Charis to prepare her equipment and to sterilize her tools using the little coal-stoked autoclave. During all that time, the messenger sat patiently. Only the occasional rattle of his chains as he adjusted his position called attention to him. Other than that, he remained silent except to answer Charis' minimal questions.

As Charis staged her surgical tray, though, he spoke up. "Did you build that yourself?" He nodded at the autoclave.

"I designed it," said Charis. "I'm untrained in smithing, though. The yurchief had it built to my specifications."

"He must trust you very much."

Charis searched the messenger's eyes for any sign of sarcasm. "No, that wouldn't be accurate to say," she corrected him with a shake of her head. "I already consume twice my energy allotment just running the refrigeration for the compounds and samples. He was unwilling to grant me more for the superheating. 'Fire or ice, biovin,' he said. One or the other. But he did eventually appreciate my ingenuity more than he did my complaints, I believe."

The messenger nodded. "A true leader."

Charis smiled in spite of herself, then clamped down on it as quick as a breath. She sat again on the bench beside the messenger and positioned her tray close to hand. "I could begin with one of the tumors on your neck, but I think I would prefer to examine your lymphs, if you'll permit it."

"Of course."

"I'll have to remove your shirt."

"If you'll do me the favor of being gentle, I have no objection."

It was hardly a shirt, more of a rough sack with holes for head and arms. "I'll have to cut it away," she said.

"Good. Let's be rid of the foul thing," said the messenger. "Burn it, for all I care."

Charis reached for her shears and turned the messenger in his chair so she could begin to work on the fabric across his shoulders. It took some effort to lift the garment away from his skin, stuck as it was with the gum of drying blood. The messenger inhaled sharply through his teeth.

"I apologize," said Charis. "I have some sugar cane, but I hoped to save that for the surgical sites."

"It's all right," said the messenger through gritted teeth. "Just talk to me. What is sugar cane?"

Charis paused for a moment, then continued at her task, cutting straight down from the middle of the neckline, following the path of the spine. "It's a compound my predecessor taught me. It deadens pain where injected."

"An anesthetic," said the messenger, nodding. "It's all right. We can save that for when it's really needed."

"May I ask —" Charis began, but silenced herself with a shake of her head.

"You may. I insist," said the messenger after a pause.

"What sort of message is worth the toll on your body?" Charis finished her cut and spread the shirt apart, lifting it with care from the messenger's shoulders. She nearly gasped at what she saw.

His back bore a few growths, rising close to his backbone, but worse than them were the dozens of whip strikes layered over his skin. Few of them had healed fully; none had healed well. Some were still oozing. The worst of them lay across his shoulder blades.

"I don't believe it was intended to take a toll at all," said the messenger. He shifted his toes on the floor, turning himself slowly until he could look at Charis in the eyes. "The 'biovins' back home did warn that there were risks, but perhaps this cancer has been fated in me since long before I was given the message, or came upon me after. It would have been nice to arrive here sooner, of course. I'm afraid I was delayed."

"Delayed by —"

Charis' words were cut off by the sound of her laboratory doors slamming open. The yurchief stamped into the room. He stood taller than six feet, broad in his shoulders but narrow in his face. Sealskins draped around his shoulders. Though he was proud of the skins, and of his own prowess in the hunting and killing of the beasts, Charis had often thought that they made him look as if he were forever carting around a pile of filthy laundry. His long hair had been stained red with choke cherries, several days ago by the smell of it.

He crossed the floor to Charis and the messenger before his two guard faithful attendants had even taken station beside the door. "Well?" he demanded, breathing in and holding it. "What is the message?"

"I have only just begun, yurchief," said Charis, lowering her gaze to the floor. "It will take time to extract the samples and then to put them in sequence. I have not practiced this, nor exercised the tech since my predecessor first instructed me in its use. And then I do not know how long it will take to decode the message into plain words, if we are able to retrieve it fully." She met the messenger's own downcast eyes and they held the moment shared between them. Charis got the impression that the messenger had told all of this to the yurchief already.

"I'm deaf to your excuses, biovin," said the yurchief. He curled one finger, rank with the smell of hide and sweat, beneath her chin and lifted her face. "Where is my message?"

"It's coming, your 'ness," she said.

"Good. You have one week. I depart this afternoon to visit the borders. Upon my return, I expect to hear my message."

"But that's —"

The yurchief's hand shifted and his fingernails suddenly bit into the soft flesh of her neck. "One week. If you are worried about fatigue, I grant you the boon of my speed. But not too much, understand?"

"Yes, yurchief."

"Good." He slackened his grip but left the tips of her fingers brushing the skin where bruises would soon form. Then he whirled, washing them in the stink of rancid oils. He snapped at his guard faithful, and the three of them swept out into the night. The laboratory door hung open behind them. A roar of laughter drifted in along with a cool breeze.

Charis went to the door, softness in her every step and motion, and closed it quietly.

"He is a storm among men," said the messenger.

She gave only half of a nod and then returned to his side. "He is not of this place," she said. "He came to us when I was young, and none among us can match him in prowess."

"I've known a few like him," said the messenger. "They do not allow for patience in the movement of things. They thrive in the center of the current, not in the eddies and back-drafts of life. Usually, I wish them well, since they will be long gone before I come to rest." He cleared his throat, which seemed to take more effort than he expected. He ended up spitting a wad of phlegm into the rags that had been his shirt. "He is one of many."

Charis withheld her hands from his skin until his shaking had subsided. Then she began to probe the sores on his back.

"What is the boon of his speed, may I ask?" said the messenger.

"It's a compound my predecessor held the recipe for. I've made some improvements. It keeps the mind alert and blots out weariness from the body."

"Ah. The good stuff," said the messenger. He gasped as Charis' thumb brushed one of the long welts.

"I apologize," she said.

"Please, don't pay me any mind. We have a job to do."

Charis nodded and continued. The signs of infection had spread beneath and around many of the welts, but the discharge was white-becoming-yellow. Treatable. "You said you were delayed reaching us. What happened?"

"It's a long story."

"Oh. You don't have to —"

"May I have some water before I begin?"

"Of course." On the way back from fetching a mug and filling it, Charis retrieved some more strips of clean gauze and a clay pot of salve. The messenger accepted the water gratefully and drank it down in one long gulp, suppressing a rising cough midway through without removing his lips from the mug.

"You shouldn't waste your time," he said, wiping his lips with the back of his hand and nodding at the salve and bandages.

"It may ease your discomfort," said Charis.

The messenger shrugged his agreement. "You're the doctor. Excuse me, the 'biovin'."

Charis moved around him and began carefully applying the salve to the worst infections.

The messenger took a deep breath and began his story. "Between here and the Calomlands, there are three great changes in the land. First, coming from my home, there is a wide plain where sharp ravines scar the flat grasses like claw marks left by enormous beasts. On the other side of those plains, there is a mountain range, peaks taller than any you have around here, but colored gray and white only. Stone and ice. Beyond them is the dwindling forest, plenty green but sparse and thinning. Then comes the mist and the deepness of the bay here — my apologies, the 'Sound'.

"I left my home at the end of winter, hoping to reach and cross the mountain range before the next winter's snow could fall. And I very nearly did.

"My path through the mountains brought me past another tribe. They were not the intended recipients of my message, and I thought it better not to announce my presence to them, so I skirted their holdings and attempted an uncharted route down to the foothills. I was... unsuccessful.

"This tribe — they referred to themselves as the Mallers — caught up with me before I could get far. They set upon me at night, while I was groggy with the cold, and bound me hand and foot. They took me to the edge of a deep canyon between two plateaus and tossed me into a hole a ways back from the precipice, three times as deep as I am tall. There were a dozen others in that hole, all of them ragged and filthy and scared. Our dialects weren't in complete agreement, but before the night was out we were communicating and I learned that I had been pressed into the service of a mighty feat of engineering. The Mallers were building a bridge between the two plateaus. It was a massive thing, indeed."

There was a brief silence while the messenger cleared his throat and gathered his thoughts. While he did, Charis refilled his mug of water. He accepted it and sipped it less greedily than before.

"How long did they keep you there?" Charis asked.

"Three winters," said the messenger, nodding as he heard Charis' involuntary gasp. "And this illness did not rest idle during that time. By the end of it, everyone looked upon me with revulsion."

"They gave you no rest, despite your condition?"

"During my time there, I saw others forced to work until their hearts stopped. My condition, as it worsened, did nothing but earn me a few lashes for my deficiencies."

"'A few'," Charis scoffed.

"Is it so different here?" asked the messenger. "I noted gibbets along the roads. And my guards may have muttered a threat or two that seemed downright believable, not to mention the indignities the yurchief impresses on his prisoners."

There was silence while Charis' face fell. "No," she admitted. "It's not so different here." She took a breath and made a decision before letting the air escape. She crossed to her work table and trailed her fingers over the tools there until she found what she was looking for. Returning to the messenger, she sat and spun him to face her, pulling his shackles forward so she could bend over them with a pick and tension wrench at the ready.

"How did you escape?" she asked while she worked.

"Through no effort of my own." The messenger chuckled. "One night, as we were returning to our pits, an electrical storm lit up the horizon. I've never seen anything like it. It takes much longer to describe than it did to witness. The flashes of lightning clawed through the sunset, but the air healed behind them in an instant. The thunder cracked from one end of the mountains to the other, but the echoes lived on — it seemed like forever. The colors and the intensity were so new, I felt curiously blessed.

"My pit-fellows and captors were likewise stunned. I don't believe anything like that has been seen before. But we only watched for a few moments before the Mallers returned to the task at hand and dumped us for the night. The storm continued, though we couldn't see it."

"Was the pit covered?" asked Charis.

"Most nights, no, but in times of inclement weather the Mallers were kind enough to lay sheets of scrap metal over us to keep out the worst of the rains or snows."

Charis glanced up into a sardonic curl of the messenger's lip and answered it with a nod of understanding. The lock clicked on one of the shackles and she moved to the other.

"So, we were covered that night, listening to the howl of wind and catching odd geometries of brilliant light through the cracks as the storm drew closer. At the height of its fury, it sounded as if we were directly under a waterfall, as if a million gallons of whitewater were bludgeoning the stone around us. We could feel it down to our bones.

"There were screams, but maybe only in my imagination. I don't know how I could have heard them over the racket. To be so small and so vulnerable dead center in the gaze of an unstoppable enemy... I was terrified. The air shook with so much chaos it became difficult to breathe. I buried my head in my hands. But then the clamor only seemed to grow louder. I looked up — I think, despairing, I was determined to stare into the eye of the storm and force it to blink, or some fool thing. Instead what I saw was that the cover of our pit was... disintegrating.

"The jailers had pinned it into the stone with metal hooks, so it hadn't blown away in the winds, but now there were holes appearing all over it. Not just holes, but slashes, rips, patches going threadbare as if the steel were no more than silk. Right before my eyes, it vanished. There was only darkness above, but I could hear a long hush, like swift water, uninterrupted, but somehow more brittle.

"While I sat there, dumbfounded, trying to understand what I was seeing, I heard a scream rise above the lessening wind and that susurrus. A moment later, a body tumbled into the pit. It was one of our captors. I, alone, edged closer to inspect the remains. I couldn't say where he had been trying to run to, or why, but he did not make it. His armor was gone, and the clothes beneath it too, blasted away. His skin and muscles had been flayed, laying open his back to the bones."

Charis felt the lock release on the other manacle and lifted the shackles away from the messenger. He rested his hands on his knees and flexed his fingers.

"What could do such a thing?" Charis asked. "I've heard reports of swarms of insects, but none have mentioned the devouring of flesh. Vegetation, only. A human enemy, perhaps, using the storm as concealment?"

The messenger shook his head. His eyes glittered; clearly, some part of him enjoyed having the information that Charis was after. "I appreciate your theories, Charis, but I'll tell you the truth of it from my observations. You see, that unusual, godlike lightning must have been strong enough and hot enough to melt the gravels and stones into glass, while the winds tumbled that glass until it was atomized, razor sharp particles flying at well more than speeds I can measure. A storm of glass, scouring the mountainsides clean..."

Charis could see it in her mind, a glittering, glowing billow of inarguable power. "Amazing," she whispered.

"It truly was. And the next morning, after everything settled, we were able to cooperate to pull ourselves out of the pit. None of the Mallers had survived the night. Their huts had been swept away or ground down to nothing. Sharp edges of the cliffside had been smoothed. Only those of us in the pits had survived.

"Us and the bridge. Mostly. All the wooden braces had vanished. The stone structure remained, though its pillars seemed thinner and — in my eyes — not equal to the task of supporting a cart. I wasn't planning on risking my own body on it. So I wished a farewell to my fellow freed men and women and headed south, toward the distance where the canyon seemed to draw its banks together.

"I have to admit, though, that I regret never seeing that bridge completed. It would have been a fine work." He retreated into reverie for a moment, then shook his head and returned to his tale. "By this time, I was very weak, so it took me several days to trace the canyon to a place where it grew shallower, then to cross it and return to my path through the forest. All that time, the world had fallen silent.

"Almost. A wind was blowing out of the north the day I crossed into the forest, cold but slow. It curled down and lifted wisps of the fine glass back into the trees. The further I went to the west, beyond the path the storm had taken, the more the trees still held their shapes, their branches, their dead autumn leaves. The sparkling breeze brushed across those leaves, a hushing much like the one from the previous night, but quieter, an unending hiss.

"It occurred to me then that it does something warm to my heart to witness things that take much less time to observe than they do to describe. Do you know what I mean?"

Charis nodded, her senses stuck on facing the external, unwilling to wrench them around and examine things inside herself. She set aside the shackles with a dull *clank* and rested her palms on her knees.

"No message could be worth all of this," she said. "None that couldn't be written on paper or hide or magnetic tapes."

The messenger shrugged. "Long, long ago we sent messengers into the skies, beyond the sphere of our knowledge, with very little hope of their messages even being read. I've already achieved more than they ever did, having met you, biovin Charis."

"Still... It seems cruel to send you into the unknown, containing the unknown."

"I volunteered."

Charis studied the messenger's face, trying to imagine how he might have looked before the corruption of his flesh.

"We should probably continue, per the yurchief's request," said the messenger softly, trying not to startle her.

Charis blinked and nodded. "Yes. Can you raise your arms?"

"Partway."

"That will do. The left side, please. I'll be quick."

"Take the time you need. I'm just dying to know what I carry."

●

Five days passed while Charis worked, recalling her predecessor's instructions and reconditioning the necessary equipment. The messenger spent most of them lying on a cot near her workstation. Charis had sent a watergirl to retrieve the simple bed from her home. The girl had stared goggle-eyed at the messenger until he had given her a little wave, then had darted away. On her return, she had stayed well away from the messenger, unfolding the cot and rushing back toward the door before the messenger could shamble over to it.

"Don't worry," he had said to the girl. "I've not made anyone else sick." The words hadn't sunk in.

Since then, Charis had isolated the helices from the sample from the messenger's lymph tumors and taken two more samples for comparison: one simply from a swab of his cheek, the other from one of the tumors visible near his spine. For the latter, she had been as careful as possible, and used the last of her sugar cane to deaden his nerves, but still his body had nearly twisted itself off the cot trying to escape the coring needle.

Now, he slept while Charis worked to amplify the fragments of the samples and render them as codes that might contain the message. In her mind, she considered the work backbreaking, because of her habit of bending close to her keyboards and displays and how infrequently she remembered to stretch and relax.

At one point, while waiting for a chemical reaction to complete, Charis felt her eyes drifting closed, and briefly considered taking the speed the yurchief had offered. But she knew what it did to the body, peripheral to the borrowed energy and wakefulness. It was fine for the guard faithful, for the warriors of the vanguard, and for the yurchief himself, but Charis intended to live much longer, much more slowly than any of them.

Gray pre-dawn light was lightening the high windows when the final strand of data resolved on her screens. The software laid the three samples side by side, eliminating the lines of identical data and presenting the differences. She tapped and clicked, reviewing each cut. In every example, the cheek swab showed differences from the two core biopsies where she presumed the message could lie.

But as she laid the data from the tumors side by side, her heart sank.

"Are you making progress?" the messenger asked. He stood a few feet away from her and spoke quietly so as not to startle her.

She bent forward and propped her head in her hands. "Yes and no. The samples from your spine and lymph nodes are significantly different. If there was a message there, it may have been corrupted by one, or by both. Most likely both, since neither is the original. Metastasis may have altered whatever was injected in your liver cells."

The messenger took this in stride, approaching so that he could see the screen over Charis' shoulder. "You have done great work already, my friend," he said. "Do you need my liver?" He said it in the pitch of a joke, but Charis shook her head, answering seriously.

"Even if we take the sample, I'm still confronted by the task of decoding the message it *might* contain. The yurchief will be back in two or three days. These conditions are not... ideal."

The messenger smiled and patted her shoulder and then retreated again to his cot, breathing heavily. The mild exertion of crossing the room seemed to have weakened him.

"Before I volunteered," he began as his lungs caught up to the demand. "Do you know what I was?" Charis shook her head. "I was a poet. I wrote verses on nature and community, real sentimental stuff. Poets are perhaps not necessary to the smooth function of society, but I do believe we are nature's codecs. Do you know that word? We decode the messages of complex systems; we encode the simplicity of life so that it will stick lengthwise in the mind. All messages, to the poet, are in all things."

"That is not a representative view of the world," said Charis.

"It is *precisely* representative. Just not very accurate," said the messenger with a warm chuckle. "I believe in you, Charis. Your successful work does not depend on knowledge you do not possess, nor on effort you are unprepared to undertake. Your only obstacle, I think, is time."

"For us both," said Charis.

The messenger nodded at that and lay back on the cot. "I'm at your disposal," he said.

Charis was silent for a moment. The messenger's breaths began to slow. There was one more piece of information she wanted from him, though. "Why did you volunteer?"

He blew a puff of air out of his nose and rolled to face her, his eyes half-lidded. "I believed there was more to life than poetry. Can you imagine that? Don't answer." The laugh that escaped him was strangely high pitched.

"I don't know much about poetry," said Charis.

"It's all right. I've proven to myself that I don't know much about anything else. It's a truth I've long avoided accepting. When the council asked for volunteers to carry messages to all the scattered tribes, I convinced myself that a humble poet would be the best for this job. All my life, I studied and practiced to draw connections between distant rhetorical points, almost like a soothsayer impressing shapes upon a scattering of stars or a clothier assembling their textures in a beautiful garment. Who better to bear a special missive to strangers than someone trained to draw together the folds of a broad idea and stitch it over a form easy to recognize?"

"Your pride compelled you?"

"My hubris, I would say. It was fueled by decades of feeling underappreciated, I don't mind saying. A poet has one eye forever locked on immortality, but nothing I composed ever would ensure my own. I suppose I felt that, in this effort, I could make a difference. One that might last."

"That was a great risk," said Charis. The messenger didn't offer a disagreement. She went on: "What did you hope you would find at your journey's end?"

The messenger gave the question its due consideration in silence, then, with some effort, shifted onto his back to stare up at the distant, shadowed ceiling. "What I hoped for back then is unimportant. What I hope for now is that I won't die lonely. And that, whatever this message in me turns out to be, it brings people closer together."

Charis looked at her hands. She wondered how many years of life she had preserved among her people, how she might quantify the difference she had made so far. "Perhaps you are the message," she said.

The messenger spluttered a laugh and moved a hand to press against his side. "Oh! Please, my friend. One more puff of conceit into this skull and I fear my head will float away. No, no. There is an end to my life and it has been written in me."

Before Charis' smile had faded, he was asleep.

●

On the morning of the sixth day since her task had begun, Charis sat and listened to the messenger groaning in his sleep. There was no place and no time where he could escape the pain of his disease. At least he seemed to recover some energy after his naps, despite the apparent discomfort.

Charis left him to his rest and stepped out of the laboratory. The mists of early morning dampened her face and clothes. The air tasted of algae, thick and green. She saw threads of smoke rising above the treetops and could smell cooking meat. A watergirl laced between the nearby trunks, two buckets balanced on a yoke, headed for the laboratory's cistern. Charis caught her eye and nodded to her. In response, the watergirl shook her head and flicked her eyes toward the deeper forest.

Now Charis could hear it: the stamp of heavy feet. An infrequent chime of metal-on-metal suggested the guard faithful. Sure enough, two of them came around a thick fir from the direction of the water. Between them strode the yurchief, back from his hunt ahead of schedule. He had a brace of otters slung over his shoulder and was using his fishing pike as a walking stick, dull end downward.

He nodded when he saw Charis, as if pleased that she had anticipated his coming. "What's the message?" he barked as she drew nearer.

"My apologies, your 'ness," said Charis, bowing her head. "I have not yet retrieved the message."

The yurchief shifted the weight of his kill and sighed. "Look at me."

Charis did as instructed.

"You look exhausted. Did you sleep last night?"

"Not well, your 'ness."

"Did you take my speed?"

"I did not."

The yurchief nodded. He gave a mild gesture with the fingers curled around the pike and both guard faithful relaxed. Charis hadn't even noticed them tensing.

"You still have until tomorrow, upon my original order. I shall leave you to it. But pay attention, biovin. If you fail to deliver the message to me before tomorrow noon, I will consider you a thief: a thief of my time and of what is rightfully mine. You will receive a thief's punishment."

"But, your 'ness," Charis protested. "Without my hands, I would be unable to compound —"

The long pike slammed into the ground hard enough to make the world seem hollow; Charis felt the beat of it rise up in her bones. "You!" The yurchief's voice hit her ears with the same force. "Your value is not in your hands! Your knowledge can be preserved through... much."

"I understand, your 'ness."

"You are burning daylight, biovin."

Charis bowed her head again and left it downturned until the footsteps had gone and the cloying scent of the dead beasts had dissipated. Then she raised her head and let the furious dampness in her eyes intermix with the air's heavy humidity.

When her heart had slowed, she re-entered the laboratory, opening and closing the door as quietly as she could.

She needn't have bothered. The messenger was sitting up on the cot, half-propped against the wall.

"You need more rest," said Charis.

"I don't," said the messenger. "It takes hours to process a sample, yes? We had better get started."

"I'm out of sugar cane."

"It won't matter, Charis." He levered himself off the cot and approached her. "He would really take your hands?"

"It's the punishment for thieves."

"Some would rather choose exile, I imagine."

"There is no exile. Nothing is beyond the yurchief."

"Come now," said the messenger. His expression shuddered for a moment and then went still, as if he lacked the energy to shift it to any purpose. His voice settled into a warm valley, though. "There is much beyond the yurchief."

Charis let her gaze fall to the biopsy needle. It hadn't gone through the autoclave since its last use. She feared there wouldn't now be enough time. "I might kill you," she said.

The messenger sighed and sat down on the creaking office chair. "I don't believe you'll have the chance, my friend. You could, of course, wait until after I am gone, but would you deny me at least the chance to see the unknown inside me? Come now. It'll be over quicker than I could write it down."

Charis looked at her hands, gray in the thin light, and flexed her fingers. They held steady. She nodded. "But give me a moment." She touched his shoulder, noting the quiver in his body that he seemed unable to still. Then she went and retrieved a portion of the yurchief's speed. She dug through the ingredients in her refrigerator and added careful measures of several to the drug, then diluted the mixture in water. She brought a beakerful to the messenger's lips. "Drink."

He obeyed, licking his lips afterward. "If I see eternity, I intend to keep far away," he said, rumbling a laugh that devolved into a coughing fit. Charis helped him from the chair onto one of the benches, laying him out beneath the strongest light. His eyes closed as the high took hold and he made barely a whimper when the needle punctured his abdomen.

●

The sun had been rising for hours before its light found Charis through the high lab windows, head bent, muscles giving up any hope of relief. By mid-morning, the cut segments of the liver sample were rendering on her display. She began to compare them to the other three, noting strings of differences, eliminating common patterns. On and on.

The symbols assigned to each piece of data began to blur together. Charis rubbed her eyes and looked up at the high windows. The branches of the trees were still, as if making an effort not to disturb her. The only sound in the room came from the hum of fans and the labored breathing of the messenger.

I could live in exile, thought Charis. *If there are lands beyond the yurchief, beyond the Mallers. I could go to the Calomlands.* She had never been beyond the Sound, had never even had to spend a night beneath the stars. *Would I have volunteered?* She had no answer for herself. Absently, she cracked her knuckles and regretted it at once as the messenger stirred.

He opened one eye and fixed it on her. The color had left his skin, his tumors ashen gray and the porous skin in the clefts between them fully white.

"How is it going?" he asked.

Charis left her work and came to kneel at his side. "Not well," she said. She calmed her voice by speaking like a biovin. "The sequences were well-extracted, but I still cannot locate the message, and even if I were to locate it now, I don't believe I could decrypt it in time. I've been giving it some thought, and since the cipher must be more complex than simple substitution, compressing our alphabet into the limited set of —" She stopped herself abruptly, the absence of the words permitting a lump to rise in her throat.

Her hands sought out his and together they held some warmth in stasis.

"I don't think I can do it," she said.

"Charis, Charis," said the messenger. "What a gift it has been to find someone who might read the messages in me —" His eyes fluttered. "Oh, eternity," he whispered, unable to focus on anything close at hand. Charis squeezed his fingers and he returned for a moment. "We are drawn together across a great distance. Do you see it?" He forced a smile onto lips unwilling to cooperate.

His heartbeat slackened, then, and stopped.

Charis tightened her grip on his hands, relaxed, then tightened again, repeating the motion over and over, as if she could urge his pulse to return. It took some time for the absurdity to penetrate her conscious mind.

Finally she stood and left him alone. She trailed her fingers over the equipment on her table, let them brush over the keyboards and controls. Who knew what accidental changes her careless touch might have made to her work? She snapped off the power. In the silence that followed, a clicking came from the high windows. Pine needles tapped against the glass.

Charis went outside, leaving the laboratory door open behind her. A breeze was beginning to stir in the forest.

One of the watergirls, headed past on her way to the cistern, noticed her standing there and approached hesitantly.

"Miss, are you alright?"

It took Charis a great effort to fix her attention on the girl, as if the thickness of the air resisted the motion of her eyes. *No,* Charis corrected herself, ever searching for precision, because it wasn't the world beyond her flesh that slowed her; it was the atmosphere within, the swirl of her intentions anchored at some midpoint she couldn't visualize. Words wouldn't come out.

"Did you find the message, biovin?" The watergirl's voice carried a lilt of excitement.

Charis turned her attention again to the trees. That riot of thoughts within her spun on and on and she realized that, though they all were tied to the eye at the center, that eye was in motion. Charis recalled the messenger's cold skin.

"Biovin?" The watergirl now seemed to be getting worried, leaning in closer.

Charis let her lips fall apart and pulled in rushing air between them. "Would you," she began, pausing as the words went out and did not return. "Would you like to learn the work of a biovin? I could teach you everything I know."

"I'm sorry?"

"And maybe I will be a poet."

The branches around them gently scraped the air, hissing. It was an inconstant sound, inward and outward, as if driven by breaths drawn and exhaled.

No, Charis chided herself. *A slackening moment like this should take much less time to describe than to observe.*

The wind moved in the trees.

●

The yurchief received Charis in his audience hall, a stone-and-thatch longhouse with three fires spaced equidistant down the length. Each fire was stoked fiercely hot, but directed mainly upward, so that as she crossed the distance from the entrance to the wooden throne her skin alternately blazed feverish and chilled beneath her damp sweat. Her mind echoed the pattern as she rehearsed what she might say, in turns raging with anger and then withdrawing to cold darkness.

As she bowed, she felt the stresses of the differentials might crack her down the middle, but in fact only her voice did as she made her decision and said, "Your 'ness, I have your message."

The yurchief looked down at her. He leaned back in his throne, the wooden joints creaking. The thick air made it hard to see his expression. Charis blinked and wiped at her face, feeling for an irrational moment that her eyes had been darkened like smoked glass.

She sensed he was waiting for her to go on. She took a deep breath. The words came to her mind barely before they left her tongue, and they quavered as they went.

"The message is a simple text of friendship, your 'ness, extended by the councilors of the Calomlands. They wish prosperity upon you and your people and invite us to reply by any means." The lie mingled easily with the grime suspended in the air between them. Charis bowed again, willing her shaking knees to calm. "They indicated landmarks for navigation to their homelands," she added, hoping that the messenger's story would supply enough detail if pressed.

"Friendship," said the yurchief, the word curling out of his mouth like smoke.

Charis nodded, fixing her attention on a whorl in the pattern of the stone floor, an image like the eye of a storm.

"Worthless. Leave us," the yurchief barked to those at his side. "You stay, biovin." A shuffling of footsteps around them told Charis that the various guard faithful and soothsayers were filing to the exit. Her flesh ignited and then froze.

"You are telling me the truth," the yurchief muttered, leaden tone absorbing all inflection if it had been a question.

"Yes, your 'ness," said Charis. *All messages are in all things.* She repeated the messenger's words to herself. It did little to bring about an equilibrium.

"Look at me," the yurchief said. Charis obeyed. "The tribe is glad for your skills," he went on. "They are a tribute to us all. Well done." A pressure wave of relief built up inside her. "Tell me, exactly: how did they address me?"

"The message was addressed to whomever leads the people," said Charis.

The yurchief snorted a laugh and rose. He clasped his hands behind his back, ambling past Charis to just within the corona of the nearest fire. He stretched out his hands to warm them and then nodded for her to join him.

"It would only be proper to compose a reply, don't you think?"

"Yes, your 'ness." She stopped herself before asking if he intended her to carry the response. The relief had faltered and dissipated.

"Entertain me, biovin. What would you say to such a message?"

"I would respond in kind. Offer our friendship. Perhaps, in the future, we might have an exchange of knowledge and equipment."

"It would not be swift enough, I'm afraid, biovin. While you have been stuck to your workbench, the world beyond you has been changing. There have been storms along our borders, brutal ones which leave nothing behind. They're coming closer. Soon, they will scour the Sound to its barren bones. We must be away from here before that happens."

"Storms of glass?" asked Charis. The yurchief nodded, turning a curious gaze on her until she explained: "The messenger witnessed such a thing near the end of his journey."

The yurchief shrugged. "Then perhaps the Calomlands are safe from them, as yet." He let his eyes drift over the flames. "They were my home, once," he said, far away. "Plains of green grass. Lakes full of fish and forests full of game. But I'm afraid my mind was not so narrow as they would have liked."

Shocked, Charis made a sound like an apology, inconsequential. The yurchief crossed his thick arms and closed himself down, eyes and all.

"Where is your gratitude to me, I wonder?" he said. "With my own strength, I have ensured our survival. I put those lands behind me, with their conceited council and the preening philosophers in their alabaster domes. This gray lump in my skull was a pitiful thing, in their consideration, and my destiny was set as a sludge-man, an offal-bearer.

"*You* would be accepted, of course, in no time at all, biovin Charis. Their sole pride was in the supremacy of their minds. They do not and would not have the strength to survive, to *thrive* as we have here in the Sound."

Silence expanded in time and space, filling the seconds and the rafters.

"Friendship, you swear?" The yurchief's throat rasped with phlegm. He spat into the fire. "There's no ambiguity in the message?"

Charis quailed, but any deviation from the message would surely bring the whole thing to an end. "There is no ambiguity."

The yurchief chuckled. "Then I know what I shall say. And I will etch my words in stone, where they might be read by anyone. And the host of us will follow just behind the messenger. We will cross the lands, ahead of the storms. They expect friendship, but they did not know who would read their message. I will return at the prow of war. You are dismissed, biovin."

He turned to face the fire and spat again. As he lowered his head, his hair fell away from his neck. Charis blinked and stared. A cyst had been exposed there, small, pale, but casting a large and dancing shadow. She opened her mouth and found no words for a long moment.

"Yes, your 'ness," she said finally.

●

Charis returned to the laboratory in silence and worry. Once inside, with the door closed, she disrobed. The cool of the evening and the threat of rain drew gooseflesh all over her skin. She examined her body in a mirror but found no lesions, no evidence of illness. Afterward, satisfied for the time being, she wrapped herself in layers and sat in front of the messenger's body for a long while.

There was so much she didn't know. She realized how desperately she wanted to confess just that to the messenger, to hear him offer his interpretation of her words and her world. *If I were smarter, or faster, or had better tools*, she thought, but silenced the voice inside before reaching a conclusion.

Being there, in the unknowing, was not unusual for her. It was part of the job of the biovin to learn, to build small answers upon each other until they reached a larger one. But for the first time in her work, she felt tormented by the blank void of unanswered questions, questions which *could not* be answered. At least, not there in the laboratory nestled in the Sound.

If the yurchief truly intended to lead his people to the Calomlands, it would take time for him to assemble them all. There would be bustle and confusion and little for Charis to contribute unless he ran out of his speed, now that he believed he had his message and his purpose.

If there are answers for me, she thought, *they are beyond his reach. Now and maybe forever.* She could slip away in the night and be ahead of the vanguard by days, turning to weeks if his condition followed the course of the messenger's. She could reach the Calomlands, a little storm of her own, full of swirling questions and fears and warnings.

Or perhaps the glass storms will sweep through and scour the lands clean of all our complexities, our imperfections.

The decision rose in her like a sudden gust. She filled a satchel with medicines that would travel well, and retrieved a stash of dried meat and nuts. Almost as an afterthought, she crammed the hard copies of the data extracted from the messenger alongside the provisions. When she stepped out into the evening, the damp wind hit what little skin she had left exposed like a bloody lash. She turned her back against it and set out for the Eastern path. Her path would take her through the drying forest, over the mountains, over the plains, to the Calomlands, bearing with her the unknown and the unknowable, and the hope of crossing bridges to meet those who might help her find the soul of the message inside her.

Ian Donnell Arbuckle's story "The Hissing Trees" was originally published in Metaphorosis on Friday, 12 August 2022. See magazine.metaphorosis.com

About the author

Ian Donnell Arbuckle lives deep in the desert half of Washington State with his wife and children.

@IanArbuckle1

The Unlucky Few Who Must Not Cast

J. Tynan Burke

"Hi, my name's Dennis, and I'm magic —"

Dennis stopped before the last word. It didn't apply to him, and he resented the suggestion that it did. Unfortunately, nobody had told the other people in the basement of that run-down Victorian. They looked up from a half-circle of folding chairs, eager for him to finish the line. And finish it he would: doing so was part of the meeting, which he had to attend, by Guild order, that night and nine more times that month, as punishment for his recent magic 'abuse'. Dennis took a centering breath. The air was vaguely moldy.

"...and I'm magic-dependent."

"Hi, Dennis," the basement chorused, out of sync.

Over at the sign-in table, a woman made eye contact. Henrietta, she'd said her name was. Mid-forties, short purple hair, studded collar. Compared to her, Dennis felt decidedly unhip with his Muji khakis and backpack. She gave him a thumbs up; she knew it was his first meeting. Dennis's eye twitched. If magic hadn't been forbidden at MA meetings, he would've cracked open his emergency invisibility potion. Instead he sat back down on his creaky chair, and took a sip of the awful coffee he'd gotten from a dented urn at the snack table. Was it a little late for caffeine? Sure. But he'd need it. He'd been exhausted in the weeks since Phoebe had dumped him, and the meeting was bound to be boring. He planned to stay up late doing spell research anyway.

The man next to him — and it was mostly men, in that basement — stood up. He was dressed like a contractor and shedding the dust to prove it. "My name's Sam, and I'm magic-dependent."

"Hi, Sam," Dennis muttered into his flimsy paper cup.

After everybody had said hello, the facilitator introduced a birdlike woman, "with a reading from the Codex," MA's self-help bible. He passed her a laminated page; she held it in unsteady hands. "How MA Works," she recited. "We are the unlucky few who must not cast. For us, magic is little more than a way to cheat at life. Such a road leads only to destruction. Some end up in prison; some find their bodies wracked with cramps and seizures; some die. Some overindulge and empty themselves so completely, hungry spirits come to fill the void within. The stories we share attest to all of these; they also attest to how good things can become. If you like what you hear, we beg of you to abandon casting and follow our path. You stand at a turning point. You must be fearless in pursuit of abstinence..."

Dennis wanted to scoff. None of that had ever happened to him, but the Guild still thought he belonged with these freaks, just because he'd cast a little while drafting that commodities report. The rule forbidding actuaries from using magic at work was dumb. Who cared? His boss was never going to find out, and it wasn't like he'd acted on some addictive compulsion. The spell had just been an expedient way out of a jam. That was hardly magic dependence.

The woman finished reading and handed the page back to the facilitator, who stepped into the center of the semicircle of chairs. He scratched his careful beard and said he was pleased to welcome that night's speaker, who went by the name of Shisk. Dennis clapped politely as a hulking man came to shake the facilitator's hand. Shisk looked around at his audience. He flashed a smile and tugged down on the hem of his hand-knit sweater.

"My name's Shisk," the big man said, "and I'm magic-dependent." His voice was heavy, either slightly stoned or permanently so.

The room: "Hi, Shisk."

Shisk cocked a wave. The hand he used, his left, moved oddly. Maybe it was a trick of the light. "Hey. So. Who am I, and how did I get here? I can tell you how I got here easily enough: by being a dumbass, then being responsible instead. A few of you probably know what that's like."

Polite chuckles. Dennis rolled his eyes.

"To make the story a little longer. I grew up in northwest BC. My family is Tlingit. I was seventeen when I got my first taste of *x'aséikw*, and I was hooked. *X'aséikw*, that's Tlingit for —"

Aether, Dennis thought, using the Hermetic term. Shisk finished his sentence with the nondenominational version, *mana*. Not for the first time, Dennis marveled that it could be harnessed by such diverse traditions. The Guild's chaos magicians theorized that human mystics were like blind men trying to describe an elephant: touching on some fundamental truth but failing to see its whole.

"It happened while we were getting ready for my grandpa's memorial party, arranging his stuff for a display. Drums, tools, things from his early life as an *ixt*, a shaman. I'd never put much stock in it... until I picked up one of his old ceremonial masks. What a rush!" He smiled; it faded. "The Guild found out, like they do, and set me up with a master to study shamanism, or what's left of it..."

While Shisk babbled about his training, Dennis's thoughts drifted to his own awakening. It had been similar in spirit. He'd been a freshman in college, wearing too much black and recreationally reading *Magick in Theory and Practice*. Trying out one of Crowley's rituals had sounded fun, so he had. A small water elemental had appeared in its summoning circle and begun to meander. Dennis had dropped the book in shock; eventually he'd thought to pick it back up and dismiss the creature. Not twelve hours later he'd been contacted by the Guild. They'd sworn him to secrecy and set him up with a master in the anthropology department.

The parallel with Shisk's story was no coincidence. Scooping up the accidentally-awoken was one way the Guild kept magic *sub rosa*. Dennis was also familiar with another way: the Guild monitored its members closely and intervened whenever things threatened to get out of hand. By keeping the magic world self-governing, the theory went, the Guild could avoid telling anything to the actual government. The only problem was that the restrictions could be stupid; sometimes harmless actuaries had to attend boring meetings for people with no self-control.

Shisk went on about how casting had crept into his carpentry business, and eventually taken over his life. Dennis held in a yawn, half bored, half exhausted. How was listening to this guy supposed to help him with his 'problem'? He sipped his lousy coffee, and regretted it.

"Alright," Shisk said eventually. "So that's where I was at in life. I was casting first thing when I woke up and last thing before bed. I'd jones hard for a spell whenever I was in polite company. And I was chronically low on x'aséikw. My hands would tremble so bad I couldn't use a saw. My feet would cramp up and stay stuck that way; sometimes I couldn't even get my shoes off. Never did get a full-on seizure, thankfully, but..."

Further evidence that Dennis was not like these people. He'd had some tremors before — who hadn't? — but nothing like what had happened to Shisk. No, Dennis always stopped with a solid amount of *aether* in the tank. Using too much was unpleasant; being half-empty made him feel half-dead. More importantly, it was dangerous, and could make him all-the-way-dead. *Aether* wasn't just fuel for casting; it was also natural protection against spirits. A mage with too little risked possession.

Aether was found in all things, though Dennis wouldn't have been surprised if it were absent from his coffee. It flowed into a caster when they ate, drank, and breathed. Methods of recharging faster were complicated or unsavory. Dennis had never cast enough to need one. Shisk, it seemed, had never been meticulous or evil enough to use one.

"But I still wasn't happy," Shisk said. "Wasting my ancestors' gift on making canoes for lawyers wasn't cutting it. I ended up doing freelance hero stuff. You know: find something wrong in the spirit world, go fix it."

Dennis sighed and rubbed his temple. A sob story from a caster with a hero complex — how *novel*. Heroism never ended well — hadn't Shisk known?

Dennis knew, and his path to learning it had been short. Like most newcomers, he'd been ready to save the world after his awakening. The feeling had lasted about three months, until one evening when he and his master had summoned the wrong spirit. The monster had almost killed them; they had beaten it back, but spent days just cleaning the ichor off the walls, and they never had gotten it all out of the carpet. And for what? If you zoomed out, getting rid of one evil spirit was nothing more than a rounding error.

Shisk's ominous story made Dennis glad that he'd had this revelation when he had. His life would have been very different without it. For starters, he might have actually belonged at this meeting. *There but for the grace of The One...*

"One day I read that a few camping groups had gone missing in the Kitlope Conservancy. This is primeval rainforest, sacred to some, and full of *jeks* — spirits. The sort of place where a missing person can be more than just lost. A quick divination showed me the spot where they'd vanished. I grabbed my toolbelt and headed out.

"Around twilight, I got to the clearing I'd identified. I recognized a threshold on one side, between two tall cedars. A bloodless prickling in my fingers and toes reminded me how little *x'aséikw* I had, but I went through anyway. I was a badass monster-hunter, right?"

Entering the spirit world with low *aether* was even stupider than everything else Shisk had described. On this side of the barriers, monsters generally had to be invited; on that side, all bets were off. Dennis leaned forward, grimly fascinated by the direction of Shisk's story. It was like a good horror movie.

"A river burbled on the other side of the threshold. In front of the river... the *jek* had the shape of a man, except his mouth was too big for his skull, and his eyes moved independently. He was humming to himself, and bending a length of raw wood. Next to him was an unfinished canoe. Its naked ribs seemed like grasping fingers." Shisk illustrated this by making a claw with his left hand. Dennis again noticed something odd about it.

"I rested my hand on the handle of my grandpa's copper dagger, and asked the *jek* about the campers. The jek frowned, and then in a blur he was on me. I stumbled and cracked my head on a rock. Saw stars, heard ringing. He rushed to stand over me, one eye on me, one darting around the clearing. 'You've made a powerful enemy, *ixt*,' he hissed, with a voice like a blade scraping over bark."

Shisk's play-by-play of the fight was brutal. If this had actually been a horror movie, Dennis would have watched from between splayed fingers. Yes, he'd fought monsters before, but he hadn't *enjoyed* it. At least the brutality wasn't senseless — Shisk had been on a rescue mission. That counted for something.

"He wore me down until my hands were so bloody I couldn't even hold the dagger. With all that blood, I'd lost nearly all my *x'aséikw*, too, so I didn't dare cast. I'd never felt worse in my life. Heavy, like my heart was pumping sludge."

Shisk frowned deeply and grunted.

"The *jek* had me pinned against a tree. He was choking me with both hands. But I had one trick left, an old piece of Tlingit lore. I snapped a chunk of sap from that tree trunk and jammed it into my gasping mouth. I mouthed an incantation and grew as sturdy as a cedar. The pressure on my neck... stopped mattering.

"I put my palms on the *jek*'s tattered shirt and willed roots and branches to grow. They tore through him. His whole body shuddered. His hands fell from my neck as he went limp. I heaved in breath after ragged breath, and my throat burned. For a while I sat on the damp leaves and panted. When I finally stood up, it was too dark to search for the campers. They were probably long dead anyway. I hung my head, and my face burned with anger. After all I'd been through, I hadn't saved anybody. I decided to head home."

Dennis felt his body deflate. Shisk had risked his life for nothing. That wasn't how stories were supposed to go, and was far more upsetting than most horror movies. He felt faintly ill.

"When I got close to the threshold, something started probing me, trying to find a way in before I left. Probably the *jek* I'd just fought — killing the skin isn't always enough. I moved as fast as I could, but not fast enough. He — the *jek*, what remained of it — had one last go at me. I don't know how long I spent fighting him inside of myself. Too long. I managed to cram his presence down into my forearm, then my hand, then…"

Shisk held up his left hand and unsnapped what Dennis had assumed was a bracelet. He peeled it from his wrist and palm; his three least important fingers came off along with it. A prosthesis. He wiggled his remaining thumb and forefinger. Dennis's nausea grew; he averted his eyes. "I'll just say it was good I still had that dagger. I put the fingers in a warded Ziploc and hauled ass to the hospital.

"I spent the next few days getting stoned and pretending it had been a carpentry accident. Pretty soon there was a knock at my door. You guessed it: a representative from the Guild. I'd been sentenced to twenty MA meetings. They thought it would give me some perspective, make me less likely to release a dangerous spirit in the future. I was pissed, but in a weird way, I was relieved, too. I obviously didn't have things under control — I'd almost become that *jek*'s next skin. I wouldn't wish that on my worst enemy, so why was I living a life where it might happen to me?"

Shisk said that his path to enlightenment had come through working the steps at MA. Dennis happily sank back into annoyed boredom; Shisk's rock-bottom had been hard to hear about, but the pseudo-religious trappings of 'the program' were easy to scorn.

At length, the shaman concluded. "So yeah, that's my story: how things were, what happened, and how they are now. If I can make it, so can you. *Yan tután, aagáa yéi kgwatee*: have faith and it shall be so. Thank you." Shisk gave the slightest bow and efficiently refastened his prosthesis. After shaking the facilitator's hand, he sat down on a front-row chair. Everyone clapped. Dennis joined them, and not only to be polite: as sermons went, it had been a good one, with a triumphant ending, and a vivid low point that lingered in his mind.

The facilitator opened the room up. People spoke for a minute or two about their own lives. None held Dennis's attention; addict-talk was boring, and all their mistakes were stereotypical. One had tried to cast his way out of gambling debt; another had developed crippling anxiety from too much divination. Instead of thinking about these people's problems, which were not his, or Shisk's story, from which he was still recovering, Dennis focused on nursing his coffee. *How is it even possible for the coffee to be this bad?* he wondered. *It seems like it would take a lot of work. What did they use, fresh scrapings from the street?*

Eventually the facilitator asked them all to stand and link hands. Sam held Dennis's left hand in a callused grip. The man on his right had clammy skin. Dennis mumbled along with a prayer that he vaguely knew: *Grant me the serenity to accept the things I cannot change, the courage to change the things I can, and the wisdom to know the difference.* Then the attendees sat again while the leaders went over administrivia about the next meeting. They collected volunteers for set-up and teardown and refreshments, and Dennis's very first MA meeting was over.

The lights rose. The room filled with the rustling of jackets and the metal noises of latches and zippers. Sitting still in the flurry of bright activity, Dennis felt nailed to his chair, not because anybody was paying attention to him, but because somebody might. He didn't like talking to strangers in the best of circumstances; he definitely didn't wish to right now.

Part of him wanted to spring to his feet and dash to Henrietta, to leave as soon as possible, to get away from this dusty and depressing basement. This urge went away when he saw somebody do just that — somebody who was a twitching wreck. Bad company to keep. With hunched shoulders, he remained seated and checked his email, waiting for Henrietta to finish signing out the other mandated attendees.

Soon it was only him and mingling stragglers. He retrieved his backpack and hoodie from under his chair, then slipped them on. On his way to Henrietta, he slunk between groups discussing happy hour plans and passages from the Codex. Once at her formica table, he produced a folded paper from his backpack and smoothed it out in front of her. She tapped the back of her pen on the gridded form, which was empty except for the first half of the first row.

"What'd you think, first-timer?" she said, looking up at him, pen poised over the page.

"Ah…" Dennis flashed a terrified smile. "Not as bad as I thought it would be?"

She gave a single *ha*. "You know, we get that a lot. Makes me wonder what people expect."

"Er." He swallowed. "Better coffee?"

"I know, right? Jenny — she's on refreshments — she means well, but, yeah. Don't worry, I won't tell." She looked around the basement, then took a crumpled pack of Lucky Strikes from her leather jacket. "Hey, you smoke?"

Dennis's eyes flickered to her pen. She still hadn't written anything. "No. I should get heading home, anyway. The cat'll want dinner."

"Oh, what's her name?"

"*His* name is Oscar."

"Why don't you come show me pictures while I burn one." She glanced at the form. "Dennis."

Dennis gave a low, mirthless chuckle, even though this hostage situation wasn't funny. "You're trying to trick me."

Henrietta smirked. "Is it working? I like to talk to all the newbies. Come on. Five minutes. You'll thank me later." She put her pen into a canvas zipper bag, which she used to weigh down the page, then walked upstairs, waving at Dennis to follow.

Blinking furiously, Dennis stared at the receding woman. *What the hell?* He entertained filling out the form himself, but he didn't know how to fake her initials. Also, it wasn't like him to cut corners; that he'd done so at work recently was the exception that proved the rule. What was he so afraid of, anyway, that he couldn't bear a five-minute chat? He groaned at himself, then hurried over the scuffed hardwood to catch her.

Thanks to the cloud cover, the night was dark and warm, even though a half-rain spat from the sky. Henrietta stopped at a tree on the front lawn. She leaned against the trunk and plucked a cigarette from the pack. She lit it with a Zippo, and the air filled with the reek of naphtha and unfiltered tobacco. Dennis scrunched his nose.

Henrietta pointed the business end of her cigarette at him. "Let me guess. You don't think you belong here."

Dennis opened, closed, opened his mouth. Apparently she didn't like to just talk to newbies, she also enjoyed haranguing them. "Is it that obvious?"

"There's a reason the Guild gives you guys sign-in sheets. Admitting you have a problem is a tough step." She blew out smoke. "Pun intended."

"Yeah." Not planning to take this first step himself, Dennis left it at that. Henrietta smoked; the silence grew heavy and awkward. He had to say something — but what? He supposed he might as well say what was on his mind. "You know, if I'm being honest... I'm not sure casting *is* my problem. I've never had the cramps or gotten possessed or anything."

To his surprise, Henrietta shrugged. The snaps on her epaulets briefly reflected a nearby sodium street light. "Hey, maybe it isn't. Not everybody here's an addict. For some people, like, casting makes their real problems worse. The community here helps them maintain their abstinence."

Dennis half-muttered, "Sort of seems like we didn't hear from any of them."

"Eh. They're not that vocal. Some of them are as embarrassed as you seem to be."

Dennis felt himself blush. Embarrassed, yes; *one of them*, no. "But I don't even have... other problems. Nothing casting makes worse, I mean."

"Hm." Henrietta looked him over, then leaned in. The smoky smell intensified. "Shisk left something out of his story, you know. A year before his life went to hell, he did a first stint in MA. Got sent here for vigilantism; some jackass was robbing houses in his neighborhood, and the cops didn't care, so he used a charm to get the guy to confess on tape.

"We all thought he had a hero complex, and a shitty attitude, too. Nothing was ever his fault. Thought he knew better than everybody else. Could've saved himself a lot of trouble if he'd stuck with the program long enough to get over himself." She rested her back against the tree again and took a leisurely drag. "What I'm trying to say is, the real problems aren't always obvious at first."

"Why would he leave that out?"

"I dunno, vanity? Pretty screwed up, right? I mean, what's the point of speaking if you aren't going to be honest."

"Yeah."

Dennis knew she was trying to manipulate him, but that didn't blunt his surprise. Shisk had had an *early warning* about this? He could have kept those fingers, if he'd only gotten over himself? A vision of the shaman's self-mutilation came to mind. Dennis's stomach ache returned.

Did he have more in common with Shisk than he'd thought? They'd both had hero complexes, however short-lived Dennis's might have been. And they'd both landed in MA because of penny-ante rule violations. It wasn't a perfect parallel, but it didn't have to be to make him anxious. Could his situation escalate like the shaman's had? What sort of violent horrors might be in his own future? Even the less tragic options weren't great; he might become an emotional cripple like the divination addict they'd heard from.

But no, no, of course he wasn't the same as these people. He and Shisk had both broken rules, but the rule Shisk had broken had made sense; Dennis had broken a stupid one. An actuary casting at work was like a driver pumping their own gas down in Oregon. Sure, it was a violation, but it didn't mean they needed Gas Pumpers Anonymous meetings. Just like Dennis didn't need *this* meeting. He should have been at home, having dinner with Oscar. Instead he'd probably have to clean up some passive-aggressive cat vomit. He checked Henrietta's progress on her cigarette. Still half remaining. He grunted.

She held up a palm. "Alright, alright. You heard me out. Thanks. I'll finish quick. How about you tell me how you ended up here, and we can get you on the road."

Dennis sipped his coffee and grimaced. Other than his chat with the Guild rep, he hadn't talked about this with anybody. But if it would help get him home — fine. "I got caught casting at work. A divination. I'm an actuary, so I'm monitored. And here I am." He laughed bitterly. "It's a stupid rule. So I know what next quarter's PNW rainfall will be, so what?"

Henrietta's eyebrows rose. "That's actually kind of a big screw up. You might not want to hear this, but the Guild has those rules for a —"

"I *know* why we have those rules. I just think it's dumb. It's not like I was a cop setting up a pre-crime division. We're talking about lumber futures here."

She looked at him like he'd told her he had not one cat, but fifteen. "Christ, man. If every jerk-off who could read the *I Ching* felt the same way, the foundations of modern finance would crumble. Doesn't sound too bad to me, but I get why others feel different. Even if —"

"Oh come on, nobody cares about —"

"Let me finish." She paused to glare at him, then shook her head. "*Even if* this rule is totally bogus, you knew it was a rule, you knew you were monitored, you did it anyway. What gives? You don't seem like the type to break rules just because you don't like them." She waved a hand vaguely, perhaps indicating his subdued head-to-toe Muji.

"Not every rule is the same!" He pointed at her leather coat, her torn jeans. "You look like you've probably bought drugs before. Does that *mean* anything? No!"

"Maybe you need to talk to Shisk."

"Maybe I need to go home." He folded his arms.

She rolled her eyes. "Easy there, cowboy. God, listen to yourself."

The cigarette's cherry glowed between them as she took a drag. Dennis watched her face brighten and fade. She looked scared. No: worried. For him. He couldn't remember the last time somebody had looked at him that way. It gave him pause.

Listen to yourself. He took a deep breath and slowly released it while he replayed the conversation. His arms fell to his sides as he realized that Henrietta had been right to call him out. He'd been radiating anger and entitlement. He'd sounded like an excuse-making know-it-all, just like Shisk had been at his first meeting. He'd sounded, to borrow a phrase from that earlier recitation, like somebody who used magic to cheat at life. Even his body language had been juvenile and petty. But he wasn't that person — or he never used to be. If he was now, well, that was unacceptable.

"I'm sorry. Let me try again. I hadn't planned to cast that morning. I just... did. I was tired, on an unrealistic deadline... it was an easy out." He sighed; more excuses. His hands fell to his sides. "I was so exhausted. Still am. I haven't been sleeping well lately."

"What's keeping you up?"

"I'll stay up late casting some nights. I know how it sounds, but it's not like that." Henrietta raised a skeptical eyebrow. Dennis scrunched his nose again, but it was from self-consciousness, not the smoke. "I've just been sort of angry. I got — *dumped* isn't even the right word..."

The rain moved from spitting to drizzling. After the first drops struck his forehead, he put his hood up. "I'd been seeing this woman, Phoebe. Pretty casually. She got serious with somebody else, and that was that. I'm sort of mad, but not at her or anything. It just sucks. What do other guys have that I don't, you know? I work hard, I make jokes, I —" He laughed at himself, sunk his hands deep into his hoodie pockets. "I have a cute cat. I dunno. Casting is something I can do that other guys can't. So lately, a lot of nights, I've stayed up late working on a spell. Not like I'll ever be able to show it to a date. Which is silly, since it's just a modified will-o'-wisp summoning, optimized to look nice in a city... I probably sound like a loser."

He shook his head. He barely recognized himself right now. The real Dennis was neither pitiable nor an arrogant prick. Maybe he really did have some things to work out. The cost of not doing so could apparently be dire; he made a mental note to check if his insurance covered therapy. In the meantime, it was possible there were worse places to be than these meetings.

Henrietta smiled kindly. "Sounds pretty, actually." A drop of rain struck the nub of her cigarette, and hissed. She frowned at it, then flicked the remnants into the street. "Let's head back in and we'll get that form signed."

"Okay. Thanks."

He followed her into the old house, into the dingy basement, to the formica table, where his form still rested under her bag of pens. Seeing the mostly-empty sheet of paper reminded him that he'd have to spend many more hours in this musty room, sitting on a folding chair that had long since lost its padding, listening to lectures.

Henrietta crouched at the table. Her knees popped; Dennis winced. She selected a pen from her bag. After scribbling something on his form, she handed it to him. "There ya go. See you Wednesday?"

"Is that the next one? Yeah, I guess." He slipped his form into a document sleeve in his backpack. A few drops of coffee spilled from his carelessly-held cup. "Ah! Crap."

"Careful now, you don't want to waste your favorite drink."

"Ha." There really was no excuse for how bad it was. *Nobody deserves coffee like this*, he thought. *The meetings would be so much easier if we had the right refreshments. Maybe we will next time. Er, not 'we', like I'm a member, but I'm, you know, in the room, and... who am I kidding.*

"Hey," he said, "before I go. Snacks and stuff are handled by volunteers, right? What if I offered to bring... you know... *good* coffee? Wouldn't be much trouble."

Henrietta straightened and looked him over with a curious smirk. "Didn't expect *that*. You'll have to run it by Jenny. I think she's still here. Let's check the kitchen. C'mon."

A few minutes later, Dennis stepped out into the rain and hurried to his car. He opened the door to his Civic and sat on the gray cloth seat. *All Things Considered* came on when he turned the key; Audie Cornish began a story about a blight affecting California strawberries. Dennis pulled away from the curb, then mashed the volume button, killing the sound. He had a lot to think about. That word, *we*, was as good a place to start as any.

J. Tynan Burke's story "The Unlucky Few Who Must Not Cast" was originally published in Metaphorosis on Friday, 19 November 2021. See magazine.metaphorosis.com

About the author

J. Tynan Burke is a software engineer and writer. Lately, he's been working on the script and code for a cosmic horror video game. He lives in Denver with his husband, their enormous cat Samwise, and their tiny cat Momo. His dream is to one day be an old man futzing around in the garden. You can find more about his writing at www.tynanburke.com, and find him on Bluesky @thearchduke.bsky.social.

A Song Without a Voice

Brad Preslar

Dahlia traced the melody on her tablet and her song poured from speakers hidden around the subway station. It burrowed into Jonah's ear and asked a question only she could answer. It dug into his brain and found his memories of her. The melody scraped and scratched until the scars gave way and some trace of what he once felt for her leaked out. At least, she hoped it did.

He cocked his head. In the darkness underneath the hooded sweatshirt she wore, a smile warmed what passed for her lips; he would love her again. Even if he was the only one.

He brushed his dark hair to the side and paused on the subway platform, searching as he strained to hear the next musical thought. Good. She'd worried the synthesized tones would be a poor substitute for the voice that once captured his heart.

"It's the edges that make it special, the raw parts," he'd said. "It gives it depth, makes it, I don't know, more real." That was back when she had a voice, before the cancer and the surgeries took it away.

Her fingers danced across the glassy tablet screen while the Monday morning commuter crowd bustled around him on the subway platform. Jonah waited for the 3 train that would take him to Manhattan. He looked around, searching for the melody. Dahlia pulled the hood up further; she couldn't let him recognize her yet. Not until she had him hooked with the circle progression that drove her song from chord to chord.

She hoped her choice of key would be prophetic; F-sharp major rang of final victory over painful struggle. The particular circle progression she'd chosen created a sense of inevitable return to its root, the F-sharp. That chord would be the one in her one-four-five-one progression, where she'd begin and where she'd return.

She longed for a return to her days as a performer, singing to packed venues, seeing the echoes of her voice on the enchanted faces of her audience. Her subway audience reflected no such joy, but she reminded herself that Jonah's reaction was all that mattered.

With the F-sharp chord as the one, her song went to the four, a B-major. It sang of adversity, including the F-sharp note for a vague sense of familiarity, but otherwise complicating the expression. Dahlia felt a particular fondness for this chord; she heard the same disfigured familiarity that she saw in her bathroom mirror.

Jonah winced at the discord, and Dahlia let her fingers dance on the piano keys displayed on her tablet, driving the discordant notes deeper into his ear. It hurt to hurt him, but not as much as it hurt to want him. She let him feel the pain she lived every day.

Dahlia's haunting melody sang from both above and below the audible range of sound. The lower sounds came from the infrasound generator hidden in the darkness below the subway platform, a black box she'd mounted down by the tracks that siphoned power from the same third rail that powered the subway cars. The sound played so low that Jonah (and everyone on the platform) would feel it instead of hearing it. They'd feel awestruck, afraid, even cold. All without knowing why.

She sent other notes to the dummy security camera she'd mounted high overhead. It looked like all the other cameras mounted on the dirty yellow platform columns in Grand Army Plaza subway station. Except hers had a focused parametric array inside. It rotated to follow Jonah, aiming the tight beam of sound directly at his ear; that note played only for him.

Finally, the rest of her song played from a street performer's small amp twenty feet down the platform. As he did every day, Uriah played '60s, '70s, and '80s pop on an electric guitar for tips. She had the sense that he was capable of more, but knew from watching him that nostalgia was what put money in his guitar case.

She practiced when the station was deserted and she knew Jonah wouldn't pass through, mid-day and late at night. She'd begun with her own small amp, playing for tips whenever the station wasn't deserted. But during rush hour, when Jonah *would* be there, so was Uriah. Rather than try to overpower his guitar, Dahlia chose to make his performance part of hers.

Earlier that morning she'd given him a wad of cash and a note asking if she could play through his amplifier during his smoke breaks. When he agreed, she had him plug a remote-controlled MIDI device into that amp.

However, as it now did for Jonah, her device could also change the music Uriah played to include notes Dahlia wanted performed, shifting key as necessary so that his song became hers. He squinted at her, obviously not appreciating her musical addition. But since the song wasn't for him and her extra cash made up for any lost tips, she ignored his glare. This concert had an audience of one.

She had ten seconds before the train arrived to move to the C-sharp five chord, where the climax of the progression would happen, capturing Jonah's imagination and setting her hook. The chord would create an insatiable need, planting an earworm deep in his brain that he'd ache to resolve. She'd set his body vibrating all the way down to his core. And then she'd send him off into the world.

He'd leave her again, like he'd left her before. Only this time he'd come back. He'd have to. Her song would guarantee it.

She let the song breathe, pause for a moment. Dahlia watched commuters cross between where she sat on the wooden bench and where Jonah stood on the platform. Tension spooled in her lungs. It tightened around her chest, reminding her of the empty ache inside.

She held her breath and counted beats in her head, teasing him with the melody, waiting to play the next chord in the progression. This was the pause she'd always adored. This was how she'd captivated her audiences, back when people lined up to see her instead of turning away from her deformed face.

When she couldn't stand it, when she absolutely couldn't wait any longer, she shifted to the C-sharp five. She added a complicating note and inverted the chord, intensifying the need to resolve back to the one.

Dahlia wanted him to need that resolution, to crave it, even beg for it. She wanted him to want it as much as she wanted him, to feel the same kind of need that gnawed at her insides day in and day out.

Jonah would know the kind of need that came from craving something you once had, the most familiar ache. That hook would bring him back. Only, instead of setting the hook, the chord unraveled.

A tall man passed between Jonah and overhead camera, interrupting the focused sound beam. At the same moment, a nearby phone rang, discordant tones slicing through her chord and cutting it in half. Dahlia cursed, her fingers flying across the tablet. She had only seconds to re-start the progression, only moments to re-cast the hook.

She moved back to the first chord and began again. Dahlia glanced up to check Jonah's position just in time to see him step into the subway car and out of her grasp. The doors closed behind him and the train accelerated into the tunnel, leaving her song behind.

She let the tablet fall into her lap. Failure settled onto Dahlia's shoulders and she let herself slump under its foul weight.

Taking a deep breath, she shrugged it off. This wasn't her only chance; he'd be on this platform again tomorrow morning. Truthfully, if she really wanted to, she could wait here all day. He'd take the 3 train home again and walk back through this station shortly after six. No, she decided. She'd waited this long, and she could wait another day.

Dahlia lifted her scarf to her mouth, arranging it about her neck before pushing back her hood. She put her tablet into her bag, and then stood and walked down to where Uriah played. She watched and waited for him to finish "Strawberry Fields Forever."

He ended with a bright riff, resolved to the final note, and held it. He said, "You're the only person I know that pays to hear songs that don't sound right, you know that?"

She shrugged, smiled with her eyes, and pointed to the MIDI controller patched into his amp.

Uriah rolled his thumb across the volume knob, fading the note out. "Go on."

Dahlia bent and unplugged the device. She stood and put it in her bag. Uriah inhaled and her stomach dropped; she knew that sound too well.

"Wait, are you Dahlia?" he asked.

Her hand flew to her scarf, which had slipped down as she'd stood, revealing her surgically reconstructed lower jaw. She hurried to rearrange it, covering her disfigurement. Recognition brightened Uriah's face. He smiled.

He said, "You *are* Dahlia."

The expression on his face was something she hadn't seen in so long she didn't recognize it. Most people looked away, and the ones who didn't struggled to hide their revulsion. He looked genuinely happy to see her; his eyes wrinkled at the corners.

Unsure how to react, Dahlia chose to retreat. Scarf in place, she turned and hurried off down the platform, through the crowd and up onto the waiting New York City streets.

●

The next morning Dahlia feigned confidence as she approached Uriah, forcing a nonchalance she was sure fooled no one. He was warming up with a series of scales and fingerings when she stopped in front of his amp holding two cups of coffee. He glanced up, finished his scale and rested one hand on the strings, silencing the guitar.

He said, "Listen. Yesterday, I didn't mean to" — he stopped and scratched his head —"I mean, I wasn't trying to be rude. You know?"

She held out one of the cups of coffee and he took it. She held up a finger, signaling him to wait. Dahlia produced cream, sugar, and a stirrer from her pocket. She handed him those as well.

"Thanks," he said. "We're cool?"

She nodded. His reaction had actually been relatively tame. Before she started consistently covering the lower half of her face with a scarf, she'd endured much worse.

He smiled and held out a hand. "I'm Uriah." She shook it and he said, "And you're Dahlia." It wasn't a question. "Wow," he said. "Just, wow."

She cocked her head.

He said, "I didn't recognize you with the scarf, but I was...no. I *am* a big fan. Got all your albums. Even saw your last concert at Beacon Theatre." He mixed the sugar and cream into his coffee, took a sip and continued, "That's good. Cleary not," — he motioned to the coffee machine by the escalators —"subway coffee."

She nodded, took the MIDI controller from her bag, and set it on the amplifier.

He sipped his coffee. "Where'd you get it?"

Dahlia took several tightly folded bills from her pocket and set them beside the MIDI controller.

He glanced at the money. "The coffee," said Uriah. "Where'd you get the coffee?"

She tilted her head and pointed to the name on the coffee cup. "Black Mountain Coffee," it read.

"Oh, yeah." He shook his head. "Listen, I feel bad about yesterday. And since you brought me coffee?" He bent and plugged the controller into the amp, scooped the money up and handed it back. "No charge."

Dahlia eyed Uriah.

"One condition," he said.

She lifted her eyebrows, expectantly.

"Play *with* me."

Dahlia squinted.

"I heard you yesterday with that tablet, and I know what you're capable of. You controlled my song, twisted it to play what you played. Instead of playing over me, why not play with me?" He pointed at the controller. "I hooked you into an auxiliary port instead of directly in line."

She looked away, considering the request.

"Or I can play with you. You were in F-sharp major yesterday, right?"

She nodded.

Uriah smiled. He strummed the one, an F-sharp major seventh. "I heard that one, then what, the four?" He played a B major.

She smiled under her scarf, flushed with the joy of sharing a common tongue. The feeling surprised her. She shook her head, and forgetting herself, took the tablet from her bag. She played the ninth of the chord, a C-sharp note, through the infrasound generator below the platform, leaning the B-major chord forward towards what came next.

Uriah looked around, momentarily confused. "I know it's there, but I don't hear it. It's more like I...I feel it?"

Dahlia nodded. She used her tablet to type out the words, "C-sharp. Infrasound generator. Too low to hear." She tapped her chest with an open palm.

"Woah. Yeah. I do feel it. What's next?"

She held up five fingers.

"The five?"

She nodded and started to play the C-sharp five chord.

She stopped, her hand just above the tablet. What was she doing? Jonah would be here any minute. If he recognized her too soon, he'd never listen.

Uriah strummed the chord. He looked up just as she slipped the tablet into her bag and put the folded bills back on the amp. She hurried down the platform to take a seat on her bench.

Dahlia pulled her hood up over her head and set the tablet on her lap. The opening strains of Def Leppard's "Pour Some Sugar on Me" floated down from Uriah's amplifier. She couldn't help but smile. His taste in pop songs ranged from recognized classics to guilty pleasures. This definitely qualified as the latter. She couldn't remember the last time she'd heard Def Leppard. She started to chase that thought but caught herself. Enough. She needed to focus on her own song.

Checking first to ensure none of the other people standing nearby were looking her way, she pulled her scarf down and sipped her coffee. Watching the crowd for Jonah's face, she rehearsed her song in her head.

When he arrived moments later, she began to play. He perked up, searching for the now almost familiar tune. He swung his head towards Uriah just as the musician played a note that should have gone to the tight beam array in the camera overhead. He'd played a note for the entire subway platform that Jonah should have been the only one to hear.

Damn. She'd forgotten Uriah had patched her controller in so he could play along. He leaned on the note, letting it rip through the air before starting his own dance along the scale.

With no other choice, she moved on to the next chord, building the momentum. Uriah surprised her, following her lead without overpowering the sound. They made eye contact right before she moved to the five, the C-sharp seventh.

His song moved with hers, not following but keeping pace and building on her notes, layering on harmonies she'd never imagined. When she couldn't stand it anymore, when the need to resolve the tension grew so great she thought she might burst, she led him back to the one.

Except he didn't follow. He repeated the melody he'd created. The conflict grated on her ears, ruining the resolution that should have felt sublime. She cursed Uriah. She cursed herself; she'd been stupid to trust him. She didn't even know him. So what if he'd seen her in concert and bought her albums?

She suddenly remembered Jonah. Where was he?

The subway doors closed and the car started to pull away. She stood and looked up and down the platform, checking each of the subway cars. This was his train though, he'd be onboard. After a few seconds she spotted him inside the departing car. She watched the train pull away, taking him with it.

Her head spun. She hadn't meant it to go this way. She felt nausea grip her stomach, followed by the hot flash of rage. Uriah had ruined it. Instead of a haunting melody, they'd played a clumsy, discordant duet. Jonah might remember the song, but certainly not with any fondness, and certainly not with the aching desire she'd intended.

Dahlia grabbed her bag and stuffed her tablet inside as she stormed down the platform. She glared at Uriah while pointing at the MIDI controller with one hand and holding her other out, palm up.

Uriah held up his hands and shook his head. "Sorry about that, I missed the change." He unplugged the controller and held it out. She snatched it from his hand and stuffed it into her bag.

"Whoa," he said. "It was an honest mistake."

She glared back at him. She took her tablet out and typed out, "You ruined it."

He said, "You never missed a change?"

She thought about it and typed, "You didn't follow."

He grimaced. "We were going to play together, remember?" He stared at her, letting the question hang in the air. He glanced down the darkened subway tunnel. "So you were playing for who, somebody on that train?"

She considered the question, not wanting to answer. She wanted to leave, to just go. She couldn't though; she needed that amp, she needed Uriah to cooperate. Even if she found another amp or another set of speakers, his playing would interfere with her song. Finally, she nodded.

"But you don't want him to see you?"

She hesitated. She nodded again.

Uriah squinted at her. "Why?"

Dahlia sighed. She typed out "We were together."

"And now?"

She tilted her head. She typed, "We're not."

Uriah barked out a laugh and smiled. "Yeah. I got that. Can I ask why?"

Why, indeed? She paused, considering her answer.

In short, because he'd left her. At first, facing the horror of her cancer had brought them together. It offered something to overcome, something to fight against. They'd only been together for a few months when she was diagnosed, but he'd sworn he'd stick by her.

He stayed by her side through the chemo, the surgeries, and her recovery. He'd stayed long enough to see her through it all, to make sure she'd survive. She often wondered how much of that was out of obligation.

Regardless of why, he'd stayed until her prognosis had improved, until he knew she'd live. And as she'd realized she was going to live the rest of her life looking like a monster, hating her own reflection and struggling to come to terms with the loss of her voice, he'd drifted away.

Really, she couldn't blame him. He'd fallen in love with a beautiful siren. How could he be expected to love the disfigured, silent thing she'd become?

She typed out, "He left." Those two words said the only thing she knew with any certainty. He hadn't returned her messages, so she didn't know exactly why. She could guess, though.

They stood there a moment, the commuters moving around them. Uriah strummed at his guitar. She could see he wanted to ask more. Finally he said, "And your song, it's going to bring him back?"

She typed, "I hope."

He gave her a half smile. "Let me ask you something."

She raised her eyebrows.

"I know what that progression should sound like, a one-four-five-one. And I know there are parts I should feel, not hear. But there are some I don't feel or hear. Where are they?"

She considered the question for a second. She'd told him this much, why not the rest? She glanced up at the security camera overhead. His eyes followed hers and she typed out, "Ultrasonic array. Focused beam of sound."

"That you point at him?"

She nodded.

"Huh," said Uriah. "Why?"

Dahlia wondered again why she was explaining any of this to Uriah. She probed the tiny warm spot in her chest and realized that something about sharing the song felt good.

She'd written it alone. She'd practiced it alone, or for people in too much of a rush to listen. She'd set up everything she needed to play it alone. After all that, and months of preparation, her audience of one had yet to appreciate it. Would Uriah?

She took the tablet and MIDI controller from her bag and plugged the device back in. She set the volume low enough that only they would hear, and set her tablet to play all the parts through Uriah's amp. She played, from the root to the fourth, on to the fifth, and then finally returned back to the root.

"Yeah, that's nice," he said.

She held up a finger and repeated the melody again. He listened.

"Huh. Catchy," he said.

She smiled and played it a third time, stopping just before the resolution.

He nodded. "I know that itch. It's an earworm. Can't forget that song. And I really want that next chord."

She typed out, "Subsonic and ultrasonic sound intensify the itch."

Uriah shook his head. "That's amazing."

She nodded. Then, she typed out, "Have to play the right notes, though." His face fell as he read it. She felt instant guilt and smiled with her eyes, trying to dull the sharp barb of truth buried in the words.

"Guess so." He glanced back down the tunnel where the train had disappeared and then back at her. "So why tell me?"

Why indeed? Then she realized why she had. She typed out, "So you can help."

"How?"

"Play with me," she typed. Her solo could be a duet.

They spent the next few hours rehearsing, working through the chord progression, harmonizing and improving the melody. Dahlia had known Uriah had talent, but she'd had no idea how much. Not only did he keep up, he improved the song, adding his own touches in places she hadn't known could be improved.

He twisted her song around the neck of his guitar, bending it under his fingers, making it his. The core stayed the same, but as he moved from one chord to the next, he filled the spaces with half steps and feints completely different from what she expected, and a world away from how she would have played. Dahlia felt a tickle of happiness; finding novelty in something so familiar felt amazing.

Uriah had improved what she'd created, changing the inflection of her sentence, somehow warming the message. It felt less like the sharp snap of bone, and more like a soft still-pink scar.

By the time the subway started to fill with people coming home, the song was better than it had ever been.

Familiar faces that usually passed without turning their heads gathered around them, reflecting a joy back to Dahlia that she barely recognized.

●

The next morning, Dahlia set two cups of coffee and her MIDI controller on Uriah's amp. She eyed the folding chair he'd set up next to it.

He smiled. "Yours if you want it."

She considered the offer. While she hadn't planned for Jonah's first two experiences with her song to go so poorly, her earworm had been planted. Today was the day she'd resolve the song and reveal herself, so instead of walking further down the platform to her usual spot, she set her bag down and sat in the folding chair.

As the morning crowd started to trickle in, she sipped her coffee and powered up her remote sound generators, both above and below the platform. Once they were ready, she sat still, watching Uriah until he noticed.

He said, "You ready?"

She nodded.

"Cool. I'm going to make a few bucks while we're waiting. You good with that?"

She nodded again.

He said, "You move your coffee cup from on top of my amp to down by your feet when he shows up, and I'll follow your lead."

She gave him a thumbs up, marveling over the spreading warmth inside her. Creating music again felt better than she ever imagined; seeing fresh joy on a listener's face validated her like nothing else could. Maybe she'd never sing again. Maybe that didn't mean she had to be silent forever.

Uriah played and she waited as the morning commuters rushed by in a blur, all buzz and grumble. After a while, she spotted Jonah making his way down the platform. She lifted her tablet, moved her coffee cup to the floor, and started to play.

She saw Jonah's shoulders lift as soon as he heard the first note. The music crawled into his brain, reminding him of the unanswered question she'd asked him yesterday and the day before.

As Jonah walked closer, she picked up her tempo. Uriah followed, his notes sharp and ragged as they sliced through the smooth even tones she played. She felt a lump in the back of her throat, a tightness in her chest.

Jonah was just ten steps away when they moved to the climax. Infrasound thrummed in her chest. She could see the tension on Jonah's face, almost feel the ache she'd created. She had him. He stood balanced on a pin, his face begging for release.

She held the chord, drawing it out as Uriah's guitar wailed, plaintive, begging to move on.

Still, she held it.

Jonah was almost to them when, finally, she let go and led Uriah back to the beginning note, resolving the insatiable need she'd created. Jonah's shoulders fell; he'd been holding his breath. She gasped, realizing that she had too.

She'd planned this moment for months. They'd make eye contact and rather than turning away she'd stare back, she'd let him see her. He'd stop, he'd listen, and he'd be hers again.

He did his part; he looked right at her. Her hood hid her face in shadow, she only had to look up. Except something tugged at her to play on, to dip back into the song.

That song that should have bored into his ear instead wrapped itself around her. It dug for the Dahlia she used to be.

Her breath caught in her throat. The tension sat heavy on her chest, pressing down hard. She felt the weight of a thousand stares, heard the inhalation of a million breaths. She remembered what it was to sing.

Jonah hesitated in front of her, cocking his head to one side. "Dahlia?" he said.

She swallowed the lump. With a tap on the tablet, she powered down the sound generators, releasing their hold on Jonah. She felt the tension fall away, felt the subway spring back to life. Uriah glanced back and forth between her and Jonah, watching carefully.

She lifted her head and made eye contact, her scarf still covering the lower half of her face. He faked a smile that she returned with her eyes.

"Hi," said Jonah.

She lifted one hand and waved.

He stood before her, obviously unsure what to say next. Her song no longer bound him. Yet, he remained.

She felt something inside her chest she barely recognized, but didn't see it reflected on his face. Dahlia felt the echoes of her song wrap her in an embrace. It had slipped through her self-loathing and breathed a gasp of life back into the lungs that once enchanted the world.

She typed out, "Good to see you," then tilted the tablet so he could read it.

"You too," he said.

Dahlia looked at him, not used to seeing him up close. She could reach out and touch him, if she wanted to. Except, she didn't. But she didn't want to run from him either. And that surprised her.

She typed, "Take care."

He smiled and said, "I will." He turned to go, but stopped. He looked back and said, "I like it. Your new song." Then he turned and left.

She watched him head down the platform. After a few seconds she looked back to Uriah. She typed out "Thank you" on her tablet.

He nodded, smiled, and then she sat back down.

They played on together, Dahlia's newfound voice rising in triumph above the subway noise. A small crowd gathered as Uriah joined in, magnifying her song into something more than she ever could have created alone.

Brad Preslar's story "A Song Without a Voice" was originally published in Metaphorosis on Friday, 13 May 2016. See magazine.metaphorosis.com

About Brad Preslar

Brad's fiction has appeared in *Analog, On Spec, Cast of Wonders,* and *Amazing Stories,* and is forthcoming in *Ares* magazine. Find him on the web at bradpreslar.com, where he wrote 52 short life lessons for his son (6), to read when he's 18. You can read them before Sam learns how.

Brad Preslar writes from Asheville, NC, where he lives with his wife Ellie, their son Sam, and their dog Stella. Brad has anxiety and depression.

The Big S

David Hammond

It was another New Year's Eve at my brother-in-law's house on the lake. Aunt Margaret sent me to the kitchen to retrieve the chocolate-covered strawberries, her eyes glassy and cheeks flushed from champagne.

The kitchen lights were off, but moonlight from the window illuminated the tray of strawberries on the countertop. By the sink, a chef's knife lay across an unwashed cutting board. I was about to rinse them off and put them in the drying rack, but I was struck by the reflection of icy blue moonlight on the blade. I leaned down for a closer look. The cutting board was slightly damp. It smelled of onions.

Perspiration broke out on my forehead. I teetered momentarily and steadied myself with a hand on the counter. Had I drunk too much champagne myself? After delivering the strawberries to the stuffy living room, I stepped outside to cool off.

Pipe smoke wafted from a corner of the porch. I couldn't identify the man's face in the shadow of an overhanging pine but recognized the plaid shirt, rumpled jeans, and thin hands of my brother-in-law's uncle, Tim.

"Hi, Tim."

Tim tapped his pipe on his knee. "Hi, Glen." He leaned forward to rest his elbows on his knees, and as his face moved out of the shadow of the pine, moonlight glistened on his wet cheeks.

He had been weeping.

So what? Aunt Margaret, just a half hour earlier, had burst into tears of joy when her two-month-old granddaughter, sleeping on her lap, had suddenly smiled and kung fu-gripped her na-na's finger. "So strong! So precious! And she smells like ambrosia! I can't stand it!"

But Tim's tears were different, his face contorted, his eyes evasive.

"The last thing I said to her was, 'Don't buy the *goddamned* light beer this time'," said Tim. "She hated it when I cursed. She just took the car keys and left without saying anything."

Consulting my earpiece at that moment would have been rude, so I dredged my brain and managed to pull a pertinent fact from the muck: Tim's wife had died in a car crash. "Irma," I said.

Tim's eyes snapped on to me. "Inga."

"Right! Inga. It was on New Year's Eve too, wasn't it? What, three years ago?"

"Five."

"Right. She was such a nice lady." I smiled at him and sat in a patio chair, which creaked under my weight, preparing to reminisce about Inga's bacon-spiked potato salad and seal-bark of a laugh.

Tim tilted his head to the side and gave me a quizzical look.

I froze. Had she been not so nice, her seal-bark cruel, her potato salad spiked not only with bits of salty pork fat but resentment and vindictiveness? Could my memory be that bad? But then Tim looked out on the lake and sighed, and a word came to me that had been absent from my vocabulary for years, which I had hardly heard spoken since I was a boy.

Sad.

Tim was sad. He was remembering his late wife on the fifth anniversary of her death, and it was making him feel sad.

I scooted my patio chair a few inches closer to Tim and lowered my voice. "Tim, are you feeling *sad*?"

He looked back at me. "You *do* remember."

I stood up. "I'll call an ambulance," I said, tapping my earpiece.

"No, goddammit!" Tim grabbed my arm and pulled me back into my seat. "I want... don't you see? I *want* to feel sad right now."

I studied his pleading face. Was this insanity? Sadness was a disease of the past, one of the worst, responsible for countless deaths and more senseless suffering than any other brain malfunction. It had been cured decades ago. I had gotten the nasal mist when I was eleven years old, and nowadays it was administered to one-year-olds along with their hepatitis A and cold vaccines.

Nobody *wanted* to feel sad.

Did they?

"I didn't know what to do with myself after she died," said Tim. "I mean, for a few days there were things to do, flowers to choose, an urn to buy. I didn't have to think; I just said 'sunflowers' whenever anyone asked me a question. 'Sunflowers for the memorial service? Are you sure?' they asked. 'Sunflowers,' I said. 'Sunflowers on the urn?' 'Yes, sunflowers.' She liked sunflowers, you know? It was something I was sure about." Tim took a long puff. "Maybe it was the only thing I was sure about. The lawyer... he had a stack of papers for me to sign with little yellow Post-it tabs poking out where my signatures were supposed to go. 'It's like a sunflower,' I said to him. He smiled and nodded. I thought he had done it on purpose. That's how feeble-minded I was at the time. I thought the nice lawyer had turned the paperwork into Inga's favorite flower."

I chuckled experimentally. Tim let out a wheeze that may or may not have been a laugh.

"Anyway, after the remembrances were done, and the papers were signed and filed, and the social media condolence pings had died down, I waited. I sat in an armchair, and I waited. I skipped my lifelong learning group, and I didn't go to the movies the way Inga and I used to do. I didn't go for hikes around the lake, even though I could have used the fresh air."

After a pause, I asked, "What were you waiting for?"

"That's just it, Glen. I didn't know *what* I was waiting for. It was like there was something I was going to do, but I couldn't remember what it was. And at some point I just forgot that I was waiting, and I resumed my life without ever having remembered what I was going to do. I took an ornithology class, and I bought some binoculars. I became a birder."

"Yeah, I heard that you —"

"What a dumb hobby that was. If I never see another rufous-bellied thrush it will be too soon."

"Oh."

"But I met another birder. Carmela. And, you know, sitting all day in a field with your binoculars and your bag of roasted cashews... Between almost spotting some fucking bird or other, it all came out. About Inga; about the light beer; about the yellow Post-its; about the waiting without knowing for what. And Carmela turned to me and said, 'Maybe you just need a good cry.' And then she said, 'Shhh,' and raised her binoculars, so I couldn't tell her how batshit crazy she was."

"Yeah."

"No, Glen. She wasn't crazy. As I sat there thinking, I realized she wasn't crazy. And then she asked me if I had heard of The Big S."

"The Big S?"

●

That was the first time I heard the drug's street name. It was usually called PIDS, an acronym of a complex, difficult to synthesize, and impossible to pronounce chemical. Some kids in Pittsburgh had been caught taking it.

On the ride home from the party, I leaned my forehead against the window and let my eyelids droop. The Big S. What was so big about it? My conversation with Tim had left me with an impression of something internalized but forgotten, like a dream whose details disintegrate in the morning light but whose pithy emotional core lingers through breakfast. It was enticing and frightening, and it smelled like... onions?

Clearly, I'd drunk too much champagne. I'd even asked Tim to put me in touch with his drug dealer. My wife would not approve.

I leaned towards her. "You know PIDS?"

"Pids?"

"You know, that drug…"

"Oh, right. The Big S." She shook her head. "It's so —"

"Hey, how do you know it's called The Big S?"

"What do you mean, how do I know? Everybody's talking about it."

"Everybody?"

"I just can't believe anyone would *want* to take it, you know? Imagine, *wanting* to feel *sad.*"

I didn't respond.

"You know?" she prompted.

"Yeah." I said, while thinking to myself, *1212 18th Street. 1212 18th Street. 1212 18th Street.* The drug dealer's address, whispered by a birder in a bramble of blackberries to Uncle Tim, and passed along beside a moon-streaked lake to me. "Yeah."

●

1212 18th Street turned out to be a narrow, tinted-glass door tucked between a Noodles-2-Go and a mattress discount store. Scotch-taped inside the window above the door was an index card with the letter 'S' written in black marker, giving me confidence I had found the right place. I pressed the button five times in quick succession, as instructed, and peered into the nearly opaque glass. The door clicked. I pulled it open.

Leading up from the entryway was a burgundy-carpeted stairway, old but well-tended and lined by a brass railing, mottled with wear. On about the fifth step, high enough for her doleful eyes to be even with mine, sat a Cocker Spaniel. "Hello?" I said as I looked for evidence of a human presence. Finding none, I smiled at the dog's golden fur and long, ruffled ears. "Hey there, pup."

She turned to climb the stairs and I felt compelled to follow.

Red-paneled walls and yellowish lights gave the stairway a sinister, warm glow. I stopped on a landing after the first flight and the spaniel looked around. "Lead on, Virgil," I murmured. "Lead on." What was that from? Hamlet following the ghost? No. Dante, on the way to purgatory? Yes.

I entered a room lit with recessed sconces and furnished in antique cherry. The dog curled up at the foot of a velvet couch and huffed a sigh.

"Hello?" I said.

"Who is that, Daisy?" A silver-haired man entered the room from a dark hallway. "What have you dragged in off the street now?"

"Hello. I was given this address for... to get..."

"Yes, yes. Have a seat."

He didn't quite look at me, waving his hand dismissively. I hesitated, embarrassed, and suddenly wished I hadn't come. It was a bad idea after all. If my wife knew... But I was comforted by Daisy, lying croissant-like by the couch. I sat and leaned down to pet her.

The man reached to verify the existence of an armchair and lowered himself in. Blind, I guessed. He rested his hands on his knees. The cuffs of his shirt looked freshly ironed but slightly frayed. "So, first things first. Did you get the memo? No recording devices?"

"Yes," I said, distracted by the discoloration of his open shirt collar where it met his creased neck. "I mean no. No devices."

"No earpiece, no iris implant, no micropod?"

"I left it all at home."

"Good, good." His shoulders settled and his face softened. "So, you and Daisy are acquainted. My name is Bartholomew."

"I'm Glen."

"You came for The Big S, correct?"

"Yes."

"Good, good. How much do you want?"

"Uh..."

"You don't know, of course. You're a novice. Maybe you're not even sure you want it at all. Hmmm?"

"Well..."

"It's okay. Daisy, bring us a ten, please. Daisy, TEN." The dog didn't move. "She'll wait a moment just to prove to herself she's nobody's servant, and then she'll go get it. Watch." A note of warning entered his voice. "You're a good girl, aren't you, Daisy?" She got up and trudged from the room. "Yes, a very good girl."

"What a sweet dog."

"You try one, and if you like it, you buy the rest, okay? Simple, simple, simple. Free samples are key. Always. Have you ever sold drugs?"

"Me? No."

"You sound a little shocked by the question. Delicate soul. Ah, here's Daisy." The dog rattled back in with a bottle in her mouth, which she dropped in Bartholomew's outstretched hand. "Good girl." She slumped by the couch again, her body sounding like a small sack of potatoes being dropped on the wooden floor.

Bartholomew turned his face towards Daisy, and they sighed simultaneously. "She's a sad dog," he said. "And that sounds like I'm anthropomorphizing, but I'm not. She's had real sadness in her life."

"Oh?" I dug into the downy fur behind her ears to give her a good scritch. "Poor dog."

"What do you remember, Glen?" He shook the pill bottle. "About sadness."

"Not much, really. Just that..."

"Yes?"

"I was eleven when I went to the doctor for the mist, and my mother told me I wouldn't feel sad ever again. And that made me sad." Bartholomew raised his eyebrows. "I don't know why. Then I got the mist and I tried to hold on to the feeling, just to see if I could, but it was gone."

"Gone. Poof." He had a wry smile as he raised his hands magician-like in the air. "And what did feeling sad feel like? Do you remember that?"

"I really don't. That's what's been driving me crazy."

"Ah." He popped open the bottle and shook a pill onto his palm. "Well. So here we are. There's water on the coffee table."

I eyed the pill in the thin-fingered, slightly shaking hand. "How long does it last?"

"An hour, maybe two, the first time."

"The first time?"

"It builds up, so it goes on a little longer after that."

"Oh? Is it addictive?"

His hand dropped to rest on his knee, still holding the pill for me to take. "I don't think so."

That hung in the air for a moment.

"The Big S," said Bartholomew, clearing his throat, "has not been approved for sale by the Food and Drug Administration. I am not a board-certified pharmacologist. I offer no warranties, no assurances, no scientific studies showing short-term efficacy or long-term safety, no whitepapers, no testimonials beyond what the person who sent you here provided, without which you wouldn't be here, right?"

"Uh..."

"Word of mouth. That's another key to success in my line of work, along with free samples and making sure nothing gets recorded. But you didn't come here for drug-slinging advice. What you *came* for, what I *offer*," he shifted in his chair and leaned forward, "is that feeling your eleven-year-old self tried to hold onto but couldn't. That feeling that's too volatile, too dangerous, too *thrilling*," he closed his fist on the pill and pulled it away, "for society to let you feel it. You came here because you believe your feelings are your own to feel, that you can't be human without them, all of them, and this one," he opened his hand back up and pushed it in my general direction, "was stolen from you."

After a pause, I cleared my throat. "That was a good sales pitch."

"Thank you."

"I'll try it, of course." I leaned forward and took the pill. "It's what I came here for, I..." The tiny white hockey puck rolled on my palm.

"Yes?"

My feelings swirled: apprehension, curiosity, embarrassment, excitement. Bartholomew's creased brow tried to communicate openness and concern but couldn't hide an underlying impatience. "Never mind. Down the hatch!"

I popped the pill in my mouth and washed it down with water. I put down the glass and settled back on the couch.

"How long does it take?"

"A few minutes. Usually. While we wait, I could tell you about Daisy." Bartholomew crossed his arms and leaned his head to the side. "I find it helps set the mood."

"Okay."

"So, Daisy here was born to a Cocker Spaniel breeder in Greensboro, North Carolina. She was a friendly pup, or so I've heard, though she had a particular hatred for percolating coffee makers." He shrugged. "Still does; I switched to French press. Anyway, at eight months old, during her first heat, for reasons that were never explained to my satisfaction, the breeder thought it would be a good idea to breed Daisy with her father."

At the word 'father', I felt an unaccustomed tightening or twisting or burning sensation in my sternum and up around my rib cage. Like a lime being squeezed and the acidic juices leaking into my chest cavity.

"What?"

"Yes. Her father. Against all recommended breeding practices, moral codes, and plain old common sense, she was bred with her father while she was still, really, a puppy, and she got pregnant, and a couple months later she gave birth to something."

The feeling in my sternum spread out in thickening waves to my limbs.

"A poor, misshapen little something, that she clutched and cuddled and licked even though it showed no signs of life. When the breeder came to take it away and dispose of it, Daisy growled and whined, very out of character. She bit the breeder, hard, which would have gotten her put down but for the dram of compassion lingering in that breeder's shriveled heart."

The feeling grew heavy and warm — fleetingly, inadequately warm — like those lead jackets they used to make you wear when they x-rayed your teeth.

"That night, she howled out her pain, hour upon hour, while the breeder wore industrial grade foam earplugs she kept for just such occasions."

It was a big feeling. I groaned under its weight. The Big S.

"Daisy was not the same after that. She roamed the house in search of her lost baby. She was ruined for breeding, so she wound up at a shelter in Virginia, where I found her. Four years ago or so."

Looking at Daisy, watching the rise and fall of her breath, I slid off the couch and began to pet her from the crease in her forehead to the tip of her tail. She lifted her head at first in mild surprise, but then let it drop with a sigh.

"She had a sock. The shelter volunteer told me it had come with her from North Carolina. She would stow it in her bed and lick it in her quiet moments. I think it was her replacement baby. But we've lost it, and my socks aren't good enough for her, apparently. I've felt around, under the couches and chairs. It must be... but anyway, how are you coming along there, Glen?"

"Poor Daisy."

"Yes, yes. Poor Daisy. Ach, well, I may have embellished the story a bit over the years, but the general outline is accurate. If you do see a sock, a cotton athletic sock... But, you know, maybe I am anthropomorphizing a bit. Who knows what's in that little canine heart of hers?"

My hand paused on Daisy's back, and she raised her head to admonish me for slacking off. "What if the sock," I said, "was only a painful reminder?"

"Could be, could be."

Bartholomew folded his hands on his lap. From my vantage point on the floor his face looked distorted, like an ill-fitting mask. Tufts of salt-and-pepper hair poked from his nostrils. Under the coffee table I saw ratty slippers, toes poking through a broken seam.

I refocused my attention on Daisy and probed the width and breadth and height of my drug-induced sadness. I had thought that I would burst into tears, but that didn't happen. The feeling was comfortable, familiar, satisfying even, like picking a dried scab on my knee as a kid.

I was eleven again, holding the feeling close, watching my mother's face as she watched mine. Watching her watch the creases in my brow smooth out. Watching her watch me watch the worry in her eyes fade away.

Remembering her, pre-mist, lying beside me on my bed, shushing me softly, and at the same time encouraging my tears. A boy had pushed me while I was at the urinal, and I sprayed pee on the floor. The other boys laughed like cartoon donkeys. They hated me. "No," she said. "You're my sweet little boy. Let it out. It's okay." Let it out, get it out, spill it out...

Remembering another night when daddy said mommy was feeling sad. I tried to comfort her the way she had comforted me. "You're my beautiful mommy," I said. "It's okay. Let it out, mommy. Get it out." Her eyes dry and blank, not letting it out. Her body a lead weight, so heavy I thought I would roll into the well she made there on the bed. Daddy in a chair with his hands on his face, dragging them down. "I love you," he said to mommy, like an accusation, almost.

Let it out, get it out, spit it out, work it out...

I love you, but...

The edge of a bottomless pit...

Visiting mommy in the hospital, the machine with the colored graphs and lights and numbers, the needle in her arm, the smell of medicine and doctors, dim gray lights in the ceiling, watching her watch me watch her watch me...

Daddy, taking her hand. "I should have locked up the pills," he said.

Locked up the pills...

I love you, but...

Sliding, grasping, flailing, falling... my very own pit... my eyes dry and blank.

Later, after the mist, walking into the kitchen, and daddy saying to mommy, "Well, it saved your life." He diced onions while mommy stirred something in a pot on the stove.

"Maybe," she said.

Daddy scraped the onions into the pot. He sniffled and rubbed his eyes. It was the onions. It was just the onions that made that happen now. He placed the cutting board on the edge of the sink and laid the knife across it, its blade flashing.

I realized that this memory had been an unanswered question lodged in a crevice in the back of my mind all these years. What had saved her life? The mist?

"Bartholomew, what about sadness that is *too* strong or lasts *too* long?"

He had been sitting stoically, hands folded on his lap, hairy-knuckled thumbs twiddling. How much time had passed? He opened his mouth but paused a moment before answering. "It's a risk, but I haven't heard any complaints."

I scooped my hand under Daisy's body as I stroked her from head to tail, head to tail, head to tail. Her eyelids fluttered. Little by little, the sadness lifted, until I found myself cooing and chirping, "What a nice dog you are, Daisy."

"So," said Bartholomew, "what do you think?"

I blinked at him. The feeling was gone, but the dark cloud of memory lingered. I got up and sat back down on the couch and eyed the pill bottle on the coffee table between us.

"Quite an experience, right?"

"Yes. Wow. Quite an experience."

"So, I accept Q-bucks or Singaporean Aphids." He leaned down and retrieved a card reader from a drawer in the side of the coffee table.

"Well, I…"

"You can start with the ten, or I do have the thirty-thirty deal — 30 percent off a bottle of thirty. That's three times the experience for only twice the 'phids." He tapped the card reader on the edge of the table.

"I don't…"

"You don't what?"

The leaden weight; the eyes watching, hoping, fearing; the slippery-edged pit. "I don't think I want them."

"You don't *think*?"

"I mean, it's quite an experience, as you say… but for me, it's not a good idea."

"Not a —" The card reader clattered on the table as Bartholomew leaned back and crossed his arms. "Daisy, bite him. Bite Glen on the ankle for wasting your master's time. Go on. Daisy, BITE."

Daisy rose and yawned nervously. She looked from Bartholomew to me and back again.

"She won't bite you, will she? She thinks she's not my servant, doesn't she? But who feeds you? Huh?"

Daisy sniffed my pant leg and nudged my hand with her nose.

"I should have stuck with smack and weed." Slapping his knees and rising, Bartholomew sang under his breath.

"*Weed and smack and a little bit o' crack*. The good ol' days." He left the room, knocking his knee on a chair and cursing softly, bitterly. "Fuck."

I rose to apologize, to say goodbye, to say something — maybe to say I'd buy the pills after all. Nothing came out of my mouth. Instead, I knelt down to pet Daisy some more.

"I'd better go, Daisy."

I wanted to get out before Bartholomew came back. With Daisy at my heel, I headed for the stairs. By the door, a rolled-up sock behind a vase on an eye-level shelf caught my eye.

"Oh. A sock. Could this be...?"

I lifted it off the shelf, and Daisy tensed. She sat and pinned the sock with her gaze.

I had theorized earlier that the sock had been an unwelcome reminder. Maybe it would be better for Daisy if I put it back on the shelf? But with her intent, pleading eyes drilling a hole in my hand, that was out of the question. Would it dredge up sorrowful memories of unfulfilled motherhood, or would it soothe the ache of a barren womb? If she could speak, could she explain it? Would I understand? Or did she only know she wanted it?

And what about me, retreating, tail tucked, to a present of forgetful bliss?

I held the sock in front of her snout, and she enveloped it in her mouth. I let go, and she rushed behind the velvet couch and out of sight.

"You're a brave soul," I said, turning to descend the stairs.

David Hammond's story "The Big S" was originally published in Metaphorosis on Friday, 2 April 2021. See magazine.metaphorosis.com

About the author

David Hammond lives and dreams in Virginia with his wife, two daughters, one dog, three rats, and a multitude of insects. During the day, he makes websites. oldshoepress.com, @hammond13

Through the Middle

J.B. Kish

There's a woman driving slowly down highway 27 in their direction, and every couple of miles, she opens her window and lets a handful of something human-tasting scatter in the wind. Ashes, Rory suspects. She misses the man who's now dust and cries a little as she goes, singing Bill Withers because the radio doesn't play much more than static and gospel out this far. Bump thinks the powdered man must have liked Bill Withers very much.

At the speed she's going, she'll reach the diner in about thirty minutes. Rory presses a finger into the countertop and thanks Bump for the heads up. Then he puts on a fresh pot of coffee. Coffee's a good start for sadness like this, Rory thinks, and he should know. He's only just found happiness again.

Rory sits behind the counter, shaped like a farm egg. He's put on weight that rounds him. Muscular legs stick out beneath his body like a pair of clearance sale limbs not intended for him, and he wears the rest of his skin like thick diving dress, rich with small folds that retreat from his ribs and neck. His body is a game of hide and seek: American traditional appearing around each corner. There's a woman in a bathing suit diving down his forearm. A faded anchor on his bicep. Twin sparrows on his chest that no longer fly straight.

Half an hour passes, and her Civic pulls up to the far-flung roadside diner. Rory plays "Grandma's Hands" on the jukebox and pours a fresh cup of coffee. The woman walks in with a newborn puppy, and he greets her warmly. When she hears Bill Withers, she buckles a little, and Rory helps her to a nearby booth. "Here," he says, placing a ceramic mug in front of her. "This will make you feel better."

Rory disappears into the kitchen and fixes the woman — her name is Aliyah — something to eat. For a long time, Aliyah reclines in the booth and stares at the sunset with the puppy in her lap. Her t-shirt is cotton-white, floating elegantly above a pair of cut off shorts and some skateboard sneakers. The skin of her cheek is pocked with dark acne scars that she's not covered up. She looks like the subject in a Rockwell painting.

Bump asks who Rockwell is and Rory places a finger on the wall like he's using a walkie talkie. Silently, he explains Norman Rockwell was an artist who used to paint restaurants like theirs. Then Rory slides a turkey sandwich in front of Aliyah and asks if she'd appreciate company. She accepts politely, and he wonders for one terrifying moment what he — an old man in his seventies — can offer this woman, if anything. He knows nothing about being young or black or growing up in these times. But he has an ear, which is all she seems to need, and Aliyah explains she's wandering southern Oregon, spreading her father's ashes. He was one of the west coast's most celebrated archeologists, and he died peacefully of old age a month ago. After an hour, Aliyah makes an embarrassed face. She's been talking this whole time and hasn't asked Rory one question about himself.

Rory prefers it this way. He doesn't like talking about his father or the Navy; he's not the kind of discarded thing that complains. Anyway, nothing before matters because this is where he matters most. Of course, Aliyah doesn't understand that at all and surprises him by asking, *What's next*.

Rory laughs through his nose. "The only way this diner shuts down is because I've died and there's no one left to open it."

"Suppose you win the lottery."

He sips his coffee too quickly and wets his mustache; Aliyah grins as he dabs his mouth dry. "I grew this thing in the Navy because I had a baby face. My commanding officer said it would make me look smart."

"Did it?"

Rory nods and sits back. "In the Navy, you know exactly where you matter most. They tell you where to be and what to do. How to shave, how to dress. After I got out, I spent a long time searching for value again. When I found this restaurant and its customers, I *did* win the lottery. I don't think I could ever walk away from that."

Aliyah ponders his words a while before dismissing them with the wave of a hand; he can't help but fall in love with her a little. *Aliyah's* value, she explains, chases her like the puppy on her lap. She gets job offers because her father had important friends and they think her trowel was destined to continue his legacy. But she doesn't want a life in the dirt. She wants to start a vegan bakery. "But is that a terrible idea?"

It's not, and Rory envies how clearly she sees herself.

"You know, I've heard of you," Aliyah says. He points to his breast, and she nods. "They say there's a hermit in the desert that helps people. That's you, I think."

He shrugs. "Most folks know what they need. Sometimes they have to hear it a specific way."

On the way out the door, she thanks him for good company and happy coincidences. "Bill Withers was my father's favorite, you know."

Rory holds up a finger and fetches a cup of coffee to-go. "For the road," he explains, and then he grabs a handful of sugar packets from the table. "And for the bakery."

Aliyah chuckles at the gift and gives Rory a squeezing hug. "We'll see."

His heart beats like a young man's as she heads down the road. It was a nice cup of shared coffee, he thinks. Coffee's always a good start for sadness like that. Then Bump asks if Norman Rockwell can come paint their restaurant, and Rory laughs before turning in for the night.

●

Bump came through the middle.

That's the only way he's able to tell it. One day, he 'passed through the middle and surfaced here', just about the same as most customers. He could be extraterrestrial, but Bump didn't come from the great above. He came from deep, deep below, 'through the middle', and burst up against the ground like a pimple on the cheek of southern Oregon's desert.

Rory never tries to dig him up because it wouldn't be polite, and Bump seems satisfied enough to exist under the asphalt bloom behind the diner, which houses him like a geodesic dome. Besides, Bump says the asphalt is what connects him to the road and the people traveling their way. It's through this that he can feel the vibration of human emotions, touch palms through cracked leather steering wheels, and read Rory the prologue of their customers. It's what makes the pair a uniquely wonderful team, and why Rory is truly happy for the first time in a long while.

This is why Rory's stomach drops when Bump says someone is coming, but he can't sense anything about them. Bump can perceive the subtle weight of their body through the driver's side tires, but the rest feels eerie and quiet. It's almost as if there's no one there at all. *Can Mustangs drive themselves on this planet?* he asks Rory realizes he's not breathing and tries to inhale casually.

Anyway, says Bump. *They should be here tomorrow afternoon.*

●

But first, there's a man and a woman — a college couple in their twenties — coming down the highway, and whenever she brings up his temper, he wrings the steering wheel in a way she can't see. His little outbursts are growing more frequent, and even though he apologizes, they seem to be dancing around an incident — something like a *push* or maybe a *fall*, Bump says. They can't agree on which. The woman is assertive, but occasionally her voice is nervous around the edge. Rory thanks Bump for the heads up. With a frown, he puts on a fresh pot of coffee. Coffee's a good start when dealing with men like this. As it drips, he can't help his mind wandering to his tools out back and finds himself asking how hard it might be to dig a man-sized hole.

You'll not stick him down here with me, Bump jokes.

A while later, the bell rings, and without asking, Rory pours two fresh cups of coffee.

A tattooed woman appears at his counter, looks down with a smile, and dubs him a saint. She holds the ceramic mug under her nose with both hands and breathes deep. She's brunette and diamond shaped, with as much life as a fresh battery. When the boyfriend appears over her shoulder, he has a square head and practiced neutrality. A chameleon: Rory spots it right away. Polite. Jovial. Makes pleasant conversation all the way up until he leaves for the bathroom, which is outside around back. Rory forgets to mention the very specific jimmy required to unlock its door from inside, and that buys him a while to chat.

He places a pastrami sandwich in front of the tattooed woman with a roll of silverware. Her jaw drops playfully, and she asks why Rory owns a diner in the absolute middle of nowhere.

"Pills," he says candidly because she needs to hear this a specific way. She doesn't follow. "When I got out of the Navy, I took a job as a line cook and spent thirty years making people happy. And then we got bought out; I was fired by a hot shot celebrity for not understanding molecular gastronomy. No one in Portland wants to hire an old cook with bad knees, so when I hit the bottom, I drove down here to eat enough Oxycodone to put me in the ground."

Her eyes grow wide, and she has the packed cheek of a squirrel.

Rory smiles, easing a bit of this uninvited tension, "I found this restaurant instead."

The woman smiles uncomfortably. "Good for you." She tries to end the conversation on a high note. "So many five-star ratings online, you must be doing something right."

Suddenly Bump is there, in Rory's mind. *The mustang is going much faster. It will be here sooner*, he says.

Rory's heart skips a beat. What *is* all this nonsense about self-driving cars and phantom drivers? He discretely presses his right fingertip into the counter. The entire finger has vibrated with heat since the day he met Bump, when he pressed down on the asphalt dome curiously, and their connection was calcified. He theorizes it's a kind of foreign energy that comes from the other side — through the middle. When he presses down, he can sense its vein-like release, connecting him from the counter to the floor below, which joins with the building's foundation, the earth around, and ultimately allows him to project thoughts to his friend out back. *You're imagining things*, he tells Bump, and then he lifts his finger, ending the conversation.

Rory returns to the woman, distracted. "The point is," he continues, "it wasn't good enough to keep telling my family I'd change. People tell themselves they can just wake up tomorrow and *do better*. But I had to work at it. Leave an unhealthy environment, change my life. Otherwise, all those good intentions were just smoke and vapor."

The woman's eyes narrow slightly.

He makes a noise in the back of his throat, then nods toward the bathroom. "What I'm saying is, people don't magically wake up and *do better*. Unless he does the work, his apologies are just smoke and vapor." Then Rory tops off her coffee. "Understand?"

The blood drains from the woman's face and the bell rings over her shoulder. "Old man," her boyfriend growls. He walks up to the counter and throws the key into Rory's chest. It lands against the floor with a jingle. "Bathroom door is broken as hell." Then he nudges the woman with his elbow. "Hurry up and pay."

The whole interaction was a bit heavier handed than Rory prefers. When they've left, he walks out to the road and stares into the distance. He envisions a Mustang blowing fire from its tailpipe, riding a cloud of smog. And then, for reasons he cannot explain, he thinks of constructing a white tower for the first time in years.

●

What would you do if I passed back through the middle? Bump asks.

The sun is tangerine-orange and quickly fading. Rory flips a chicken breast on the charcoal grill he's rolled out back. With an elderly groan, he touches a finger to the ground. *You know it's rather unfair that I must speak through my finger, but* you *can project your thoughts directly into me.*

Humans are surprisingly complex, Bump answers. *Would you stay at the diner?*

Rory is annoyed and tense. *I'd climb the white tower and throw myself off,* he snips.

Bump is quiet a while, then says, *The mustang will be here soon.*

"Lord!" Rory shouts with his actual voice. "What is all this about?"

When Bump doesn't respond, Rory splays his fingers in frustration. "Fine," he says, "Let it come," and he walks inside. He grabs a large piece of parchment paper and writes 'PERMANENTLY CLOSED', then tapes it to the front door and kills the lights. There's not a single glowing bulb in the entire dining room. Out back, he waves a dismissive hand at bump and takes his dinner to bed.

●

He's here, Bump whispers.

Rory opens his eyes with a start, then sticks his head out the trailer door and spots a light in the restaurant. "He?"

The one driving the Mustang. He's waiting for you inside.

"It's nearly five in the morning."

You should go in, is all Bump says.

Inside, there's a handsome man sitting at the counter eating a bag of potato chips. He looks like he stepped off a Hollywood movie set, but Rory can't decide why. His features are elusive: Latin American one moment, Eastern European the next. There is a fresh pot of coffee on the counter, and he invites Rory to join him.

"Who are you?" Rory whispers, looking down at his parchment paper sign, which has been folded into a perfect square on the counter.

"Name's *Very Hungry,*" the man says with a punchline smile. It's a joke, but Rory's not laughing. The stranger reaches into his pocket and pulls out three one-hundred-dollar bills. "Can you make the perfect burger?"

Well now, just what in the hell is this? Rory wonders. *And why are you suddenly so damned quiet?* he asks Bump through the countertop. Bump doesn't answer.

"Every time I come here, I can't wait to get my hands on a real American cheeseburger." The stranger makes two fists. "But you can't go to a drive thru. What's the point of anticipation if the food's no good?" He slides the money forward. "Three hundred dollars for the best burger you can make."

Rory scowls. Breaking into his diner — scaring his friend — that's one thing. Questioning his ability on the grill is another entirely! He takes the money and draws up his torso. "I'll make it to-go."

Rory returns with possibly the greatest hamburger he's ever made. Carefully sculpted. Cooked to perfection. Golden French fries that could usher in the seventh trumpet! Lettuce so crisp it looked plastic!

And what does he find waiting for him? Nothing.

The Mustang is still parked outside, but there's no one sitting behind the counter.

Rory, says Bump.

He closes his eyes. *Shit*, he thinks, keeping this particular thought to himself. Cautiously, he walks out back and finds the handsome man standing above Bump, looking down at the asphalt dome with a mouth full of potato chips. Rory licks his lips and presses a finger into a wooden railing. "What is this?" he asks.

Rory, says Bump, *this is Hadrian. Hadrian, this is Rory.*

Hadrian waves and smiles. It's not unkind, and Rory hates him for that.

Hadrian is my grandchild, adds Bump.

●

Inside, the to-go box is empty. Rory is three hundred dollars richer, and he's never felt worse.

Hadrian is here to take Bump home. Bump left without telling anyone, and at his age, he really needs to be looked after. A depression drapes over Rory like a series of blankets, one after the other. He feels heavier the longer Hadrian talks.

"But," Rory whispers. "We're quite good friends."

"That's a funny pair," suggests Hadrian. The sun illuminates the diner with a warm glow. Dust floats along the rays of light like sad poetry.

"I've come to care for your grandfather very deeply," explains Rory. He finds himself appealing to the man's sense of empathy, but who's to say if Hadrian has any to begin with. His kind comes through the middle and takes on a form that emulates the planet's inhabitants. That didn't necessarily mean they possess the same emotional capacity. "Perhaps he could stay here with me?" Rory's smile is desperate.

Hadrian shakes his head. "Grandfather got stuck trying to emerge. It happens occasionally. I'm here to help." He takes a long sip of coffee and sighs gratefully. "Have you considered what you'll do when Bump passes back through the middle?"

Rory's too scared of the white tower to answer, so Hadrian adds, "Would you like to pass through the middle with us instead?"

Through the middle — it's a terrifying notion! Timid, he whispers, "Your grandfather's never told me much about where you come from. And this is my home."

"So, you wish to stay here?"

"I wish for things to stay as they are!"

"They cannot," Hadrian says in a way that's not unkind. "We leave tonight."

Tears gallop down Rory's cheek. It's just like life to do this to him again. The bell over the door rings, and Rory jumps. Quickly, he dries his cheeks and waves hello to a pair of men with a young boy. Farmers perhaps? "Be right with you," he calls. "Grab a seat anywhere."

Rory plucks his apron from the counter, pausing long enough to ask Bump why he didn't give a heads up on their new customers.

"'I've suspended your connection to my grandfather," Hadrian whispers. "Only temporarily."

Suspended their connect — how dare he! What kind of game was he playing? Rory's face is beet read. He opens his mouth to shout when —

"Hey fella," one of the men calls. "Coffees and a juice."

Rory is shaking. Gradually, his expression lifts upward and he fetches their order. Standing above them, he withdraws a pad of paper and a pencil, clears his throat, and wonders why he's so uneasy.

"Y'all from around here?"

Neither man looks up from their menus. They're vaguely like one another. Brother's maybe? Or perhaps it's just coincidence. The youngest, a boy of ten or eleven, stares out the window thoughtfully. He has a book on his lap — *The Spectator Bird* — but never opens it. The eldest, a leathery man with ruddy cheeks, looks down at his wristwatch and speaks in a way that's not intended for Rory. "Two hours," he whispers.

The other nods and looks up from his menu. "Three omelets, bacon, white toast all around."

Rory notes the order and retrieves the menus. "Beautiful day out there."

The younger man slides his cup forward. "Top off, please."

As Rory steps back into the kitchen, Hadrian raises a polite finger. "I'd love one of those omelets, if it's not a complete bother."

The kitchen door swings shut, and for a long while, Rory stares at the range. Slowly, he begins making the order. It's easy. It's muscle memory. He could make omelets in his sleep, and without meaning it, his mind drifts to the white tower. He makes sure his index finger isn't touching anything that connects him to Bump, and he's ashamed of it. *How much is left?* he wonders. He is pulled from the question by the distinct smell of eggs starting to burn. He saves the omelets just in time. Again, it's muscle memory. He really could do this in his sleep.

After breakfast, the man with ruddy cheeks pays and Rory asks how everything was. "Sure," the man answers. "Good enough."

The blood drains from Rory's face as their truck pulls out the lot and disappears down the road. Hadrian picks at the men's leftovers while Rory dumbly removes his apron and floats outside, into his trailer, and opens the closet door. He pushes aside a few shirts and finds a shoebox tucked all the way in the back. Inside is an orange prescription bottle with ten tablets that make a maraca sound when he shakes them. His heart pounds as if it means to crack his ribs, and suddenly Rory can't breathe. He races outside for air.

Hadrian sits on a folding chair next to Bump, finishing a side of potatoes. After Rory's caught his breath, he drags a chair next to them and squeezes the plastic bottle between both hands.

Were you able to serve those men? Bump asks.

Hadrian nods; he's allowed them to speak again.

"I was able to feed them," Rory answers. "If that's what you mean."

Quietly, he opens the plastic bottle and slides half the contents into his palm. They're heavier than he remembers, like they have somewhere important to be. He imagines them pecking through his skin and dropping out the back of his hand, so he stacks them one by one on his armrest before they can get away. Carefully, he constructs a beautiful white tower and envisions himself standing atop it, leaning out over a smooth, granite edge. The vast Oregon desert yawns beneath him, and his heart flutters at the brush of an old friend. An adrenaline he hasn't felt in years.

Rory's only closed his eyes for a moment when his chair nudges strangely, and when he looks back down, the tower is missing, and Hadrian is making a childish face. "These aren't good at all."

"You ate that?" Rory sits up as Hadrian dry swallows a white paste.

Hadrian's eyes widen. "The mints?"

"You can't have."

"Hadrian," Bump says. "Those were Rory's mints."

Rory presses a finger into his armrest. "They're not mints." Then to Hadrian, "You need to vomit."

"You mean on command?"

"Quickly."

"What happens if I don't?"

Rory doesn't answer, which is answer enough. "Oh." says Hadrian, sitting back. "Interesting."

"How exactly?"

"Well, if I don't, then my grandfather stays here, and you get what you want."

Rory's blood thickens with pressure. "I don't want your grandfather to be stuck here."

"But you don't want him to leave either."

"I don't want things to change." He's about to stand and force Hadrian to vomit himself. "What about our customers?"

"Will they stop coming?"

"How do you propose I help them without your grandfather here? Look what happened in there."

Hadrian makes a face like he finally understands the riddle in front of him. "My grandfather gives you value."

Rory draws himself upright. "Of course not."

"Is there someone else who does that?"

"His commanding officer," Bump says brightly.

Rory twists his hands anxiously. "My what?"

"You told the dust-man's daughter that your commanding officer made you grow that mustache and now you're smarter. He has given you value."

"No."

"You're not smart?"

"I was always smart."

"The mustache doesn't make you smart?"

"You need to throw up right now."

Hadrian holds out both palms like he didn't read that part of the human manual. "Do I punch myself?"

"Who then?" Bump asks.

"No one *gives* me value," Rory barks. "Stick your finger all the way down your throat until something happens."

Hadrian does as he's told.

Rory twist the cap onto the prescription bottle and stuffs the remaining pills into his pocket. "What would you have me do?" he growls. "Leave the diner tonight? Abandon my customers?"

"The diner gives you value," Bump clarifies.

"No." Rory pinches his brow and then points at Hadrian. "*Deeper.*" Hadrian grunts in acknowledgment and his finger descends another inch.

"Then what?"

"*I* do," Rory shouts. "I'm good at this. I'm good at helping people!" He stands and grabs Hadrian's elbow. He pushes upward and the man's finger disappears another inch. Hadrian gags fantastically; he vomits white bile onto Rory's clothes. It's unclear if he's disposed of all five pills, but Rory suspects it's enough. He's about to stumble backward when a small voice clears its throat: "Sir?"

They turn in surprise. The boy from breakfast peeks around the corner with a cautious expression. Rory let's go of Hadrian, who wipes his mouth and waves.

Bravely, the child asks, "You seen my book?"

"Book?" Then Rory understands. He waves the boy inside and searches the booth where they ate. He gets down on his hands and knees, hoping to find it under the table.

"What were you two fighting about?" the boy asks from behind.

"If I told you my mustache," Rory mutters, "would you believe me?"

Rory cranes his neck and spots the book wedged between the wall and booth. He reaches out and can nearly touch it with the tip of his finger, but Bump is idling there. Instead, Rory uses his ring finger to paddle at the book's spine until it falls to the floor.

Grunting, he shuffles backward and feels every vertebrae of his back unfurl. "Here." The boy takes the book and nods in thanks.

"Those men." Rory motions to the truck outside.

"My uncles."

"They don't talk much, do they?"

"Sure they do."

Sure they do. Rory's about to ask what terrible things they've been saying about breakfast when the boy turns and heads for the door.

"Wait —" Rory calls out and the child stops to look over his shoulder. Rory wants to ask; he's desperate to know, but a thick feeling of shame coats his throat. Frankly, the words are so dull in shape that even his mouth is bored with them, on top of which he's just realized how badly he stinks. The truth is, he's so insecure that this entire moment feels perfectly normal, and he hates himself for that.

The boy startles him by going first. "It doesn't matter if he doesn't like it."

Rory stops. He doesn't understand.

"Your mustache." The boy draws himself upward and walks across the checkered floor with raw, adolescent confidence. He places a companionable hand on Rory's bicep and says firmly, "I think it only matters if *you* like the mustache."

There's an inaudible *crack* of ivory-white granite.

With a radiant clap on his arm, the boy turns and jogs out. Rory opens and closes his mouth like a fish. His eyes have gently doubled in size, and there's a tangible warmth in his bicep. He floats to the window, and as the boy climbs up into the truck, he spots Rory. The boy waves and then reaches backward, withdrawing a plastic comb from his pocket. He holds it horizontally beneath his nose and smiles through the prongs.

●

Nothing here is as she remembers it. Aliyah sits in her Civic, staring up at the diner which is no longer the diner. It's *Dot's*, and Dot is a woman who doesn't allow dogs in her restaurant, so Koda waits in the car. Aliyah sits at a booth craning her neck, waiting for the hermit to round a corner.

Dot is a short Thai woman in her fifties who can carry more plates than seems possible. She tends to a busy dining room before dropping a cup of coffee in front of Aliyah. "Morning. Need some time or are you ready?"

"The man who worked here, an older gentleman."

Dot doesn't follow.

"He was the owner just a few months ago. Did he..." Aliyah tilts her head morbidly.

Dot shakes her chin no. "He sold."

Aliyah's stomach pirouettes. "He what?"

Dot smiles politely while scanning the restaurant from the corner of her eye. "If you need a little time with the menu..."

Aliyah nods and falls back into the booth, struggling to understand. She's driven all this way so he could talk her out of it. What's she supposed to do now? Take the job and play secretary for a department of PhDs obsessed with her last name? How could this have happened?

The hermit *sold* his lottery?

Aliyah sips her coffee and stares at a caddy of sugar packets and room temperature creamer. Dot returns a while later and refills her cup.

"Did he say anything?" Aliyah asks. "Or where he was going?"

"Were you friends?" When Aliyah doesn't answer, Dot nods. "He sold quickly."

Aliyah knits her brow and chews the inside of her cheek. She can feel herself sinking inward.

"He left something." Dot speaks softly as if telling a secret. "A funny note taped out front with a couple urns of coffee." Then she turns and points to a bulletin board near the door. "I couldn't bring myself to throw it away."

When she spots the note, Aliyah's skin prickles. She climbs out of the booth and walks to the board.

Passed through the middle, she reads. *Help yourself to some coffee. No matter the problem, I've always found coffee is a good start.*

"Hon?" Dot's voice appears over her shoulder. "Do you need more time with the menu?"

Rubbing her thumb over the note, Aliyah shakes her head. She pays for a coffee to-go and Dot fetches her a paper cup. As she turns to leave, Aliyah plucks a few sugar packets from a nearby caddy. She pictures the old hermit in the desert who used to help people. Who told people things they knew, just said a specific way. Without thinking, she grabs a handful more. She stuffs her jacket pockets with little white packets until they are full. Pretty soon, she's emptying another caddy over a table and scooping them into her saddle bag.

"Hey!" Dot shouts from the register, her eyes wide.

Aliyah smiles apologetically as she empties a third caddy directly into her bag. Then a fourth.

"I said stop!" calls Dot, but the bell above the door is already ringing. Aliyah is racing to her car, shouting an apology through the window. She's got to get going!

Bill Withers glides into place as she and Koda soar down the highway toward home. Aliyah's turning down the job; she was never meant for a life in the dirt. She's decided to take her sugar packets and build something brand new.

J.B. Kish's story "Through the Middle" was originally published in Metaphorosis on Friday, 9 December 2022. See magazine.metaphorosis.com

About the author

J.B. Kish is a weird fiction and horror author that helps emerging writers design a strategy to reach their goals. His writing has been featured in Underland Press' *The Cozy Cosmic, Metaphorosis' Best of 2022, Cosmic Horror Monthly*, and Unsettling Read's *Still of Winter* anthology. His author workshops have been developed based on eight years of helping clients roadmap and achieve their goals. When he's not writing, he facilitates workshops for people looking to improve their public speaking and presentation skills. Learn more at www.jbkish.com.

The Frozen Generation

Jacob Coffin

Compared to my coworkers, I didn't get many death threats. Storage, my department, was usually overlooked by fanatics and politicians.

They saved their anger for the people up front who made the Frozen Generation — the doctors and administrators who met the clients, did the scans, fed in the waldos, extracted the mingled cells, vitrified them in cryofluid. My crew in Storage were just the ones who tended them forever after.

They had their reasons for overlooking us. The Frozen were an easy demographic to advocate for, and an easier population to have when it came time to allocate votes and funds. But most people in this state would still tell you that extraction destined for cryostasis was just abortion with less guilt. Those people had gotten their way tonight, expanded the definition of abortion to include any extraction not destined for immediate gestation. And banned it.

Their new laws were going to close the clinic, maybe for a long time. But that wasn't my main concern. They'd also upped the charges for embryonic deaths in an extraction clinic and, tonight of all nights, I'd received notice of a blackout across the entire facility.

That's why I was in my truck, racing back to work as fast as I could drive after only two hours of sleep and despite the crowds celebrating in the streets.

We had backups. We were a priority repair site by law. We were seriously overbuilt for the two-hour limit the power company had to have us fixed by. But my team would be scared, and I wasn't going to let them deal with this alone. After all, they knew as well as I did that technically, under the new laws, any failure onsite could cost us our lives.

I made some calls as I got on the freeway. The front office didn't answer. No one on my crew knew what had happened yet, except that the power was definitely out and only for us.

The protestors had probably just shot out a transformer. They did that sometimes when they were celebrating. Tonight, that was really the best-case scenario.

The scattered fireworks popping low over the rooftops, the crowds in the streets around the churches, and the 3 a.m. rush hour traffic were enough to tell me tonight wasn't a night for best-case anything. But I wasn't thinking clearly.

●

Cars were already filling up vacant lots in the industrial park we called home. Armed silhouettes with posterboard signs grouped together in the early-morning dark and chill. The usuals claiming their spots early, maybe. Either way they'd have a big crowd today — some of our neighbors even rented their lots to them.

I was scanning the parking lots as I went — more from habit than because of the news tonight. I like to think I've gotten pretty good at watching my surroundings, even when I'm tired and stressed. After a protestor follows you home, you find your motivation.

The crowd got thicker once I was close enough to see the place. The clinic had already been pretty ugly, sort of a warehouse trying to turn into a bunker, but it was folks like these who had put the finishing touches on it, decorated the outside with scorch marks and bullet-pocks.

Speaking of bullets: one of them took a shot at me.

I honestly hadn't been expecting that. The crowd at the gate didn't have the usual rage tonight, though they threw some rocks when I pulled through, just to keep up tradition. I figured they were there more to celebrate and maybe burn our building down later if the police seemed amicable. They'd won, after all; no more need for self-martyrdom.

But once I made the last turn toward the garage, my back windshield exploded.

I hit the gas and slammed down the ramp and out of view before I'd fully processed the gunshot. And then it was over and I was sitting there in the red emergency light of the employee garage with more adrenalin than I needed for work problems and nothing to use it on.

I ran my fingers over tufts of foam in the new hole in my roof while I called the shooter in to our security team. Though God knew what they could do about him. After that was done, it all started to feel real, and I had to pause and get my breathing under control. I knew from experience that if I stayed focused, I could save the real freakout for after I got home and felt safe. And I had a lot of work to do.

The bullet hole was barely in arm's reach. Not a very near miss. Had he been trying to kill me or just scare me and make me run? That pissed me off worse than attempted murder. I could picture them laughing and cheering while I fled out of sight.

If they'd known what department I worked for, would it have made any difference?

I got out, slammed the door, and climbed upstairs in the dark, checking my phone for updates to the alerts that had woken me.

Power failures were the last thing we needed now. Every other supplier we relied on had been flaking for weeks, including our cryofluid producer, now fifteen days late on our delivery. I think they saw which way things were going, knew nobody was going to enforce our protections any longer. Even when a company's official faith didn't oppose extraction, there were always employees who felt that helping us endangered their immortal souls.

No updates on the power alerts. My feed was full of articles on the new laws, but I ignored them.

Don't get me wrong, things were bad, but this back and forth had been happening for my entire life. Hell, this mess of shortcuts and simple solutions was the reason I even existed. As far as I was concerned, this was just a temporary interruption of service until the law got challenged or interrupted somehow.

Even the people who had passed it didn't seem to expect this to last forever. They'd already tried gestating every unwanted embryo and that led to the government hives they then spent decades tearing down, and generations of Unwanted like me who didn't even vote for them. Doing it again with even less planning would be a horrible mess, but banning extraction with no solutions at all would be even worse.

The new laws would make things difficult, but I was trying to focus on what I could control. And for us in Storage, it would be business as usual, more or less.

From here on out it was our job to keep the clinic operational until we could reopen. And new admissions would be on pause, which would give us some time to catch up on maintenance, build some new racks, maybe even upgrade our cryofluid production capabilities if I could mooch some budget while the rest of the work was on hold.

We'd get through this.

●

Inside, the place was in chaos. Half the lights were off and there were way too many staff here for this time of night. The lobby was locked down, galvanized drop-barricades reflecting the lights back through the glass doors up front.

Ester was cleaning out her desk, taking everything with her name on it. She'd actually grown up in the same hive I did, though she was a later generation, so she was a bit more normal. I was in a hurry, but she looked so freaked out I stopped when we made eye contact.

"Moses, did you hear Dr. Quarzi quit?" she asked. She had her fake-calm, air traffic control voice going.

"What?"

"Yeah, he called in and did it over the phone right after the hearing, from London. He said this will be a huge mess and we should all get out before it starts if we know what's good for us. He'd already cleaned out his files and everything."

I blinked, tired eyes bleary in the bright light, and looked down at her desk. "Taking his advice?"

"Yeah. How about you?"

"I just came in to fix the power. If this place doesn't stay cold, we're all in a lot of trouble."

She gave me this look. "We're in a lot of trouble either way. My boyfriend has family in Canada — we're heading up there. You should get out too."

Wow.

"Uh, best of luck," I said. "Look, you'll be okay, you just do inprocessing."

Still that flat look, like I didn't get it. I guess I didn't. "Yeah. Good luck yourself."

Man, I just kept everything cold.

I hustled through the office, looking for the Operations Director. If the power loss was upstream, then getting it back was her problem. The rest of us just had to keep the outage from harming the patients.

Most everyone I saw was hurrying and worried. Some were unpacking reserve Herz-Stanton exowombs, and the rest looked like they were leaving. I didn't recognize half of them. Sure, most of my work is back in Storage, but I come up once a day to check the tanks in the clinic, write up my maintenance reports, and order parts. I like to think I'm sociable, for a hive boy anyways.

I stopped outside the Ops Director's office. Charlotte was standing over her desk, shouting into the phone, gestures and everything.

She didn't show any sign of slowing down, and with everything else going on, I couldn't wait for answers. Whatever had caused this blackout, I had to check our status.

I headed for Storage, my department. There was a reason that the only clinics left in this state stored their patients on-site: Storage facilities got guarantees. With the nation's most vulnerable citizens in our vaults, reliant on their services, the power and telecom companies couldn't drag their feet for weeks when we got disconnected. More than that, we were allowed to hire armed security, and even got an exemption to the Religious Freedom Act so parts suppliers had to sell to us as long as we could pay. They accused us of a lot; I suppose hostage-taking was fair.

Storage took up most of our site. It was the big, bulky, warehouse-looking part of the facility with the legally-mandated symbols outside, to protect clinic bombers from killing any of the Frozen. Inside, there were thousands and thousands of silver cryo flasks linked with tubes and wires resting on rows of metal shelves, elevated flood-safe, suspended and stabilized against earthquakes and guarded by the most paranoid fire suppression system in the county. Each had an individual battery backup for its sensors and pumps and a small reserve tank of cryofluid.

The manifest for each flask listed the occupants by social security number. No names or assigned sex yet. For the vast majority it was far too early to identify more than the number of cells, and you could usually count those on both hands.

In the back, rising up over it all, was the in-house cryo distillation rig. The patients' storage tanks didn't take power to stay cold; they were just fancy vacuum flasks with sensors. But their cryogenic fluid evaporated in an endless slow boil, and we needed power to monitor the levels and to run the pumps that kept them topped off. The in-house 'still was elevated so we could rely on gravity feeds if we had to.

Cryofluid is pretty complicated stuff. It's mostly liquid nitrogen, but nitro on its own can be a vector for viruses and bacteria between tissue samples. Cryofluid has a mix of additives so we could transfer it safely and to assist with vitrification and devitrification. It was actually overkill for our purposes, as most of our patients were kept in hermetically sealed straws, but our state legislature said nothing was too good for the Frozen Generation (except hives of their own), especially if it made running this place difficult.

As I looked for my crew, I automatically checked the dashboard for each rack of tanks I passed, eyeing the levels and power requirements.

All the levels were lower than I expected.

Some of my techs were shouting over by the loading dock. Zeke saw me and waved me over, calling across the warehouse:

"Mose!" He looked worried, and that worried me.

"Zeke, what's going on?" I asked. "Someone cut the lines?"

"Yeah! The fuckin' power company!"

"What, on purpose?" That cold dread started working its way down my back. They wouldn't. They fucking couldn't.

"Yeah. Told Charlotte on the phone. Can't legally provide services."

"What, because of the abortion definition thing? We're not taking patients and even then it'd only apply to the front office, not Storage." Not us. But the whole place was linked together — that was how the clinic benefited from Storage, after all.

"Yeah. Closed the loophole."

"Loophole, hell. This was their goddamn solution in the first place."

Exowombs were supposed to solve abortion. Then when the flood of Unwanted got too deep, and government-commissioned hives had to raise the kids, cryostasis was their solution for that.

I ran my hands over my face. This was bad. Without power, our reserves and battery backups weren't overkill — they were woefully, criminally inadequate. We weren't an island. Weren't supposed to be. State laws enshrined us as a priority recovery site. Hell, they'd send the national guard if there were a flood or hurricane. Send 'em right past people trapped on their roofs or buried in rubble. Anything for the Frozen Generation.

But that had changed, hadn't it?

"Charlotte's been screaming at the power company," Zeke said. "The state police, the governor, even. Nothing's got us online. Been running on our solar reserves and gas gennys ever since. I had Jimmy making runs to the charge station for extra fuel, but once they figured it was for here, they refused to sell to him. I sent him to Pembrook since they're the next closest with liquid, but I'd be surprised if he doesn't just quit."

"If the main circuit's off, we're not generating new cryo. Hell, half the tanks are already low." We had solar rigs, but like everything else, they weren't enough to make us completely independent.

"I *know that*, Mose!"

These guys were looking to me because I had always been the quick one, the first with a solution when things went bad. Some people are wired for crisis situations, and I kind of loved them. And now I was flat-footed, slow. Tired. They needed me to be better. I shook my head to clear it.

"Okay, we need to cut everything we can, try to make the reserves last. Mike, hit the breakers, cut the whole front office. Keep the clinic for half an hour and warn the docs up front — I think they've got a couple active exowombs, and they'll need time to transfer back to cryo. We can move 'em back here on the battery backups if we have to.

"Zeke, Sol, get the pumps running. Top up all the flasks and shelf reserves first, and pump whatever we got left into the reserve tanks on the 'still."

"It won't last as long once it's distributed."

"Yeah but it won't do us any good in the main tanks. Sounds like we could end up running without *any* power for a while, so we need to get the patients as self-sufficient as we can. Same for power, make sure the tank batteries are all fresh. Pull some from the vehicles if you have to."

It was the same protocol we were supposed to use if the ocean came in around us, or the building collapsed. Get all the cryotanks ready for travel and wait for the national guard to come collect us. We'd lose auto-refill when the generators stopped. Internal regulation and monitoring too, once the local batteries dried up. We could top off tanks manually, if we had any cryo left, and if we knew the tank was low. We'd have to make visual inspections.

If the outage lasted long enough, we'd have to start consolidating fluid.

After tonight, any embryonic deaths in an extraction clinic were to be charged as murder two. We could get first degree if it was the result of a deliberate action. That was starting to seem more possible than it had yesterday.

"I'll go talk to Charlotte and see about getting us some backup. Someone has to care." I tapped on a cryoflask. "They only just made a bunch of laws about these guys."

Everyone started moving, so that part of the job was done. We'd get this place set up as best we could and hope society at large would help.

●

I backtracked through the clinic, head down, through everyone's rush to prepare for whatever came next. Every now and then, security would call someone's name. Took me a bit to realize they were escorting people off-site.

I passed a couple of clinic techs opening up one of the equipment storage rooms. One had on the scrubs they all wear up front, the other just had jeans and a t-shirt. I thought I recognized them both from the day shift.

"What about the old Herz-Stanton Gen 20s?" the one in scrubs asked.

"Uh, they're not on the APL anymore," the other answered.

"But they still work fine, I mean, maybe keep them off the network but they'll do the job."

He wasn't wrong. I was born to a Gen 3 and even those were so safe that there were actual arguments over whether to ban internal birth because it killed too many Unborn Americans. It was a public health crisis, after all: when an American's life begins at conception, failure-to-implant becomes the country's leading cause of death.

They don't exactly cover that stuff in school but I guess I have an interest, since their last great idea led to me being born Unwanted, named by an algorithm, and raised in a hive, even if it wasn't one of the bible-warrior training facilities/sweatshops you see in the documentaries.

"She said all the approved units. This is just CYA, right? They're looking for ways to screw us, so I don't think we'll get bonus points for going above and beyond using illegal equipment."

"Fair enough."

If they were starting up extra exowombs now, of all times, that would be a problem. But I'd deal with it once I knew when we'd get the power back.

I didn't hear any shouting as I approached Charlotte's office. That seemed like a good sign. This had to be some local fuckup. Some anti-extraction asshole at the power company giving us a hard time.

Charlotte was slumped forward on her desk, her tablet docked and playing some news feed. The smart wall to her left showed every angle of the perimeter and most rooms in the clinic. On the cameras, cars had filled the closest lots outside. Biggest crowd we'd seen in years.

I knocked on the door frame. "Hey boss, how's it going?"

"Hey, Moses. I thought I told you to go home and get some sleep." She gestured at the news. "'Cease all extraction operations. Commence the immediate and safe transfer of all Embryonic-Americans to external wombs and begin gestation.'"

I gave her the baffled, disappointed look we'd shared through so many newsreels of hearings and debates.

"Yeah, we'll get right on that."

There weren't enough approved exowombs on the planet for that. And even if they'd all been in the U.S., it'd take decades to get through the backlog.

We had twenty on site. We'd tried to order more over a year ago, after the election, but all the domestic manufacturing companies were swamped, and you couldn't buy them from overseas for fear of foreign supply-chain sabotage. Sleeper-diseases, hard-coded loyalties, who knew what the Reds could cook into our most vulnerable citizens?

And hospitals got legal priority on exowombs, of course. Most wanted births were external these days, if only for the legal liability. A miscarriage was bad enough without the criminal investigation ripping your life apart just in case.

"All the hospitals in a hundred-mile radius are already swamped." She said, "I've called every one of them. The other sites are dumping as many cases off on them as they can. I got St Mercy's to agree to a *hundred*, a lousy hundred kids! And then some assholes parked ten freezer trucks in their emergency lane and took off on foot. Now it's all, 'sorry, now *we* have six hundred thousand to take care of, good luck with yours.' It's like that everywhere."

"Any word on the power?"

She snorted. "All the words are bad. It's not coming back."

"Why?"

"Power and Light's lawyers dusted off a couple of old state abortion laws from back around the fight over the amendment. Any organization or individual who provides aid or assistance *of any kind* to an abortion clinic will be held equally liable. Apparently, it doesn't matter that we're not taking clients anymore. Our lawyers think their interpretation is legit enough to stick until we've challenged it in court."

And if things kept going like this we'd all be in jail for mass manslaughter or negligent genocide or something by then.

"The storage facility protections-" I started.

"One law says they have to provide power, the other says they can't." She paused just long enough to solidify her composure. When you do her job, you can't ever risk it slipping — there're always cameras on you looking for ammunition. "Our lawyers are still with us, and they're raising hell best they can." She said, "The ACLU and opposition legislators too. But by the time this mess gets sorted out, it'll be too late."

"They- they realize that if we shut down all the way, the embryos will thaw, right?" I asked. "And thawing would be bad for them?"

She shrugged again, like she didn't want to give the lawmakers or God's power company that much credit. These were the kind of people whose idea of compromise had forced generations of women who'd otherwise have taken a pill to risk surgery.

"Why are they doing this? They have to know it'll blow back on them..."

She looked down at the tablet, head in her hands, and said the next part almost to herself. Like she was thinking aloud. "There's a census coming up."

"Boss?" I didn't like this line of thought.

"If six hundred thousand 'people' disappeared overnight, they could redraw the map. Eliminate this district, a progressive congressional seat, and who knows how many state-level positions. It'd change funding allocations and…" She looked up at me. "Or maybe they're just a bunch of zealots who didn't listen when we pointed out all the problems with the bill six months ago, including that this could technically happen, even if it seemed unlikely. Same results either way."

She scrolled back through the news footage, picked out a segment, and spun the tablet. The Reverend Senator Callahan was walking out of the capitol building, a wide, closed-mouthed smile serene on his face.

"It's about personal responsibility. To all those… facilities, I'd say you shouldn't have done the procedures if you couldn't take care of your obligations afterwards. The American people trusted you with their children, and if anything happens to any single one of them, we *will* hold you accountable. At long last."

"Oh."

That was all I could think to say. I'd missed something Ester and Dr. Quarzi had seen coming.

I knew they'd been trying to kill our industry. What I hadn't realized was that it wasn't about the Frozen Generation. They were after us.

Us, like as individuals, the people who worked at the clinics. Not just the politicians who supported us, or our CEO, or the other executives they dragged before congress, but all of *us*. Me.

Even after all these years in their crosshairs I'd still taken them at their word. Still internalized some gut, cultural-suffusion belief that they cared about the Frozen Generation enough not to sabotage them. No matter how much they hated extraction or us that enabled it, Storage should have been safe.

Oh. You damned idiot.

It wouldn't matter if tonight's ban got overturned if we were all in prison when it came time to reopen the clinic. Whether we were the victims of a conspiracy or yet another bit of collateral damage didn't really matter. Dr Quarzi was right. Ester was right. For all the good it would probably do them, at least they were running.

"How long do we have?" Charlotte asked.

I shook out of the reprieve; the math was fresh in my mind. We were already so low.

"Without more juice? Maybe a day or two before we start losing ones near the top of the flasks to evaporation."

With cryo, thawing isn't like you'd imagine. Everything's so cold, it's actually skipped freezing to being this ice-free glass. If it thaws unregulated, you have two problems: ice crystals will form and slice all the cells apart, and the cryoprotectants that preserve the cells by replacing their water will go toxic as they warm. Warming the cells and diluting out the cryoprotectants is a whole process you just can't manage when a few thousand flasks of enhanced nitrogen are going from liquid to gas and you have no electricity.

"I contacted our sister organizations and sent out an alert on all our social media. Described what they're doing and begged for fuel and cryo," Charlotte said. "We've got a good base of someday-parents who are organizing to help."

"Any luck?"

"Not sure if our people can even get through that riot outside. The police are supposedly here to keep things under control, but they're basically blockading us in."

My eyes were still on the muted tablet, watching our representatives. I felt a bleak certainty that there would be plenty of investigations to determine all the ways we were at fault for this.

The power cut out. The wall of security monitors went dead. The only light in the room was the screen on the tablet.

I shook out of it. "Oh, yeah. I had Mike cut everything but Storage. We'll move any clinic hardware we have to keep to the back, try to make it last."

Charlotte nodded. "Good idea."

"Could you double check the doors?" I asked. "Some of the emergencies are fail-open maglocks and we might need to barricade them."

"Sure." She grabbed a flashlight from her desk and the gun she kept holstered under the tabletop. She knew about the doors. She was probably relieved to have the distraction.

"Thanks."

Mike caught me as I left Charlotte's office.

"It's Dr. Clarke. She won't let me cut the clinic. Says she wants any surplus for the wombs."

"What? Tell me she hasn't started a new batch."

Those things suck power and they still take almost nine months per kid. Regulations imposed on the manufacturer — anything else would be unnatural. And there were only twenty of them. We had over six hundred thousand embryos and fetuses in the back.

"Sorry, boss. She outranks me."

"What, she's gonna print half a million kids before the batteries run out?"

But she had to look like she'd tried. She was the doctor in charge of production. Someday they'd be asking her, 'Why didn't you try to save *any* of them?'

We were on a sinking ship, and we were all looking ahead, past the lifeboats to the historians, trying to dictate what they'd say about us in their accounts.

Or, more likely, in our atrocity trials.

●

All twenty Securus Platinum exowombs were humming away on their pedestal mounts, and ten old Herz-Stanton 25s were sitting on the counter. All were occupied and lit.

I wondered where Dr. Clarke had gotten the kids. Were they future orders? Had she picked them at random? The front office tried anonymizing the embryos once. Give them all an equal chance at adoption. Our client rate had plummeted. People out in the world talked a big game about the abandoned, forever-frozen masses and their right to life, but when it came time to grow their new kid, they only wanted the best.

"Dr. Clarke?"

"I knew you'd show up." She looked tired and scared. She pointed her phone at me like it was a gun. Recording the conversation, proof she'd done all she could. Proof I was the bad guy here. Fine. Her jury would love us turning on each other.

"Doctor. You need to put the patients back into cryostasis." It's always 'the patients' when you talk about the Frozen, but especially when you know you're on video.

Her chin came up and her face went hard. "This is my department, and these patients' well-being is my responsibility. I have to do what's best for them. I don't answer to the cryotechs."

Ouch.

"They cut our power, and these things are draining the reserve." I spoke clear and slow for the court. "Without the exowombs running, we can get another day or so for all the patients in the back. Maybe they'll turn the power back on by then. If we don't, they'll *all* start to thaw." She didn't react, so I kept going. "We'll never have enough power for these machines either way. But running them could kill all the patients onsite."

I half expected her to say I was just trying to save my own department at her expense, but she didn't go there. She stuck to the script.

"The law says we need to transfer all Unborn Americans to exowombs immediately."

She put herself between me and them, like she expected us to fight.

I realized I didn't have to argue this out. I didn't have to say anything. The breaker was in the basement.

Antisocial hive tendencies, I guess. We always caught flack for being 'indirectly confrontational' after being raised by a monolith we couldn't affect in the slightest. As a nod to professionalism, I spoke up on my way out.

"Okay. You can put them back in cryo or you can take them someplace else. Either way, I'm cutting power to this room." I headed for the stairwell. She followed me.

"They can't leave these facilities! They're not allowed to leave the clinic. We have to maintain custody of all-"

I stopped at the basement door while I found my light. "I can spare a truck. I can't spare power."

"You don't 'spare' anything! That's not your decision to make!" I was the last facilities person here with any rank, so I would contest that.

Luckily, I didn't have to. Charlotte appeared from the darkness and stepped in. I guess we hadn't exactly been arguing quietly.

"Rachel. Stop," she said. There was an edge to her voice, but she kept it calm, authoritative. "We can't support them here. Not anymore. If you want them to make it, you have to take them someplace else."

"But they can't leave…"

She took Dr. Clarke's hand. "Listen, they, and you, will be safer someplace else. Take them to a hospital, take them to your church. Hell, take them to the governor's mansion. Anywhere'll be better." She started guiding her toward the garage. "Come on, I'll help you get a truck."

"I-"

"It's *okay*. It's okay. These are terrible times and you've done everything you could. If we had more than thirty exowombs, you would have saved even more. You've already gone above and beyond. They'll understand. Hell, you'll probably be a hero."

I hit the staircase, flashlight searching for the clinic breaker. I'd probably be able to watch her single-handedly rescue those thirty innocent lives again someday in the based-on-a-true-story dramatization. From my prison cell.

●

I made a decision on my way back to Storage. Or maybe I realized that I'd made it a while ago.

Keeping the Frozen 'alive' had always been the goal, but the way I'd seen it, my real job was to keep everything perfect back here, exceeding every regulation, so nobody went to jail.

Most of the crew I had left seemed to feel the same way. If we quit, we'd be abandoning our teammates, and the rest of the clinic.

That made what came next easier. My plans might have changed since the drive in, but I'd still be doing my job.

Zeke was manually forcing the heavy door to the employee garage when I got back to Storage.

"Jimmy's back, and he says he got fuel!" Sol told me.

Zeke grinned. "I love that kid."

The sun was up now. I saw a sliver of it as the garage door rumbled back down. The truck rolled to a stop as we all hustled over.

Jimmy shoved the door open and stumbled out, looking beat and wild-eyed. "I'm sorry, boss." He shook his head. "I couldn't get- it's bad out there."

His knuckles were scraped bloody and he had a nice shiner forming on his left eye. He'd stopped somewhere and spray painted over the logo on the truck. I wondered if it was before or after his fight.

I went around the back and looked over the bed of gas cans. Most of them were empty.

Zeke was talking to him. "Hey, hey it's okay. You're okay."

"No, it's not. They'd only sell me eighty gallons. I couldn't do more, I'm sorry. The first place, when I tried to fill everything, they figured it out and came out with a gun. I-"

Behind us, Sol swore and kicked the truck.

"Hey, it's fine!" I waved a hand at him, then looked back to our driver. "You did more than we had any right to ask. It's okay. We'll figure something out."

There was a half second of silence, and then: "I quit." Jimmy was looking down at the painted-over logo, focus distant. "Look," he said. "I just came to get my truck. Sorry." He met my eyes for a second. "Sorry. I'm done. I got to go."

And then he did.

We got as ready as we could with what we had left. We consolidated the fuel, shifted our resources around so we weren't producing any more power than we could use or store, made sure we were running everything else on the minimums.

They worked hard, though they looked scared, kept checking their phones. Couldn't hold that against them today. News updates, worried texts from families. Finally, I said, "Enough. Go home. We're as ready for shutdown as we're going to get."

After all the hassle from the government inspections, the impossible hours from being badly understaffed, the slurs and attacks and violence from the protestors, the crew I had left were here because they were loyal and they cared. With their skills, they could have gotten jobs at any lab or factory floor for more pay and less work, less stress. I was grateful for them.

"Naw, you'll need us here," Sol said.

"I need you to go get some sleep. Go home, see your families. I'll text you if we need anything else. There'll be a lot to do when Charlotte and her lawyers get the power back. They'll probably have inspectors out here before the next shipment of cryo."

"What about you?"

I didn't have kids, or anyone at home to worry about. Most of my forty-six surviving hive siblings could take care of themselves.

"I'll take the first shift here. I'll let you know as soon as anything changes, or if I need help with anything in the meanwhile."

"If the power doesn't come back..." Zeke started.

"I'll watch the levels. I got reserve batteries, reserve tanks, and gravity feeds from the 'still. If I need a bucket brigade, I'll let you know."

They laughed a little. Then they just looked tired. Finally, they took the out, headed for their trucks. Promised they'd look for gas, be back as soon as we needed them. But they weren't coming back and we all knew it. I wasn't going to text them, and they knew that, too.

Someone had to be responsible for what was going to happen next. Storage was my department. If I sent them away before the failures began, it kept responsibility for everything nice and tidy.

I waited till they were gone, then I climbed up on the pump station, set all the warning alarms to max volume, and took a nap.

●

I woke up when I started sweating through my clothes. The sun was cooking on the warehouse roof — good for our solar, not that it'd do more than pump our thin reserves around. The Frozen wouldn't notice this heat though, not in their vacuum flasks of liquid nitrogen. Out here it was too hot, but in there it was impossibly cold.

The generator's warning lights glowed amber on the dash. Nothing left to do about that.

I went for a walk around the clinic.

The place was empty, trashed in everyone's haste to evacuate. I could hear someone clinking around in one of the labs and it made me think of rats or squatters. Just last night it had been business as usual, and now this. Muffled outside, I thought I could hear voices and pops, like fireworks or gunshots.

Amerinews was playing in Charlotte's office.

"State militia units here in Godless California are mustering on the border for what they call a humanitarian mission, an invasion to kidnap and illegally transport the Frozen across state lines. It's a logistical nightmare in clear violation of state autonomy. God only knows what will happen to these helpless babies."

"Hey, Moses," Charlotte said.

"Hey. Jimmy quit."

"Everybody's quit."

We both looked at the tablet for a minute.

"How about you?" I asked.

"I'm going down with the ship. You?"

"I'll keep things cold as long as I can. After that, I don't know. Any luck on the power?"

She shook her head. Subject change. "There's a mob outside."

"Yeah? Maybe we'll get lucky and they'll set the place on fire. Take the credit." I said.

That got a little smile. "If you need to get out, the side door by client parking still opens out. Plus your loading dock."

"Thanks. Not sure there's any running away from this."

"Nope."

She sat there in the dark, lit by her dwindling tablet. "I'll be here if you need anything," she said.

I walked back to Storage and made my rounds again. Looked over all the racks and racks of flasks, batteries, reserve tanks, bundled wires and tubing. I'd configured most of these units. I'd loaded half of them. Tended them all for years, watched for even a single power or temperature failure. Soon there'd be thousands.

The last generator sputtered to a rest outside. The fans stopped. The pumps cut out. The beeps and squawks of the monitors went dead on standby. And in the silence, the Frozen Generation began to thaw.

Jacob Coffin's story "The Frozen Generation" was originally published in Metaphorosis on Friday, 10 February 2023. See magazine.metaphorosis.com

About the author

Jacob Coffin is a tech writer, woodworker, amateur electrician, and former apprentice blacksmith, with a passion for land conservation, reuse, and the world he lives on not dying. He has published science fiction with Metaphorosis Magazine, and in the upcoming Harbour anarchist fiction magazine. On the lighter side, he photobashes rural cyberpunk comics and scenes of a solarpunk future and shares them here: jacobcoffinwrites.wordpress.com

He shares his other projects, making and fixing things, here: movim.slrpnk.net/blog/jacobcoffinwrites%40slrpnk.net

And he's most active on lemmy at slrpnk.net/u/JacobCoffinWrites and mastodon at writing.exchange/@jacobcoffin

My Little Sister Brigid

Harold R. Thompson

My little sister Brigid was born when I was four years old. I loved her from the start. She was this funny little pink smiley thing with a round bald head like a baseball, and for a while I called her Baseball Head. I enjoyed talking to her and telling her things, even if she didn't talk back. She never said a thing, even as she grew older. Our parents seemed worried, but I figured that was just the way she was. She would never speak and that was that. I played games and explained them to her. She just watched me with her huge eyes, and I thought she understood.

Once, after she'd returned from a trip to the doctor, I told her, "I'll make sure nothing bad ever happens to you."

I would make Mom and Dad happy and feel safe.

One day when she was five, Brigid looked at me and said, "What's for supper?"

"Pork chops and corn on the cob," I said. I'd been looking forward to that. Then I said, "Hey, you talked!"

After that she spoke in complete sentences worthy of any six-year-old, or even an adult.

"What are all those lines?" she asked me one day.

"What lines?"

She told me she could see gold shimmering lines in the air, like the edges of curtains, or giant sliced orange peels like you see in the marmalade. She even pointed to them, and traced them with a finger, but I couldn't see anything.

When Mom and Dad found out about the lines, off to the doctor they went. They were worried that Brigid had something wrong with her brain, something serious like a tumor. By then I was ten, and old enough to understand what that meant, so I was a little scared, but it turned out there was no sign of a tumor or any kind of disease. What the doctor had said, my parents told me, was that my little sister might have a type of 'spectrum disorder'.

The word 'spectrum' just made me picture a prism, and that made me think of the cover of Pink Floyd's *Dark Side of the Moon* album.

"Why is it called that?" I asked.

Dad's face scrunched up like he had a pain in his gut or something.

"It means," he said, "that she's different. Her brain works differently from other people's. Some parts are more developed and others are..."

I waited for him to finish the sentence, but he just looked away with that pained grimace.

"Are less developed?" I said.

I didn't believe that. I knew Brigid. My little sister was perfect. Some of my friends had annoying little sisters, but Brigid was never annoying. She didn't take my things. She watched my games and didn't interfere. She went away when I asked, plunked down in a corner with a book. She was only six, but always reading. She also followed instructions well. She said whatever was on her mind, so you always knew what she was thinking. She was curious and asked questions. She wanted to understand things.

But I worried about the lines in the air. That meant she was seeing things that weren't there.

I asked her about them again one night while we were in the den watching TV.

"Are there lines here now?" I asked.

"You still can't see them?"

"No, I can't. There aren't any lines, Bridge."

She glared at me, her pursed mouth looking like a button. Before my eyes, she reached out with one hand... and the hand disappeared.

I sat up on the couch. I rubbed my eyes. I wasn't sure what I was seeing.

"I just put my hand into one of the folds," she said.

Not lines anymore, but folds.

"There are things in here," she said.

Her hand reappeared, but now she was holding an old flashlight made of shiny aluminum. It had a red plastic cowl around the lightbulb, and a magnet on one side so you could stick it to the fridge. The plastic cowl was dirty and the shiny tube was dented in a few places.

"Where did that come from?"

Brigid shrugged.

"I saw one like it once. I thought of it and there it was. That's what the folds do, I think. I figured it out a few days ago. Look!"

She pulled out other things, one after the other: an adjustable wrench, a roll of masking tape, and a jar of peanut butter. I took the lid off the peanut butter to make sure it was real.

"It is," I said, after sticking in a finger and licking it clean.

This was a relief. My little sister hadn't been seeing things. The folds were real but just invisible. That meant she was going to be all right.

I got some bread from the kitchen and we ate some of the peanut butter with it.

A few days later, I went into Brigid's room to discover her playing with a huge castle made of coloured wooden blocks. Detailed plastic knights guarded the walls.

"Where'd you get all this?" I demanded, a little jealous.

Then I remembered what she could do.

"Oh, they came from the folds," I said.

Brigid ignored me and kept playing. She could be single-minded when she set herself to a task and would get upset if she was forced to deviate, even to answer a question.

It was after this that she started building elaborate Rube Goldberg machines. Most of them involved a steel ball rolling along a track, knocking things over and causing a chain reaction that would end with a fan turning on or a radio blaring or something. Some of the machines were huge, extending into the hallway and dining room and living room and even out the window. My parents were pretty tolerant of this, just like they'd tolerated the toy railroads I'd set up when I was Brigid's age, as long as she cleaned up after a few hours.

I don't know what went through my parents' heads when they found out Brigid could pull things out of thin air. When Dad first encountered one of the Rube Goldberg machines, he just told Brigid to put everything back when she was finished. But later I overhead them discussing the possibility of sending Brigid to a special school.

I was having none of that. I stormed into their bedroom.

"There's nothing wrong with Brigid!" I said. "She should go to our regular school."

Mom came over and put her hand on my shoulder.

"It's okay, it was just an idea," she said.

That was all.

I walked Brigid to school every day after that, and she always held my hand. After confronting my parents, I was pleased with myself for having saved her, in my mind, from having to attend some strange institution, but I also began to worry what others would think, including other students, even Brigid's teachers. I felt like I needed to stay close to her, to watch out for these potential villains.

"Remember," I said to her on her first day of Grade One. "Don't tell anyone about the folds or what you can do."

"I won't," she said. "But why not?"

"Just don't," I told her.

I didn't want to scare her with an explanation.

"The government is going to come and take her away," I said to my parents one night, and I got so upset I started to shake. A few tears even started. "They're going to want to do experiments on her."

My dad gave me one of his genuinely-concerned looks and put his hand on my shoulder.

"I don't think shadowy organizations like that really exist," he said. "This is a free democracy, and every citizen has rights. No one can just take you away against your will. If your little sister has special talents, that's her business and no one else's."

Did I mention my mom and dad were both lawyers?

As far as I could tell, Brigid never revealed her powers at school, and that was good, but as time passed, I started to worry that she wasn't really fitting in. Her schoolwork was perfect, straight As in every subject, but she didn't seem to make any friends. I'd see her in the playground by herself, sometimes just staring into space.

I wanted to change that.

"Why don't we have a big party?" I said to her one day when we were all sitting at the dinner table. "For your birthday. You can invite all the kids from your class."

Brigid gave me one of her stares, but after a moment she nodded.

"They would like that," she said.

We made paper invitations and invited about thirty kids. In those days, if someone in your class invited you to a party, no matter who it was, you'd go. It was only polite. Plus you got to go to a party. So on the big day, which was a Saturday, a ton of kids showed up, each one with a present, looking for fun and cake. I acted as host. Brigid meanwhile had made her largest Rube Goldberg machine yet, one that went through every room in the house, and it became the center of activities as every kid took a turn letting the steel ball drop.

When it was all over, Brigid said to me, "That was fun, having all those kids over."

"They're your friends," I reminded her.

"Are they? Oh."

After that, nothing changed. None of her classmates seemed to dislike her, and no one bullied her, but she still stuck to herself most of the time.

I'd tried. At least she would always have me, I figured.

As more time passed, and I turned thirteen (almost a man), I decided that it was good that my little sister was something of a loner. That was safer. I still worried, almost every day, that her secret would come out, and made a solemn pledge — a reaffirmation of my childhood promise — to protect my little sister from anyone who would try to do her harm or infringe her rights, as my dad had put it, as a citizen. I knew that if the powers-that-be found out what she could do, they would be afraid of her, and they would want to find out how her abilities worked so they could exploit them. That's what always happened in the movies.

Two more years passed and no one came to take Brigid away. In that time, I never let my guard down. If I saw a suspicious car parked on our street, I would check it out. I got in the habit of telling Brigid to hide whenever someone I didn't know came to the door.

"Why should I hide?" she asked me.

I finally decided to explain that there were people who could be afraid of her, or who wanted to use her for their own purposes, and make her do things she didn't want to do. I figured she was old enough to understand.

"But I'm just a nine-year-old kid," she said.

"You're different. Not everyone likes that."

That just made her frown.

When I was fifteen, my first year of high school, Brigid stopped eating her supper. Mom and Dad were worried she'd developed an eating disorder, but one day I caught her pulling a tray of cupcakes out of the air. She'd been snacking on magic goodies. She'd tried to hide it, even from me, and that made me angry. She and I weren't supposed to keep secrets.

I told Mom and Dad.

"You can't just eat cake and candy, honey," Mom said, and then she and Dad gave Brigid a lecture about what was right to pull out of the folds, what was wrong. They didn't mind the toys, but they didn't want her eating so much unhealthy food.

"Maybe it's time to get to the bottom of this," Dad said, "before it gets any more out of hand."

By that he meant another trip to the doctor.

"You can't do that," I said, horrified.

"We just want them to run a few tests, honey," Mom said. "We won't reveal everything, but... we just want to make sure she's okay."

I thought they were crazy and was sick to my stomach with worry. I wished I hadn't ratted on her. If the doctor found out what Brigid could do, he would just have to make one phone call, and the men from the government would be on our doorstep.

"Deny everything," I whispered to Brigid as she was leaving the house. "Tell the doctor it's just a game. It's not real."

Brigid just gave me one of her big-eyed looks.

I went into the back yard to wait, just sitting in a lawn chair and stared at the sky, at the clouds.

The back door opened and Brigid came out and sat in the chair next to mine.

"You're home already?" I said, startled.

My little sister shook her head.

"I did what you said and told Doctor Heppie that it was all a game, but he didn't believe me. I asked to go to the bathroom and then I decided to come home."

"What do you mean? Come home how?"

I felt a chill.

"I found a new way to use the folds," Brigid said.

I grabbed my phone and texted Mom, telling her what had happened. She'd been worried sick and the whole clinic had been running around trying to find Brigid.

"Thank you, honey," Mom wrote back. "Thank you for letting us know!"

When Mom and Dad got home, Brigid faced them and said, "Please don't take me to the doctor again."

I stood behind her, nodding.

"There's nothing wrong with her," I insisted.

Mom and Dad looked at me, then looked at Brigid.

"Okay," Dad said.

After this, I told myself I had to live by my own words, at least a little. I'd said there was nothing wrong with Brigid, but I behaved as if there was. My high-school friends knew I had a little sister, but I never invited anyone over because I was afraid they'd see Brigid do something, and then I'd have to explain. That had to change. I had to trust Brigid to be responsible, like she was at school. I told myself I had to start giving her more freedom.

One day I invited my friend Rosie over. I was learning guitar and Rosie played bass, and we were going to form a band to perform at the school music festival. This was going to be our first jam session, in our rec room.

Rosie wore her hair super short and also lifted weights, so she had rocks in her arms. She wore white t-shirts and jeans and that was the extent of her wardrobe.

"Are you a boy or a girl?" Brigid asked her, in her blunt way.

That embarrassed the hell out of me, but Rosie just laughed.

"A bit of both," she said.

"So you're just yourself," Brigid said. "Like me."

Rosie said nothing for a few seconds, then gave my sister a smile I can only describe as conspiratorial.

"Yeah."

I watched the two of them together, and something turned over inside me. I'd been carrying the secret of my little sister's power for a long time, and I needed some help with that weight, help from someone we could trust. I wondered if Rosie could be that person.

"My little sister is different from other people," I said.

I guess I was testing the waters. Brigid turned and looked at me with her big round eyes, and something in that look stopped me from elaborating.

Rosie shrugged.

"Everyone is different," she said. "Most people don't care about that stuff anymore."

Brigid smiled, and I felt a little burst of hope. Could that be true? Was it possible that few people, including the government, would really care if they found out what my sister could do?

I wanted to believe that, only Brigid didn't just have personality quirks, but actual powers.

I decided I'd have to carry the weight of my sister's secret for a while longer.

Not long after that, Brigid announced she wanted to have another birthday party. She was about to turn twelve and thought that was special. Her idea was to have a party where she gave the guests gifts instead of receiving them.

"Please don't give them things that you find inside the folds," I told her, worried that was her plan.

It was.

"Why not?" she asked. "Where else can I get the gifts?"

"Mom and Dad can buy them."

"But I want the gifts to be special."

Brigid trusted me and always listened to me, but I was spoiling her plans and she didn't like it.

"Look, I'm sorry about this," I said.

Brigid suddenly brightened.

"I know! I can say it's a game, like with the doctor. A magic trick! And I won't be lying, because it is a game, really. Right?"

I mulled this over. I was feeling pretty down about disappointing her, and this seemed like a reasonable compromise. If Brigid trusted me, I had to learn to trust her.

"Okay, but be careful," I said, hoping I wouldn't regret my decision.

At the party, Brigid revealed her power to all, telling the other kids that she could pull anything out of thin air. That's all she said. She didn't describe what happened as a magic act, but when it was over, everyone applauded. No one thought it was real. They deceived themselves.

I was proud of Brigid, both for her amazing talent and how she'd presented herself. But later that evening, my old fears started to filter back. What if a couple of the kids realized that what they were seeing was the real thing? What if they told their parents, and their parents called the police or some other authority?

On Monday morning, as I was packing a lunch for school, a large black truck pulled up to the front door. I told Brigid to hide in her room. The truck turned out to be a courier delivering a package for Mom, but I was shaken. I'd decided to walk Brigid to school like I used to do. I'd stopped when I'd moved to the high-school, and I'd probably be late for my first class, but my little sister's life was worth the wrath of my homeroom teacher.

When we arrived at the elementary school, a large black car was parked out front. A man in a black suit wearing Aviator sunglasses opened the driver's door and stepped out.

I'd never seen that car before. I led Brigid in a wide berth around it.

"You see that car?" I murmured in her ear. "I don't know for sure, but it looks like it might belong to those government guys who want to kidnap you. Stay away from them. Don't even let them see you."

Brigid gave me a big-eyed look and nodded.

"I don't want that," she said.

The passenger side door of the car opened, and a kid got out, a boy with a camouflaged knapsack. The man in the dark suit and sunglasses said something to the boy, who waved and started running toward the school.

"That's just someone's dad," Brigid said.

I watched as the man got back in the car, but he didn't drive away at once. Was he watching us? Had the kid with the knapsack been some kind of cover?

"I'm not sure," I said. "Don't talk to that kid or his dad. Okay?"

Brigid nodded.

"Okay."

I couldn't think of anything else the entire day and found it impossible to pay attention in class. I was terrified that the man I'd seen was a government agent who'd been sent to watch my sister. I wasn't certain, but that didn't matter. The idea had taken root and was growing.

I left my last class early, claiming to be sick. The truth was, I felt sick. I was so anxious, so worked up, I ran all the way to the elementary school and waited for Brigid to come out, all the while watching out for that black car.

When Brigid saw me she broke into one of her big smiles.

"Hi, big brother!"

She held my hand on the walk back, but neither of us said much. Brigid was still generally quiet, and I was busy keeping watch.

We were almost home when I saw a large black sedan turn onto our street. I came to a hard stop, jerking Brigid's arm.

"Ow!" she said.

I didn't know what to do for a few seconds, but there was nowhere to run.

"We have to keep going," I murmured.

I felt like I was walking in glue, but when we turned the corner, there was no black car on our street. Maybe it had just driven past.

On our front step, I knelt in front of Brigid and said, "I think I just saw that car again, and think it might have been looking for you. I think you should hide. Not just in your room, but... in the folds. Do you have a place to hide there?"

"Yes, I go there all the time," she said. "I can go there if you say so."

I didn't get my homework done that night, but sat in front of the window, plucking at my guitar and staring at the street. I didn't see the car again.

The next morning, Brigid wasn't at breakfast.

"Do you know anything about this?" Dad asked me. "Did she go to that place, wherever she goes?"

I shrugged. "I guess so."

I didn't want to admit I'd told her to go. I was afraid Mom and Dad would say I was being irrational.

"She'll come back," Mom said. "But we'll have to call the school and tell them she'll be absent today."

She was trying to sound casual, but I could tell she was upset, and felt a little pang. That was my fault.

I reminded myself that this was necessary.

Brigid still wasn't back when I got home from school, nor did she return the next day. Or the next. I started to get a little worried, and sat in her room and called her name, hoping she could hear me, but I had no idea how the folds worked. I told her I hadn't seen the black car for days and it was probably safe to come out. I even felt a little stupid, and had to admit that maybe I'd been wrong.

By now Mom and Dad were a wreck, but they couldn't go to the police. Their daughter wasn't missing. They knew exactly where she was.

"What if she stays away forever?" Dad said at a joyless supper on that third day.

Mom reached out and took his hand.

"We always knew something like this could happen," she said. "She's unique. She's special, and she's just flexing those muscles. Why would she stay away forever? Don't worry about that."

My Dad just nodded. I'd never seen him cry before, but tears started running down his cheeks.

That night, I came down with a fever. I don't know if it was due to raw negative emotions or if I'd let myself get worn down and the flu had taken the opportunity to attack. When the sun rose the next day, I couldn't get out of bed. The room spun when I tried to raise my head, and I think I had visions. I saw Brigid standing next to me and asked her where she'd been.

"Come on," I heard her say, as if from a distance.

I managed to sit up. Brigid was right next to me, but half of her seemed to be missing, like she was peering around a curtain. Or a fold.

"Follow me," she said, voice a whisper.

She slid back behind the fold, but held out her hand. It looked like her severed arm was floating in the air.

I took her hand and let her guide me through the fold in space.

On the other side was a room, like an ordinary room in a house, though with no features, the floor, walls, and ceiling all resembling white plaster. In the far wall was an ordinary wooden panel door with a white doorknob. Next to the door stood a massive palace of wooden blocks, like I'd seen Brigid build years ago, its walls armed with plastic cannon. In another corner was a table covered in maps drawn in coloured pencil, and beside them were the remains of hamburger wrappers and cupcake papers. Books were stacked in little piles here and there.

Brigid let go of my hand.

"How do you like it?" she said.

"It's... nice."

My head was starting to clear and I could see there was a certain coziness to the room. It couldn't have been more safe, more secure, but I hated the idea of my sister spending her life like this, hiding from the world that was rightfully hers.

I wanted her to come home.

"Bridge, I think I might have been wrong," I said. "I haven't seen the car again, and no one came to look for you. I think the coast is clear and you need to come back. Mom and Dad are worried."

She looked at me.

"They are?"

She said it like it had never occurred to her.

"Yes."

"But they know where I went."

"They want you to come home. You don't really need to hide all the time."

She looked at me, eyes big.

"I'll keep you safe," I promised for the thousandth time.

She nodded.

"Okay, I believe you. You always tell me the truth."

I digested this as she went to the panel door and grabbed the doorknob. The door swung open, and beyond was the rec room in our house.

"Can I step through?" I said.

"Yes! Just follow me."

When I'd gone through the doorway, I looked behind me, but all I saw was the other wall of the rec room. The door and Brigid's hiding space were gone.

I felt like I'd just awakened from a dream. The fever was gone and there was my little sister, standing next to me and smiling. Safe and sound.

"What time is it?" I said. I'd been home alone, sick in bed, and something about the light coming in the high rec room windows said it was late, afternoon coming on to evening. School would be out.

"I don't have a clock in my hiding place," Brigid said. "Maybe I should get one?"

I wanted to check the street one last time, just to make sure.

"Come on," I said.

We went out through the basement door and up the concrete steps to ground level. Our driveway was empty, and I looked along our street to the left, at all the other quiet semi-suburban houses, each with its garage or car port, front lawn and shrubs and flower beds.

There were no black cars and no one was trying to take my sister away.

"I guess I'll have to go to school tomorrow," Brigid said. "And everyone will say, oh, where were you? Welcome back. It'll be like a party."

"And even if we told them where you'd been," I said, "they wouldn't believe us."

I smiled at her, and in that moment, I made my decision, the decision I'd been building towards. It was time for me to let go of the fear for good. And this time I meant it.

"You know when I said I'd keep you safe?" I said. "I'll still try, but I don't think you'll need me. You can keep yourself safe."

"You think so?"

"Yes."

I looked again at the empty street.

"You know what else?" I added. "Mom and Dad will be home later, and they're going to be happy to see you."

In this I was wrong. Mom and Dad weren't happy. They were overjoyed.

"You didn't have to worry," Brigid told them.

I watched as they enveloped my little sister in a three-way hug. I joined in.

They say old habits die hard, and over the next few months and even into Brigid's high school years, I secretly watched for black cars. I never saw one, and I never talked about them.

I did my best to stick to my decision.

After her senior year, Brigid won a scholarship to a reputable university and I faced my biggest test. Could I stand it, with my little sister away from home, living in a dorm?

Turns out I could. I kept waiting for something terrible to happen, but it never did. One weekend she came home, traveling through the folds, and told me, "I think I'd like to be an architect. I like to design and build things."

"That sounds like you," I said.

A few months later, she told me, "I'm going to switch to engineering. I like to design and build things, but all kinds of things, not just buildings."

She was a star pupil, which came as no surprise. After graduation, she got a job in another city.

Her visits became fewer.

We were both busy, but still made time for each other. By then I had two kids, six and three, and Brigid delighted in entertaining them with her 'magic tricks' when she came to dinner.

"I'm not sure I'm going to make it next week," she told me one evening, when the plates had been cleared from the table and we were alone for a few minutes. "Things are getting crazy and I might have to put in some extra hours."

"You do what you have to do," I told her. "And you know where to find me."

As it turned out, I didn't see her the next week, nor the week after. One day she sent me a text message. She was in town for business, and could I meet her for coffee? Not could she come to the house, but a coffee date. Just for an hour or so.

I was a little disappointed, but agreed to meet her.

I arrived at the coffee shop first and grabbed us a table. Brigid came in a few minutes later, tall and slender and grinning. She still wore her hair long, almost down to her waist.

We didn't talk about anything significant. We just chatted about what was going on in our lives. At one point, I wanted more cream for my coffee, and Brigid pulled a little porcelain pitcher out of the folds. It was casual and surprising, and no one seemed to notice.

"Do your work colleagues know you can do that?" I asked.

"They see it all the time. Everyone still thinks it's a trick. They don't believe it's real."

I leaned back in my chair. I wanted to ask something that I'd wondered about for a while.

"Do you… ever feel tempted to reach into the folds and grab a few bags of cash?"

Brigid's big eyes seemed to double in size and her jaw dropped open.

"That wouldn't be fair!" she said. "And how would I explain that on my tax returns?"

"Well, you've never been reluctant to find us presents in there!"

Brigid shook her head.

"That seems different somehow. I think I make those things. You're not allowed to make your own money."

I could think of a few counter arguments but kept them to myself. Her response was typical for her, and I felt myself flush with love and admiration.

"Sometimes I think I should go to the physics department at the university," she continued, "and show them what I can do and say, what do you think? But then you know how much I value my privacy. I don't need them trying to figure me out. And that's not who I am anyway. I'm not really that interested. I've got other fish to fry."

She sipped her coffee. We talked about other things. Eventually she checked her watch and said, "I'm sorry I have to dash, but I'll see you at Thanksgiving. You're going to Mom and Dad's?"

I was, and I would see her there.

We embraced, and then she was out the door. I watched her walk away, back to the life she had chosen, and wondered if, after all, we had become a little ordinary. I'd read once that extraordinary children often became ordinary adults.

Well, I decided that was a crazy thought, and turned away, smiling to myself. Completely crazy. If there was one thing I'd learned, after all these years, after all the worries and reliefs, all the failures and triumphs, there was nothing ordinary about my little sister Brigid.

Harold R. Thompson's story "My Little Sister Brigid" was originally published in Metaphorosis on Friday, 10 March 2023. See magazine.metaphorosis.com

About the author

Harold R. Thompson enjoys storytelling in all its forms. A long-time employee of Parks Canada, he develops exhibits and public programming at several national historic sites. He also writes historical fiction and science fiction and fantasy, both short stories and novels, including the bestselling "Empire and Honor" series of historical adventure novels, which include *Dudley's Fusiliers*, *Guns of Sevastopol* and *Sword of the Mogul* (published by Zumaya Yesterdays). His upcoming science fiction novel, *Orphans of Sturnus*, will be published in 2024.

Gatekeepers

Douglas DiCicco

Now she'd never get to finish her book, Elsie thought. She'd just gotten to the good bit when her train derailed.

"So what happens now?" she asked Osiris. "You weigh my heart against a feather?"

"Not personally, no," Osiris answered. "Too many dead people these days. The gatekeepers handle that now. I just get the process started."

Osiris reached into Elsie's chest and pulled out her heart. It was more colorful than Elsie would have guessed, much more luminous. Her heart was a whirl of metallic sheens and colorful glows.

"What did you love most in life?" Osiris asked, eyes on the heart.

"Stories," Elsie answered.

Osiris smiled and pressed the heart into Elsie's hands. It squelched with disconcerting wetness.

"I'd start there." Osiris pointed down one of the countless corridors stretching endlessly into the dark in every direction. Like all the others, it was lined with shadowy figures, each standing before a flickering portal. "Third on the left. Best of luck."

Elsie followed the directions. She felt her heartbeat quicken in her hands. She was nervous.

The third shade on the left hovered before a portal to an endless library. Up close, Elsie could smell tea and paper wafting through.

"Do you seek to take your eternal rest in my realm?" the shade asked.

"I think so?" Elsie answered. She wasn't quite certain how all this worked.

The answer seemed to be enough for the shade. It took Elsie's heart from her and held it up to the light. It turned the heart from side to side, then upside down. The shade shook its head disapprovingly. "No, no. I'm sorry. This won't do at all."

"Why not?" Elsie frowned.

"See this bit here?" The shade tapped at a silver bit on the heart's underside. It produced a quiet metallic ping. "Dragon scale. Or some other mythical creature. Doesn't matter." The shade passed the heart back, handling it like a scrap of rotten fish it was eager to be rid of. "If it's part of your heart, I can't let you pass."

"Why does that matter?" Elsie asked.

The shade sighed. "Because this is the portal to the Realm of Literary Readers," it answered. "Literary," the shade repeated the word, emphasizing each and every syllable. "This is a place for the souls of serious readers of serious works."

"I like serious literature," Elsie insisted.

"Yes, but you also like dragons. Or something just as bad. Something that smacks of genre," the shade said. "I'm sorry, but there's no place for you in my realm. Try the Realm of Fantasy Readers." It stretched out a shadowy limb. "Down that way, fifth on the right."

Elsie took the advice and presented her heart to the shade guarding the portal to the Realm of Fantasy Readers. It was just as unimpressed as the first shade had been. "No, I'm sorry. I don't think this is the place for you."

"The last one I spoke with thought it was," Elsie said. "They said there's a dragon scale on my heart."

"What, this?" The new shade poked at the heart's silver bit. "Oh, no. That's no dragon scale. No, looks like chrome to me. You probably want the Realm of Cyberpunk Readers. Back the way you came. Second on your left."

The guardian of the Realm of Cyberpunk Readers was no more receptive to Elsie's heart. "The hearts of true cyberpunk aficionados are wrought of naught but chrome and bleed naught but code. Look, you've got this much larger dark patch right here." It prodded a particularly squishy portion of the heart. "I'd try Horror Readers."

The shade at the portal to the Realm of Horror Readers weighed Elsie's heart and found it too light. The guardian of the Realm of Comedy Readers weighed it again, and found it too heavy. Her heart was too cold for Erotica, too hot for Cozy Mysteries. Elsie's heart was too old-fashioned for Science Fiction, too modern for Alternate History.

"Have you tried the Realm of Literary Readers?" suggested the shade guarding the Realm of Thriller Readers, after a rejection full of misdirection and shocking twists.

Elsie slumped against the wall, knees against her chest, clutching her heart tightly. She had wandered the endless halls for what felt like an eternity. She felt no closer to finding the place she belonged. Each of the realms had something which drew her in, but the shades barred her way at every turn.

"Still here?"

Elsie looked up to see Osiris offering her a hand. She took it and got back to her feet. "I don't belong anywhere," she said, barely holding back tears.

Osiris smiled gently. "Which stories were your favorites?"

Elsie considered the question for a moment. "The ones I told myself."

"Ah." Osiris gave Elsie's hand a gentle squeeze. "Come with me."

Osiris led her to a portal guarded by a squat and smoky shade.

"Try this one." Osiris suggested.

Elsie stepped forward. She could hear the scribbling of pens and the clacking of typewriters echoing from the portal. She smelled good coffee and cheap whisky. She glimpsed untidy desks overflowing with crumpled notes and obscure reference tomes. The portal beckoned to her like none of the others had.

"Do you seek to take your eternal rest here, in the Realm of Writers?" the shade asked, holding out a shadowy tendril.

"Yes." Elsie said, handing over her heart.

The shade inspected the heart. The parade of rejections had drained Elsie's heart of much of the energy and vigor it once possessed. It was a dark, shriveled thing now, hard and bitter, like an especially withered raisin.

"It certainly looks like a writer's heart," the shade said. It placed the heart on a shelf beside the portal. "Thank you for your interest in the Realm of Writers. You can expect an answer in six to eight weeks."

Elsie sat before the shade and waited. She waited, and waited, and waited. Six weeks passed. Then eight. Then twelve. It was somewhere around half a year when the shade finally picked her heart off the shelf, eyeballed it for a moment, then tossed it back to Elsie.

"Thank you for your submission to the Realm of Writers." The shade sounded very rehearsed. "Unfortunately, your heart does not meet our realm's needs at the present moment."

"What?" Elsie cried. She'd really thought this would be the one.

"We receive many quality hearts of the recently deceased," the shade continued. "I'm afraid your heart didn't quite win me over. I wish you the best of luck finding another placement for your eternal soul."

Elsie sat there a moment, stunned, staring at the withered lump her heart had become. She had no idea what to do now, where to go. This was the only place that had felt right for her, and now it was closed off. Not knowing what else to do, she got back to her feet and prepared to resume what felt like a futile search.

"Didn't like this one after all?" Osiris was back.

"I don't belong here either," Elsie said, holding back tears.

Osiris arched an eyebrow. "Says who?"

Elsie pointed to the shade in front of the portal.

"Ah." Osiris smiled. "You know... they're only as strong as you let them be."

Elsie watched the shade for a moment. When she turned back to Osiris, they had already disappeared.

She looked down at the heart in her hands. She saw a flicker of light somewhere deep in the core. A spark that hadn't quite been snuffed out. She turned back to the portal and marched forward.

"You again." The shade seemed both surprised and mildly annoyed. "I'm sorry, I can't provide personal feedback on each and every heart I examine. If you'd like to try again with a new core personal identity, maybe something a little more mainstream, I'd be happy to review another submission."

Elsie ignored the shade and kept moving toward the portal. Her heart glowed brighter.

"Wait!" The shade moved to block Elsie from the portal. "You can't go in. You aren't a real writer. I haven't approved you yet."

Elsie held up her heart. The light shone straight through the shade. She walked through it, ignoring the guardian's wailing as she entered the portal.

"This time…" Elsie said as the light enveloped her. "I'm going to write my own ending."

Douglas DiCicco's story "Gatekeepers" was originally published in Metaphorosis on Friday, 24 December 2021. See magazine.metaphorosis.com

About the author

Douglas DiCicco is an author of speculative fiction living in Clovis, California. He has worked as an attorney, a teacher, and a Renaissance Faire performer.
@CiccoDouglas

Catching College

Maggie Slater

Hilltown's peace of mind shattered as the first whisper seeped out of a wristclamp autoreader over lunch, and before long, every device crackled with the news. Work stopped, students gathered, primed ears bent low to catch every detail. The collective heartrate skyrocketed. Inhabitants collapsed into chairs, eastern windows groaned as they were shoved open and eyes strained for something beyond the horizon. The dull old line where the plains cut the sky in half had always been present but unimportant. Not now. Promise lingered beneath its lip; opportunity raged towards town at fifty-five miles an hour.

Beneath the Hill, lodged deep in the rock where it had hidden for three hundred years, the Hilltown Energy Beetle's turbines spooled up, preparing for the increased demand on the grid. Far above it, in every room, the people of Hilltown laughed and cried and hugged and danced.

Parbrier College was coming. There was no time to waste.

●

All my life, I'd planned — no, *dreamed* — of catching a college like Dad. I'd heard his Wakereach boarding story so often at bedtime it felt like I'd been there, tasting the sea foam and feeling the burn of desperate paddling in my own arms. And now, I was going to get a shot at one. I wouldn't have to spend weeks or months hunting it down, tracking its paths, living out of a backpack. Parbrier was *coming to me*.

After classes were cancelled, I'd bounded down the Hill, expecting Dad to have beaten me home after catching the announcement at work and bolting, but nobody was there. I paced our tiny apartment from deck to kitchenette, looping around the sitting area Dad used as his bedroom and back, around and around, seething with the nervous energy the radio announcement had injected straight into my chest. Three weeks!

I couldn't even remember what Parbrier College looked like, though it was probably in Dad's Encyclopedia of Modern Behemoths. I stopped pacing and made for his sagging bookshelf. He had over three hundred books about behemoths, but the one I wanted was wedged right in the middle, acting as a pillar for the shelf above. I wriggled it out carefully, making sure nothing came crashing down on me.

The Encyclopedia was fourteen hundred vellum sheets, grouped into chapters on various locomotion styles and native locale. I'd pored over the section dedicated to ocean behemoths as a kid, obsessed with the googly-eyed, spiney, deep sea machinations that often people only learned existed when their metal shells washed up on shore, rusted out and covered in barnacles. The land-based education behemoth section was pristine.

After a little searching, I found Parbrier College. Even in a palm-sized sketch, it gave me a shiver of dread. Seven stories tall, three hundred feet wide, built like a porcupine with a plow head, its towers fanned out like quills across its back: Parbrier was no joke. It looked downright vicious.

I looked up at the paper-mâché model of Wakereach I'd made in seventh grade. I'd spent hours working on it, recreating every hatch, every rivet, with cardboard, paint, and paper. Dad had been so impressed, he'd rigged it up from my ceiling so that it looked as if it were beginning a dive to the depths. It was sleek where Parbrier was sharp; it was beautiful where Parbrier was ugly.

Three weeks. I shut the book and slumped back on my bed, mind racing. How could I possibly be ready in time? Everyone at school was talking about their plans, their trainers, their theories and gameplans. I didn't have a plan. I didn't know anything at all about catching a land-based college.

The apartment door opened, and my heart jammed itself up into my throat as Dad's shoes scuffled on the floor. Something rustled as he set it down. The sink sputtered on.

"Kai? You home?"

He sounded so calm. I crept to my door, staring as he dug through a canvas sack of groceries and started putting things away. He glanced over at me, smiling like the world wasn't about to shift into high gear.

"Ah, there you are! How was school?"

He couldn't not know. Everyone, everywhere, was talking about Parbrier. There was no way he hadn't heard.

His brows arched as he pulled out the battered cutting board and set it on the counter. "What's up?"

I was just about to explode when his eyes suddenly twinkled and his straight face broke into a huge grin. The restrained horror burst out of me in giggles, and he ran over, scooping me up into a bear hug.

"Three weeks!" he cried, and I clung to him like a life raft. He thrust me out at arm's length and looked me up and down. "When'd you grow up, huh? You excited?"

My face locked in a grin. "It's crazy! Three weeks!"

"God, I can't believe it. When I heard, Kai!" He pulled at his thinning hair and waved me towards the kitchen table. "And Parbrier is a great school. World-class in Behemoth studies, if that's what you're looking for. But also pretty top-notch in agriculture and history. Oh, and their Arts program!" He kissed his fingertips and turned back towards the counter, unpacking the groceries. I recognized the ingredients for my favorite curry and a six-pack of light lager. He was planning a celebratory dinner.

"The last time a college passed Hilltown, it came within half a mile," Dad was saying, "but — and you didn't hear this from me, because Neil said they haven't finished running the simulations yet — but a few of the path models are saying Parbrier's going to come a *lot* closer."

"How close?"

"Close. Possibly even hitting a street or two. But like I said, it's early days and they won't have a clear projection for a while."

I thought of that huge, spiny machine barreling towards town on its tracks as wide as a roadway, and choked down a lump in my throat. This was real. This was happening, *now*, not in some mythical future. Parbrier would be here in three weeks. How could I possibly be ready by then?

"Hey."

I pulled myself out of tunnel vision to see Dad stooping in front of me at the table, a warm smile on his face. "Don't worry. I know this is a lot, and there's a lot to do, but we're in this together, all right? You're not alone."

Dad winked at me, and I felt my fear evaporate under the confident gleam in his eye. I might not have a team of strategists or a jetpack like some of the kids from school, but I had Dad.

The knot in my chest released and I leaned forward, the nervous energy converting into excitement. "So where do we start?"

●

No quiet place existed in Hilltown anymore. Its living rooms buzzed with excitement; its streets with swarms of vendors setting up temporary shops. Banners snapped in the desert wind, advertising coaching services, specialized training, lucky talismans, every kind of trick and placebo. They caught even the most skeptical eyes. No one could afford to be too confident.

On the outskirts where the town bled onto the flats, tent fabric squealed as applicants and their families from neighboring towns built encampments, jamming themselves into every unclaimed bit of sidewalk and courtyard. The Hilltown Energy Beetle grew feverish as every spare outlet was overloaded with extension cords and portable grills and radios and TVs and chargers. The streetlights at night fluttered, gasping to remain lit. High on the Hill, the Beetle's internal heat made the asphalt as hot as high noon, and the dainty lights strung on the sculpted trees writhed in the shimmering air.

●

The next night, after we'd cleaned up from dinner, Dad dropped a pile of schematics on the kitchen table. The giant sheets crinkled as he unrolled them and smoothed them flat in front of us. Dad weighted the corners with mugs and a shoe.

Here was Parbrier in every detail, no longer a tiny sketch in the Encyclopedia. Thin grey lines dissected it, measuring it, picking apart its fundamental features in minute detail, down to the number of links per tread. In such a close-up view, with a tiny human figure silhouetted for scale, I felt my stomach flip on itself. It was vastly taller than our apartment building. Its tracks were wider than our street. Its underbelly, forty feet above the ground, was pocked with manholes and webbed with catwalks.

I looked again at the tiny scale figure and tried to imagine what it would feel like to stand so close to such a thing. Parbrier wouldn't even feel a bump if it crushed me screaming into the dust. I shivered.

Dad pulled at his jaw, frowning at the schematics. "The main difficulty with Parbrier is the treads. It should slow down as it approaches town, prior to its turn, but probably not a lot slower than twenty miles per hour. That's still going to be pretty fast for our purposes. We might be able to hook it, if you get close enough, but without getting up to speed, that'll be pretty risky even if you *do* snag it…"

I slumped in my chair. This was impossible. If I had a jetpack or a paraglider, sure, I could just sail over to one of its towers and drop onto it, but from the *ground*? It was a mountain. Climbing it at a standstill would be challenging, but moving? How could I ever have thought I could do this?

I'd always imagined that I'd choose my own college after graduating, and then spend months or years hunting it down, and that somehow, in-between, I'd become brave enough, I'd grow up, I'd be ready.

I wasn't ready now. My fingertips throbbed from my racing heart. I swallowed to wet my throat enough to speak, and then said, embarrassed by the slight waver in my voice, "I heard a Parbrier specialist on the radio. They said the last time Parbrier passed close to a highly populated area, six people died."

"The average is nine."

"What?"

"Most colleges have an average of nine deaths per season. Parbrier's a little better, actually." Dad was still frowning at the paper, his finger tracing the tracks. He sighed. "Maybe hooking it is the wrong angle. If it slows down enough, maybe you could ride the track up and over, jump off it to here." He pointed to a series of doors along the left side of the school where the track passed a broad, low balcony. "That might work, but we'd still have to *catch it...*"

I cleared my throat, trying to banish the idea of nine kids like me who weren't around anymore. "H-how many people made it? Onto Parbrier, I mean."

"Hmm?" Dad looked up at me as though he'd forgotten I was there. "Oh, um. Well, when it passed Moschberg about a year ago... Let me think. Three, I think. But I'm not sure what its overall season total was."

"Three?"

Dad shrugged. "Plenty of applicants just don't catch it, Kai. If everybody who wanted to succeeded, it wouldn't be special, would it? Wakereach has an even lower annual admittance ratio."

He frowned back down at the paper. "Ah! I've got it!" he shouted, the paper crashing like a firework when he slapped his palm down on it. He bounded to the balcony and scrambled over the railing onto the fire escape. I followed. "My old motorbike! That thing'll do forty-five, easy, and it's junk, so you can ditch it and it won't matter! You'll be right up next to Parbrier in no time!"

He swung around the last post, missed the top step, and through some miracle, managed to dance down to the ground without falling. He laughed and disappeared around the side of the building.

I thought of the motorbike, stashed in the communal garage, buried under boxes of forgotten things. It'd been years since he'd taken me out on it, perched in front of him, his arms bracing my eight-year-old body from shaking off.

My butt would go numb from riding, and even a bath wouldn't get all the sand off my skin, but I'd loved it.

The garage door far below rattled open; boxes groaned and hissed as Dad moved them aside. I scrambled down the fire escape. I came around the corner just as he rolled out the battered old bike and set it on its kickstand.

"Ta-da!" He grinned at it like it was a custom jetpack instead of a crumbling bucket of bolts with two flat tires and chipped paint.

"Does it still work?" I asked, running my hands over the dented fuel tank, the ripped leather seat. Dirt came off on my palm.

"Oh, it'll work. These bikes are tanks. A quick tune-up, new tires, fresh fluids, gas, a couple of filters — it'll run like a dream."

I bit my tongue. Never mind that I'd never driven it before and now hardly seemed like the time to learn a whole new skill, I could see by Dad's dreamy gaze that he was already sold, and nothing I could say would change that. And maybe he was right. I took a deep breath and tried to invoke his confidence. Wakereach had a worse admittance ratio than Parbrier. Yes, people had died, but a lot just hadn't made it. If I was smart, if I was careful, maybe, just maybe, I'd be one of the lucky few who got on board. Dad believed in me. Now I just needed to believe in myself, or at least fake it until I could believe it for real.

Forcing a smile, I slung myself on and gripped the handlebars.

"That's my girl!" Dad slapped the bike's front fender, and it fell off with a clatter.

●

Every word in Hilltown was about Parbrier. Voices raised in arguments over strategies, over pros and cons of approach techniques. Everyone had an opinion. Everyone's opinion was right and wrong.

Parbrier had closed plenty of lives instead of opening them. Not all seeds landed in fertile soil. Some baked on stones. Some were consumed by birds. Life didn't offer guarantees. But the opportunity to spread its liveliest citizens beyond its borders, to chance at even just one of them finding great financial success or fame or a scientific or artistic breakthrough so that Hilltown could become The Place Where They Started: it was worth the risk.

●

Dad frowned at his wristclamp when I pulled up after my latest test run on the motorbike. We'd been practicing for almost two weeks. Parbrier was due to arrive in less than six days. Hour after hour, we'd run its expected paths. Dirt crusted my nostrils and caked the corners of my eyes. Grit chaffed my feet raw in my boots. My butt ached from the barely-padded seat, and I couldn't clench my hands from gripping the handlebars so tightly.

"You can't fear speed," Dad said, shaking his head. "We've been through this. You've got to *push*, Kai. Parbrier's not going to slow down just to make you more comfortable."

"I'm trying!"

"Well, try harder. This is a once in a lifetime opportunity. Go again. I want to see at *least* thirty-five. I don't care what the scientists are predicting, there's no way Parbrier is dropping to fifteen. And this time —" He squinted at me, and I withered inside. " — I want you to jump."

"What?"

"We've got six days, Kai. Six. Days. You need to practice jumping off the moving bike."

"What if I get hurt? I won't be able to catch Parbrier if I'm injured!"

"So don't get injured. Come on. We don't have time for theatrics. You need to be comfortable jumping."

I bit my cheek, willing tears from my eyes. Theatrics. Parbrier was just days away, looming in my mind like the end of times. My whole life stopped at that threshold, after which nothing would be the same, after which I couldn't even envision what life would be like.

Whether I caught Parbrier or missed it, whether I lived or died, its coming was the most momentous thing that might ever happen to me. Catching Wakereach had been the highlight of Dad's life. It gave him proof that he was capable of taking his destiny into his own hands, wrangling the fear of his mortality, and proving himself worthy against the biggest, scariest thing the world could throw at him.

I was just scared. It was normal to be scared. Everyone was scared, weren't they? I took a deep breath. I could not give in to self-pity. I'd never pull myself out and Parbrier would be as good as gone.

"Okay," I said, the dirt crunching between my teeth. "But can I work my way up?"

Dad sighed. "We've practiced tumbling. You can't run from speed forever."

"I'm not running." I almost shouted. "I'm just...trying to be logical about it. Build up speed, build up confidence. If I mess up at thirty-five, it's going to be hard to get into the right headspace. If I work up to it, I'll be ready for the speed."

My stomach unclenched as he nodded slowly. "Okay. Yeah. That's not a bad idea. But start at fifteen."

"Tuck and roll!"

He rewarded me with a smirk and I yanked down my goggles and kicked off.

●

The rumbling through the bedrock intensified with each passing day. Hilltown felt it. Its people felt it, too, radiated up through bed and table legs, through streets and floors, setting their stomachs on edge, making them short-tempered, nervous. The skies, irritatingly clear, provided no relief from the sharp horizon line burning its shadow-double across the backs of every eye. Every whirl of dust or smudge of shadow made breaths hitch. No one could risk being caught off-guard.

Within the metal fungi of City Hall, machines blipped and squealed as Hilltown's best and brightest ran simulation after simulation with each new shred of information. The path models converged, solidified, bound themselves into something like certainty. Their voices whispered in hushed concern, as new paths drew closer to the outskirts of town.

Barring a miracle, some fluke of chaos theory that governed the mechanisms that drove the school, Parbrier

College would hit town. Evacuating neighborhoods would spare civilian lives. There was time, thankfully. Parbrier was still some distance away.

But it was closing in fast.

●

Two days. I sat in the living room alone, looking at the pile of boxes and bags Dad and I had packed after the evacuation order had come down the Hill. In two days, Parbrier would crash through our neighborhood and destroy everything.

I hadn't slept well last night. We'd stayed up past midnight strategizing, testing the makeshift radar Dad had rigged to the motorbike to help me find my way when the dust cloud made it impossible to see. I'd collapsed into bed like a sack of concrete, the dust from the plains still clinging to my scalp because I'd been too tired to take a shower. Even with my eyes burning, my body shaking with exhaustion, I couldn't sleep.

I lay awake, thoughts swirling over things that only half made sense but seemed so important to puzzle out, to fit into real life. My inner monologue devolved into self-loathing. How could I be so stupid as to think I could catch a college? Not everyone was my dad. *I* wasn't my dad. He'd faced down one of those enormous behemoths, not side-by-side with a dozen other applicants, but *alone*. If waves had swamped his kayak, if he'd been caught in a rip-tide, if he hadn't gotten on board before Wakereach dove, he'd have drowned. He'd had to risk everything, knowing he wouldn't make it back if he failed, so he didn't fail.

But me? Did *I* have that in me?

I stared into the gloom where the Wakereach model arched gracefully from the ceiling. The fairy lights glittered on its scales, on the curves of its fins. Parbrier seemed nothing like Wakereach. It was bulky and sharp and frightening.

I dragged the covers over my head and stuffed myself under my pillow where everything was dark and muffled, smothered like deep water. At last, whether from slowly suffocating myself with my own CO2 or from actual exhaustion, I finally fell asleep.

Then came morning, and the announcement of the evacuation orders, and Dad and I had spent every second since scrambling to pack up what we could. I wouldn't be taking the bulky Wakereach model, but the fairy lights made it into my backpack. I packed a week's worth of clothes, my old stuffed whale Nemo, and my journal. I couldn't fit anything else, and I couldn't weigh myself down on the motorbike. Dad set aside a box for me to put anything else I wanted, but I quickly realized that everything I wanted wouldn't fit.

Defeated, I helped him pack a few kitchen supplies, bathroom things, his clothes, and his books. I paused at his old copy of The Encyclopedia of Modern Behemoths, thinking of his boarding story. It changed a bit each time he told it, as personal memories do, but the core remained the same:

My father, in his early twenties with all his hair in dark tousled waves, scrambling barefoot across algae-slicked rocks along the southern shoreline for a hundred miles. Eating limpets and clams as he could find them. Wincing from the infected cut on his hand that kept getting sand and saltwater in it. Jotting down notes on Wakereach sightings from local fishermen in his damp pocket notepad. Calculating that its next ventilation flush would be close enough to shore for him to board, if he could get to it fast enough. Buying the leaky kayak, barely seaworthy, that whitecaps filled with water before he'd gotten three hundred yards off shore, soaking his belongings, freezing his feet and hands. Paddling harder as Wakereach's massive metal spine arched up from the depths and settled on the surface a quarter mile ahead, its foghorn moaning, its blast of spray arching up into the sky and raining down on him. The kayak foundering. Casting the oar aside and plunging into water so cold the fishermen had warned him he'd only survive ten minutes before drowning. Hauling himself up the iced metal rungs with the last of his strength and pounding, screaming at the porthole for someone to open it, to let him in. Finding himself face to face with a student horrified to see him and getting dragged inside mere seconds before the school dived back to the depths.

That was the kind of story I'd always wanted for myself. Proof of my unflagging determination, my strength, my bravery. Secretly, I'd always thought I had that in me, but sitting in the living room, waiting for Dad to come back, I felt every last drop of confidence ooze out of me.

I just wanted things to stay how they were. I wanted to live with Dad, go to school, work a part-time job over the summer, and keep falling asleep under my Wakereach model. I wasn't ready for everything to change, and yet it would, whether I caught Parbrier or not, whether we evacuated or not: nothing, in two days, would ever be the same.

I clutched my head in my hands and willed myself not to cry. I wasn't ready. How could anyone, any of my classmates, be ready for this?

The footsteps on the front stairs made my heart sink, and I sniffed hard to choke down the dread that threatened to break me into pieces. The door burst open and Dad swept in, sandwiches under one arm, and a bright green pair of goggles dangling from his other hand.

"Hey, kiddo!" he said, beaming, practically dancing on his toes as he dropped lunch on the bare table. In two days, the table would be gone. The room would be gone. Everything, everything —

Dad came over and dropped with a huff onto the couch beside me. "Here. I got them printed just for you. Look! It's got the Parbrier logo on the side."

I looked and looked.

"Hey." Dad's arm draped over my shoulders, squeezing gently. "What's up? You look like you've got something stuck in your throat. You okay?"

The concern in his voice broke me. I couldn't stop it, couldn't hold it back any longer. I curled up against him and burst into tears. It was like the ocean and all Dad's saltwater stories were pouring out of me. I cried and cried, but eventually the water dried up, leaving me numb as Dad hugged me, shushing softly, whispering, "Hey, hey, hey. It's okay. It's okay."

"I can't do it," I croaked at last, mashing my face with my hands to wipe the tear tracks from my cheeks. "I can't, Dad. I'll die. I just know it."

Dad turned in his seat and gripped me by the shoulders, giving me a little shake. "Hey. You listen, and you listen closely, okay? You can do this. Kaiya, you're strong and you're brave and you're smart."

"No, I'm not!" I could feel the tears surging again. "I'm not brave and I'm not strong. I'm terrified. I've been terrified for weeks, ever since they announced Parbrier's approach."

"Of *course* you are!" Dad cried, and I looked up at him.

"What?"

"Kai, I'd be worried about your sanity if you weren't terrified. Parbrier is a massive, powerful school. It has and will destroy people, good people, smart people, brave people. I was terrified of Wakereach, too."

"Really?"

Dad nodded and a small, comforting smile slipped across his face. "Yeah, Kai. I don't talk much about that part because I don't like remembering. I was shitting myself in that kayak. I almost turned around to go back to shore. A part of me was absolutely sure I was about to die, that Wakereach would dive before I got close and that its wake would drag me down behind it." He rubbed his warm hand up and down my arm. "Catching a college is terrifying, Kai, but you are fully capable of doing it. I know you. I wouldn't let you do this if I didn't think you had it in you."

The dread clenching my stomach loosened slightly. "Why does it have to be like this?" I whispered. "Why does it have to be so hard?"

Dad shrugged. "Who knows? But I promise you, no matter what happens, I'll be here for you, okay? I don't want you to let your fear stop you, because I know you'd regret it. This is the experience of a lifetime, a chance to bloom into the person you'll be from here on out. It's a rite of passage, proof of your adulthood. Kai," he said, taking my hands, "you're braver than you think. You don't have to do something stupid just to make it, okay? Healthy risks. Don't dwell on all the things that could go wrong. Think instead about what it's going to feel like when you climb up onto Parbrier and the other students sweep you inside. You're going to *love* it. Libraries the size of City Hall, dorms filled with ambitious kids like you, world-class professors to drive and inspire you!" He laughed. "Oh, Kai, the future will be yours! You'll be able to do anything you want, go anywhere you like! And wherever you end up, know —" He held me apart from him and peered lovingly into my eyes. " — I'll be here. Always. Okay?"

His enthusiasm infected me, set my heart soaring. This *was* my chance. Yes, it was terrifying, but wasn't that part of the appeal? To prove myself? To show that I could manage on my own, carve my own path in the world?

"Okay," I said, and he hugged me tight again.

"Good. Now let's eat and get this stuff packed up, okay?"

The warmth and confidence that had enveloped me while safe in his embrace began to trickle away as I watched him unwrap our sandwiches, softly chanting, "Two more days! Two more days!"

I looked again at the piles of belongings we needed to move. I looked at the apartment's peeling paint, its uneven walls, the way the floor sagged under the weight of his bookshelf. The fold-out couch Dad used for his bed; the side table piled high with his stack of notebooks. The small but tidy kitchen where I'd eaten almost every meal of my life.

I took a long, shaky breath, absorbing the smell of coffee, sawdust, and paper. I'd been lucky to grow up here in Hilltown, even if it was boring. I'd never realized it until now. After tomorrow, I would never stand in this apartment again.

I choked down the thought and went to the table where Dad was already tucking into his salami sandwich.

Yes, I told myself, *everything will change. But it'll be for the better.*

It had to be for the better.

●

It appeared as a dark cloud on the horizon, as a warning tremble that sizzled the sand in the gutters and clattered glasses on shelves. Hilltown's concrete teeth rattled, and in a burst, its sirens screeched over the rooftops: IT'S HERE.

Eyes snapped open, exhaustion wiped from every heart as Hilltown's citizens gathered at their eastern windows to peer out at the drifting darkness, like volcanic smoke on the horizon.

The city, after a breathless pause, a moment between heartbeats, exploded into activity. Citizens scrambled for supplies. Jetpacks whined, engines warming. Earpieces and hand-held radios squawked as frequencies synced. Parasails strained in the breeze. Boots pounded down Hilltown's steps, beating their way to strategic spots.

This was it. The city's walls echoed with shouts of encouragement and people mobbed the guardrails high up on the Hill. Cardboard banners danced above their heads. Flags lunged and shivered in the breeze. The air filled with the smells of roasted nuts and fried dough and spicy street noodles.

Through the haze of dust far across the plains, Parbrier College began to take form, a shadow of spines, roaring closer.

●

Dad sagged against the deck railing, a beer clutched in his hands even though the sun was hardly above the horizon. He looked thin and tired, his hair ruffled up like he'd tossed and turned all night like I had. When I pushed the sliding door open, he pivoted to squint at me, and over his shoulder I saw it: a dark cloud of dust billowing up from the east. Inside the unearthly plume, a knot of shadow made me catch my breath.

Pushing off the rail, Dad came over and wrapped his arm around my shoulders, and we stood like that, watching the cloud grow, feeling the deep rumbling as it shook its way up through the ground, the floor, and into our feet. The warning sirens shrieked, echoing off the courtyard and the surrounding buildings.

The cloud swirled in hypnotizing spirals, coiling up into the sky. It drifted higher and higher, its veil wafting over the sun, blotting it in and out of sight, turning it red as a blister. Beside me, I heard Dad take a trembling breath, but when I glanced up at him, he was grinning.

"Let's get you ready, huh?"

Following Dad down to the courtyard where the motorbike waited, I felt every step jam up into my hip, making me suddenly aware of how my muscles and bones connected to make walking happen. It was such a strange process, walking, I realized; it took so much thought, so much mental work, all of it tucked away in my subconscious, forgotten by ease of practice. But it was a complex movement.

The bike looked fragile in the vague light, patched together with duct tape, its paint pitted, its crevices jammed with dust from weeks of practice. I slung onto it, took the small rubber grips in my hands. Parbrier's approach made the bike's body rattle softly, like it was shaking. I brushed a film of dust from its fuel tank, felt the gentle shushing from my lips before remembering it wasn't a living thing. It couldn't be afraid. It couldn't die.

Dad stood with his hands deep in his pockets, hunched and peering as he paced around the bike. "I checked over everything," he said. "Spent all night making sure it was good to go. It's rock solid."

I nodded, swallowed the muddy spit that had started pooling in my mouth. The rumbling was making me nauseous. I needed to get moving, get distracted.

"You're heading straight up Hill when I go, right?" I asked. He didn't look at me as he stooped to pick at a flake of something on the rear tire. "You'll have a better view up there. And better reception on your clamp, so when I call..."

Dad nodded, stood, cleared his throat. I felt a shudder run through me at the shimmer of moisture in his eye. "Yeah. Yeah, that'll be perfect." He nodded, and I saw his nostrils flare as he glanced up at the sky over the courtyard wall. The dust cloud was drifting towards us now. Parbrier was getting nearer. The fire escape rattled against the building.

"I gotta go." It came out as a croak, and Dad lurched suddenly, catching me up tight in his arms.

"Be careful, okay?" he muttered as he pressed a fast, dry kiss to my cheek and ruffled my hair as he stepped back. "Don't let fear get in your head, but don't do anything dumb, all right?"

I nodded. "Thanks, Dad."

He forced a grin that muffled the wetness in his eyes and threw up his two thumbs. "Go get 'em, kiddo!"

I revved up the bike and the tires spun out on the asphalt, shooting me forward as I wrestled to keep it under control. It was like everything I'd learned, everything I'd practiced had flown out of my head, and suddenly, I needed all my attention just to stay on the bike and keep it going straight.

Swerving around chunks of masonry shaken free from the buildings, I cut through a side street and out onto the plains. The landscape folded flat around me, and I saw it: Parbrier, its spires rising up out of the gloom, its windows glowing in sooty twilight, not more than two miles away.

I gunned the bike to its top speed, thirty miles per hour, forty. The wind filled my ears, its soprano screaming cutting through the roar of the school. I swung out in a circle to get around the worst of the debris cloud. Far to my left, I caught a glimpse of tiny figures scuttling up into the trees at the edge of town, ropes and harpoons dangling like delicate strands of spider silk beneath them. Would they be too close when the college turned?

I shivered and swung out farther. I needed to pass the college in order to get behind it, attack from the rear. The bike engine squealed as it pushed forty-three. A stone stung my cheek. Off to my left, the college formed a cliff of darkness. It was no longer a uniform mass, but a complex of recesses and protrusions, projecting thousands of interior corridors and laboratories and community rooms and private spaces. High up on the spires, silhouettes gathered, waving.

I'll be up there with them tonight, I thought, and yanked down my goggles.

Leaning low over the handlebars, Dad's attack plan raced through my head. I had to keep up the speed to stabilize the bike for the jump. One shot, one jump, one chance. If I missed, I'd land hard and probably scrape off most of my skin, if I didn't break a bone.

The dust cloud boiled ahead of me. It'd be impossible to see inside. I'd have to turn, line up, then drive into the fiercest debris, all relying only on radar.

Overhead, a flash of movement drew my eye, and I watched as a kid with a jetpack raced towards the school, vapor trails streaming behind him. He was almost there when the jetpack's left engine sputtered out in a billow of smoke and he plunged. My heart lurched into my mouth as he tumbled, arms and legs flailing, out of sight on Parbrier's far side.

Then the cloud caught me. Sand sizzled against my windbreaker. I switched on the radar and turned hard. The fist-sized screen started blinking, showing a large cobalt splotch sliding into place ahead of me. My bike jittered over ravaged dirt. I had to focus.

The dust thickened as I gunned forward, barreling towards where I hoped the track was. I tugged up my muffler. The debris burned my cheeks and sand-blasted my goggles, and then I sensed it: a bulk in the darkness, coming up fast. I couldn't hear anything but the bone-numbing roar, the squealing earth, the percussion of rocks. A stone punched me square in the shoulder, making my hand go numb. I yelped and choked on dust.

I aimed into the raging storm. A pebble cracked my goggles. Almost there. Grit stabbed into my eye, blurring everything to the right. I had to jump soon, but couldn't tell where. I couldn't see anything in the chaos, couldn't even detect a shift in sound to find the tread. Rubble flew at me, bounced off. I'd be speckled with bruises later. One chunk clipped my lip, sending a shooting pain up behind my nose. I tasted blood, and felt the knife edge of a cracked tooth with my tongue.

I couldn't get close enough, I realized. Dad hadn't considered how many rocks would be mixed into the soil, that it'd be too dangerous to get close enough to jump. I couldn't see, my goggles were broken, I couldn't breathe!

His plan wasn't going to work. I dropped back to where the dust thinned, ripped off my hazed goggles, and fought back a sob of frustration. This was my boarding story, and this was how would it end? That I'd gotten scared of getting hurt and given up? I imagined riding back to town, weighed down by dust, walking the gauntlet of spectators recognizing failure. Would they laugh? Would they try to comfort me, clap me on the shoulder, say *Nice try*? And then Dad's face, the forced smile, the soothing hug, all the words that would spill out of him trying to convince me it was fine, that there'd be other chances, that sometimes luck just wasn't on our side, but deep down, I'd know — and he'd know — that I'd given up. That when faced with the same terrifying choice he'd made a hundred yards from Wakereach, I'd turned around and run back to safety.

The dust thinned for a moment around me, and I saw the gap between the tracks, Parbrier's underbelly. It looked clearer there. I thought back, searching my brain for some small piece of info, and remembered with a jolt the portholes on the underbelly.

I revved up the bike again and gunned forward, breaking out into the clear and eerily muffled space under the school. Above me, the college was a vast inverted horizon. The size of it gave me vertigo, like I was falling headfirst out of the sky towards the darkened land below.

With a nauseating lurch, my perspective whipped right-side up again as I made out the latticework of catwalks above me. If I could get up there...

Movement caught my eye, a fluttering line, dangling from a grappling hook snagged on a railing. I started towards it, but just then, the college shifted, the right track arching towards me. I veered, and missed the rope. Looking back over my shoulder, the rope was gone. Had it been there at all?

Up ahead, through the broad gap, I could see the buildings of my neighborhood racing nearer. I scanned the catwalks for anything that could help me. There! A broken walkway within reach.

I had to get up and get inside before the debris from town started bouncing around the undercarriage. Ten feet. Five feet. My boot slipped off the saddle as I tried to get it under me, the leather slick with dust. I gripped the handlebars, just as Dad had taught me, and leveraged myself up again. The bike wobbled. I accelerated a little to keep it stable, and then jumped!

I crashed onto grating and felt the twisted metal bite into my thighs. I cried out and shifted to take the cutting weight off my legs, felt hot, sticky liquid soaking my pants. I clawed higher. I could hear the sirens from town again. I had to hurry.

A hand clamped onto my wrist, and I looked up to find a pale lady dangling from a climbing harness. "Welcome to Parbrier!" she shouted, throwing a safety line around my waist. Hauling us up to a stable platform, she unclipped me and shoved me towards four waiting kids.

A concrete chunk buzzed past us, not twenty feet away.

"Inside! Now! We're gonna hit!"

Someone dragged me inside with them, and the woman slammed a steel door behind us, cutting the roaring noise to a whisper that rang in my ears. Then everyone burst out laughing. I sat trembling as someone applied pressure to the gashes on my legs. A girl with black curls hugged me.

"Congratulations! You made it!" She grinned. "Let's get you registered, okay?"

●

And then it was over. The last chunk of stone flipped up from Parbrier's tracks, and Hilltown felt the roaring subside as the college cut off to the north, its dust cloud once more shrouding it from sight. The city watched, stunned to silence, until one bold voice shouted out in joy and the streets erupted in hoots and howls and Parbrier's fight song which everyone had learned by heart.

Details trickled in, reports from the ground. Of the thirty applicants, eight had gained admittance, ten missed their chance, and twelve perished. The school had crushed two streets deeper than predicted, forcing citizens to scramble to escape. Some didn't get out in time. Parbrier had left its mark on Hilltown once more.

But what thrill! What destruction! It made Hilltown giddy and loud and boisterous. Champagne corks popped, and there was dancing and music and joy and among all that, huddled in dark, quiet rooms, failed applicants and the families of the dead clutched their heads in their hands and wept or stuffed their mouths with bedding and screamed in rage.

The Energy Beetle hummed quietly to itself, pleased to make the strung lights glow, the stereos pound, the griddles sizzle. The town swelled with pride, having launched its seeds of future prosperity at the raging college, and having successfully landed many. For those who failed or died, Hilltown chose to believe if they'd only tried harder or been smarter, if only they'd made better choices, they'd have made it. It was easier that way.

●

I lay on the bed in my dorm room ,which was little more than a cube with a cot and a storage locker that doubled as a desk. The bulb overhead cast flattening light into every corner, erasing the shadows. I switched it off, preferring the reddish glow of dusk seeping through the slotted window.

On my legs, bandages tugged on the school-branded sweatpants I'd been given in the Parbrier infirmary. Thirteen staples, all told, and filler for my chipped tooth. The painkillers helped, but I was sick with exhaustion and bruised to my core.

I kept waiting for the thrill of triumph to hit, for my version of Dad's victorious whoop to burst from my chest and fill me with joy and pride, to feel changed, worthy. But I felt nothing.

I'd met with advisor after advisor, all of them trying to puzzle out what I wanted to study, what I wanted to do with my life, and I couldn't tell them. I didn't know. I'd never thought about what would happen after I caught a college.

In the end, they signed me up for behemothology. It was the only major I could remember Dad talking about, and lost as I felt, it seemed to make sense to study the thing that had baffled me: this giant machination that came and destroyed and left, without malice or kindness, without explanation. It simply existed, as all behemoths did, without question. Who built them? Who controlled them? But even more, why didn't we question it?

Maybe I was just ungrateful. I tried to conjure up the enthusiasm I'd felt at our kitchen table, but that only made me remember the table was gone. Our plans were gone. Our apartment, our deck, my room, my model of Wakereach, everything.

I thought of the kid with the jetpack spiraling out of control, and my stomach lurched up into my mouth. There'd been four other kids in the medical center when they brought me in, blooded and scraped raw from the ordeal of catching Parbrier. The medical techs chatted around us while they cleaned wounds and patched torn skin. A dozen kids had died trying to board this year. One of the techs said it was the highest casualty count in Parbrier history, and would no doubt increase its desirability.

My wristclamp buzzed with another message from Dad congratulating me, asking me to call, to tell him everything. I stared at its cracked screen, then looked back up at the slotted window. Wind wedged silt under the sill, leaving a film of dust on everything, including me.

Dad wanted my boarding story, the one thing I'd dreamed of ever since I was a kid. But all I wanted to do was sleep. I clenched my eyes shut and tried to squeeze pride out of my heart. How could I feel nothing? How could I not sense how I'd changed?

I'm just tired, I told myself. *Tomorrow, I'll wake up and squeal in delight*, I told myself. *It'll all be worth it*, I told myself, but Parbrier's rumbling engines lulled me to, I was more certain than ever that I was wrong.

Maggie Slater's story "Catching College" was originally published in Metaphorosis on Friday, 2 June 2023. See magazine.metaphorosis.com

About the author

Diagnosed with depression in 2019, Maggie Slater lives in an 1800s farmhouse in New England with two half-tamed boys, a half-trained puppy, her husband, her parents, and at least one benign ghost. When she has an almost quiet moment, she enjoys Haruki Murakami novels, sampling craft beer, and hoarding cheap notebooks.

maggieslater.com, @maggiedotwrites

Shortcut to Happily Ever After

Ben Wan

Dedicated to Dr. Larry Yip

"Wanna grab coffee sometime?" Daniel Woo looked across at the cute cashier with the big glasses for her reaction. Her name tag read 'STEPH'. As he watched her surprised expression form into a smile, he logged her name into his memory.

"You're awfully forward, aren't you?"

Daniel smiled back. "I just don't like wasting time."

Steph laughed. "Alright. Phone?" Daniel handed it over to her as she typed in her number. "When's your day off?" he asked.

"Tuesday."

"How 'bout next Tuesday then? Five o'clock? The place next door?"

Steph laughed. "*Wow.* You really don't waste time."

You have no idea, he thought, as he took his phone back, said good-bye, and walked out. To Steph, Daniel must have seemed incredibly confident. But had she met him months ago, she would've met a completely different man. A timid man. Because back then, he hadn't had *the watch*.

Outside, he unrolled his sleeve to reach it; his key to finding love, his shortcut to 'happily ever after', conveniently wrapped around his wrist.

He made it a habit now, when asking someone on a date, to set up a specific time and place. The women usually thought he just liked to plan. But really, it was so he'd know where to tell the watch to go. *Next Tuesday. 5PM. Place next door.* He finished with the settings, took a breath, and pushed in the dials on the watch.

In an instant, he was standing on the same street, but the cars and pedestrians had all changed around him. He still hadn't gotten used to jumping between the present and the future. It felt like skipping from chapter to chapter on a Blu-ray disc. Except he was actually *in* the movie.

He peeked into the window of the coffee shop. Sure enough, his future self and Steph were inside. *So she shows up to the first date*, he thought. *But how* well *does it go?*

He programmed the watch again and jumped forward an hour later, where he saw the two of them outside the shop. Together, they were laughing. He overheard himself set up the next date at a restaurant next week.

Daniel knew exactly where it was. He took a long walk over to it a few blocks away and programmed the watch again. This time, he watched himself and Steph walk out, nervous laughter from both of them. As they stopped by the street, there was a pause. He had to cringe just watching the awkwardness, along with the fact that for some reason, neither of them seemed to be as happy as on the previous date.

He hid, hearing his nervous future self ask, "So, uh, want a ride back?"

There was a pause and Steph awkwardly said, "Listen, Daniel...you seem like a great guy..."

He didn't need to hear more. He had heard it all before.

'We just don't seem like a fit.'

'I'm just not feeling the chemistry.'

'Maybe we could be friends.'

He watched his future self's expression change to disappointment. It was that same expression that made Daniel feel relieved. So it wouldn't work out. *No need to go on this date, then. Saved myself from getting my hopes up.*

His other self, after a minute, regained his composure and told her, "I understand. It was, uh, it was fun." As Steph walked off to her own Uber, Daniel turned away from his future disappointment and set the watch back to the present day.

Now, he was outside of the shop again, looking back through the window at Steph, who had just given out her number to him. A Steph who had no idea what he had just seen.

A few hours later, Steph got a sincere phone call from Daniel.

"I know this is gonna sound really weird," he said, "But I'm gonna have to cancel next Tuesday. It's not you, it's just...I realized I'm just not in a place to date right now."

"Oh," said Steph, who was more surprised by the sudden news than hurt. "Uhh, no problem. Thanks for not wasting time. Again."

"Of course."

"See you around the shop?"

"Sure," said Daniel. After hanging up, he sighed in relief. He always felt bad about doing this, but in the end, he knew he was dodging a bullet. Just like he had done with the others.

Steph was the third woman he had canceled on before even the first date. There were no hard feelings, especially given that none of these women had a chance to develop any attachment to him. It wasn't selfish either. He had spared all of *them* the same hurt too. The hurt he saw from simply looking into their futures. No more failed relationships. No more heartbreak. He would keep peeking into the future until he *knew* for certain that he had found a relationship that would last.

He set the phone down on his dining table. Only to jump.

There, standing in his living room, was a tall woman with a ponytail. She wore a long black coat of a snakeskin leather material. And she was pointing something that looked an awful lot like a gun at him.

"What have you been doing with that watch?!"

"What?!" Daniel put his hands up. *Oh fuck*, he thought.

He looked at the gun. It didn't look anything like the firearms he was familiar with. And then he saw it on her wrist...the same 'watch' he wore. Just in a different color.

He had wondered about the origin of the 'watch' when he found it. Now it was catching up to him.

The owner of the 'watch' was here. And she wasn't happy.

He stammered. "Okay, okay, I can explain..."

Six Months Ago...

The night Chloe left him wasn't the worst part. Sure, Daniel cried after it was all over. But it was just a couple hours until the mercy of sleep took him. Asleep, he could forget what happened. Asleep, he and Chloe would still be together...

No, the worst part of the breakup was the day after.

Because now he had an entire day to remember that she had walked out on him. He'd wake up and look across at her empty spot in bed, knowing he would never see her face there again. He had spent their entire relationship in this one bedroom apartment, yet now it felt even smaller.

It seemed like this was always something that happened to him. Ever since he was a child, he had wanted to live out the stories he grew up with, where the hero would always find love. Yet whenever he found someone special and got attached, she'd inevitably leave him. Chloe was just the latest in a series. Once again, he was left with unfulfilled dreams and fantasies. Trips they would never travel together. Movies he would never get to watch with her. Gifts he would never to give to her. The worst, of course, was the feeling of being chronically unwanted, that all he would find was rejection, heartbreak, and loneliness. And yet, there was always a part of him that hoped that he'd find someone who'd help him prove that wrong. Someone who would prove that he *was* wanted and could be loved.

Chloe had felt like that 'someone' at first, but something had been holding her back. She had admitted several times that she had trouble getting close to the guys she dated. He had hoped, or rather expected, that as he continued to show he cared, she'd see that he was different, and gradually be as intimate and vulnerable with him as he was with her.

Instead, all he did was drive her away. Maybe she was afraid he'd hurt her the same way that the other guys did. Yet the more he tried to forgive her, the more resentment he felt towards her for punishing him for the sins of her exes. *She could at least have punished me for my own sins,* he thought. *That at least would have been fair.*

The pain carried over from one day to the next.

He started burying himself at work in the morgue to distract himself. Suicides, unfortunately, spiked during the holidays. There was a common depression, triggered by a yearning to be with others and a realization, for many, that the yearning could never be fulfilled.

He looked around at the dead around him. He knew he should feel grateful to be the only one in the room breathing. But instead, he felt like he could relate to them, at least on the inside. Cold. Numb. Nothing left to care about.

1:30 came around. Daniel had heated up his lunch, a can of clam chowder that he usually packed because it was easy to microwave in the kitchen.

He took it back to his office, only for his boss to barge in.

"The cops have been asking about this John Doe for way too long. I need you to perform the autopsy *asap.*"

The John Doe was a man in his forties. Nothing unusual about his appearance. But there was an ID card that was unrecognizable from any state's driver's license, giving the name John Tempest.

To everyone, it seemed fake. The police were at a loss. The fingerprints matched no database. Neither did his DNA. Nor, strangely enough, did his teeth match any dental records.

The man was a complete ghost.

Daniel performed the autopsy, as requested. It seemed that the cause of death was a heart attack. No murder or suicide. Just his heart giving out. (In a way, he could relate.)

It was about halfway through the autopsy that he remembered the clam chowder sitting back at his office. Probably cold and likely spoiled by now.

He went back to his desk and tossed out his lunch. The *thud* as the bowl hit the bottom of the trash can felt satisfying, but it wasn't enough to quell the anger he felt.

Now he'd have to wait until dinner to eat. Which pissed him off further. Work was supposed to be his distraction. But now it had become such a distraction that he was skipping lunch. And skipping lunch would just remind him of Chloe and how she always packed lunch for him...and well, work wasn't such a distraction anymore now, was it?

Towards the end of his shift, he looked through the belongings that were found on 'John Tempest'. Perhaps he could help the police find a clue to the man's identity.

Among the belongings was a watch. It didn't match any brand that Daniel had been familiar with. Instead of a single dial to adjust the time and the date, there were multiple ones. There even seemed to be ones to adjust the month and the year, which made it even more unusual.

Daniel played with one of the dials absentmindedly. *It seems like a good watch*, he thought as he turned the hand back a few hours.

Lost in thought, he snapped the dial back in. That was when he felt *the jump*.

He was still in his office. But his surroundings felt... different.

Because the clam chowder was now back to sitting on his desk. Still warm, steam rising from it.

That was strange, he thought. How could that be back there? He hadn't had it out since lunch time, which was...

He looked at the dead man's watch. Sure enough, it had been set to lunch hour. *1:30PM.*

There was no way. Or was there?

His mind must be playing tricks on him. And yet, here was the soup, as it would have sat. But if he had really gone back, where was his past self? He snuck out into the hallway, towards the lab, took a peek in the window...

And *there he was*. Performing the autopsy on the dead body, forgetting all about his lunch back in the office.

He had traveled in time.

Which likely then explained John Tempest. Tempest. As in *Tempus*. As in *time.*

The man was a time traveler. A *dead* time traveler. He wouldn't have any record. Was he from the past? The future? A different world entirely?

Daniel didn't know. All he wanted to learn about now was the watch.

He turned the dial and adjusted it a few hours further back. Then a few hours forward. Each time, he kept adjusting, spying on his past self in the lab or office, and testing the watch further. *Shit, what time was it when I first started jumping around?* he wondered. He needed to go back to his present time. His *real* time. He remembered it being towards the end of his shift and estimated that it must have been around 5:30. He set the watch and jumped once again, finding himself back in his office at the end of the day. The clam chowder was gone and John Tempest's belongings were all on his desk. He had returned to the present. Daniel wasn't sure whether to sigh in relief or cheer in excitement. It *worked.*

What now? Anyone he reported this to would think he was crazy, until he demonstrated it. But then they'd surely take it away. Examine its functions. Use it for their own purposes. No, he had a unique opportunity here.

John Tempest, whoever he was, seemed to have used this watch for time travel. So far, Daniel could only move through time in the same spot. Which probably meant that if he wanted to go back in time to watch the Beatles debut on the Ed Sullivan Show, he'd have to physically *go* to the Ed Sullivan Theater in New York in the present before setting anything.

Tempest had wound up in this timeline where he died. He certainly wasn't using it anymore. So if Daniel took the watch...who would miss it?

Plus, who would even find out? The police might have a record of the watch's existence, but with other cases preoccupying them, they probably wouldn't notice if he kept it to himself. And considering that Tempest probably wasn't even from this time period, the police would never find any leads about him.

It was settled, then. He was going to keep it. But what would he do with it? It didn't take him long to think about it. He knew deep down what he wanted…

He was going to use it to find the love of his life.

At first, he was tempted to go back and undo the breakup with Chloe. But what exactly would he undo? Would he even be able to convince her to stay with him? If he couldn't, he'd just be opening up an old wound. He wanted to make himself feel *better*, not worse.

No, he'd only use the watch to take peeks into the future and come back, rather than change his past. And this time, the watch could help him know that he was moving on with the *right* person, rather than wasting any more time with the *wrong* person.

So Daniel started putting himself out there.

First, he met Ann at a party through his co-worker Simon. "You're not seeing anyone. She's not seeing anyone. I'll set you guys up," he told Daniel.

"Why don't you go for her?"

"Already tried," said Simon. "But she goes for nice guys."

Daniel shook his head. That was a backhanded compliment if he knew it. But he was intrigued.

Simon gestured him over. "Hey, Ann. Meet my buddy, Daniel."

Daniel looked over at a cute girl in a leather jacket. Okay, he wasn't hating this experience so far.

"Hey Daniel," said Ann.

"Alright, you two talk. I'm out."

Daniel watched Simon go. Ann said, "Well that wasn't an awkward introduction at all."

"Not at all," he agreed. "So how do you know Simon? Other than him trying to hit on you?"

She laughed. "Is that what he said he did?"

"Clearly he wasn't that successful."

"I'm friends with his roommate. We met that way, unfortunately."

Daniel nodded. He could tell that she was wondering what his connection was. "Well, I work with Simon," he said.

"With the dead people."

"Yep, with the dead people. Which kinda sucks, actually. Because I thought that meant I wouldn't have to deal with anyone annoying. But then I met him."

She laughed. Once they hit it off about classic literature, she gave him her number and he decided to take the watch for a spin.

The planning was simple. He'd make it a habit of scheduling each new date at the end of the previous one. As an observer, he'd bounce around and spy on how the date went. Then, he'd overhear his future self set up the next time and know exactly where and when to pop up.

After calling Ann to schedule a meeting at a local bookstore, he used the watch to jump to the first date. Then the second. The third. Then months of dating until the night he asked her to be his girlfriend.

Daniel had been tempted to stop peeking then, already satisfied with the future. But he didn't just want another relationship. He wanted *the* relationship. The last relationship he'd ever be in. He wanted to know the *whole* future. So he watched Cliff Notes of an entire relationship unfold. Their first time meeting the parents. Their first fight.

And then, after a year of dating, the breakup. Another girl out of the blue who would leave and break his heart.

And once again, he'd find himself alone in a one bedroom apartment that was starting to feel even smaller.

He wound the watch back to the day after the party when they first met. Then he called Ann, telling her that he'd have to cancel their date at the bookstore and that he just wasn't really in a good place to see anyone. Maybe he'd just see her at another of his friend's parties again and save her from Simon trying to shoot his shot a second time. She found his honesty refreshing and genuinely wished him luck.

There was a wave of relief in what he had done, not to mention pride. He hadn't wasted Ann's time and she hadn't wasted his. They could move on to the right people without baggage. He felt ready to use the watch again on the next girl he met.

That was Kristine.

They had matched online. Daniel wasn't really a fan of online dating and trying to make conversations on the apps.

But, as a change, Kristine had started the conversation first.

She seemed like the opposite of Ann. For one thing, she wasn't a book nerd at all. For another, she was less sarcastic and more direct in her interest. The day after they started talking, she was already messaging him, 'Hey, handsome', and before he could float the idea by her first, she was the one proposing, 'Wanna get drinks this week?'

Still, Daniel wanted to see what would happen. So once again he used the watch to skip forward.

A couple of dates in, he saw that he'd invited her to his place. They both seemed to like cooking and he had wanted to show off his pasta maker. Though for some reason, it wasn't in its usual place and he'd had to buy a new one. That was odd. He could have sworn that he always kept it in the same spot in the same cabinet.

He knew this relationship would last longer than the previous one once he saw that, two years in, he and Kristine were still together.

Then eventually, engaged.

But he just kept pushing and jumping forward. Would she marry him? He had to *know*. Even when the wedding was already planned, a date set, invites sent out...he felt that he needed the confirmation. He needed to see himself married before he'd go on that date.

So it was discouraging, but not at all surprising that, when he jumped forward, he saw Kristine call off the engagement.

He overheard himself from the other room, asking, "What did I do?"

Kristine replied, "I just feel like...you don't put in any effort with me anymore."

At that point, Daniel stopped listening. He couldn't stand the sound of his own future voice breaking and crying. And he couldn't stand to keep watching Kristine break his heart even further.

If he was feeling that from just witnessing everything, he could only imagine what it'd be like to *live* it. And it made him even more grateful. This watch from John Tempest was a gift that spared him from pain.

He didn't even want to hear the rest of the argument or wait until Kristine had left. He knew her well enough, at least from observing their relationship, that she wouldn't change her mind.

And he'd be alone, once again, in a studio apartment that was still feeling smaller.

Better to just go back in time and end it. He reset the watch so the sound of his crying in the background would stop.

A month later, he went into the shop and met Steph.

The Present

Daniel finished his story. The woman with the gun had settled in at his dining table, drinking coffee that he had brewed for her. She had put the weapon down too, though the barrel was still pointed in his general direction.

She sipped the coffee in silence, thinking over Daniel's story. He cleared his throat.

"So...you must have known John Tempest, then. Miss...?"

She set down the cup, staring down at it and seeming to ignore him until she finally answered.

"Call me the Overseer."

"Overseer...so what, is that a title or something? For, like, time travelers?"

"Something like that. We're the ones assigned to stop the time ripples."

"Time ripples?"

Then, as if on cue, the coffee cup disappeared from the table.

It wasn't a magic trick. But it felt like one. Almost as if something had just *edited* a jump cut from a movie into reality. Even stranger, the Overseer had looked satisfied, almost having expected it to happen.

Daniel sat up, alarmed. "What...What just happened? What the hell is this?"

"Like I said. Time ripple." She stood up. "Mr. Woo, I tracked you down because your apartment appears to be the center of a set of time ripples."

"What are those? Some kind of butterfly effect?"

"In a way. When time gets undone, your environment changes around you. Usually, you don't even notice the changes. They usually start with your living arrangements..."

Daniel thought it through. He'd been living in a studio apartment for the last six years...but had it always been a studio?

Hadn't he been in a *one bedroom* apartment at some point? Or had he just dreamed or imagined that? No, that couldn't be right. Was she causing him to remember new things or was she causing him to *think* he was remembering new things?

She continued. "Then, certain things go missing. It's probably happened to you before. You can't find something. You don't know where you put it. And if it's not where you last put it, you chalk it up to a bad memory. But it's not. It's actually the beginning of a time ripple."

Things go missing...like a pasta maker? he thought.

"Because for just a few moments in time, whatever's missing actually *stopped existing.* You get residual memories of something that's no longer there and the mind just rationalizes that it's lost or misplaced. Until you stop remembering that it actually existed at all."

Daniel looked alarmed. The Overseer noticed. "Don't worry. Sometimes, what's lost gets found. Sure, it's not where you remember it. But you're so happy you found it again, you don't really question how it got there. You chalk it up to bad memory or just being forgetful. But you didn't forget. Time just set itself right again. And it took an Overseer to bring it back."

Daniel thought of all the times he had found something that he had once lost and how it never seemed to be in the last place he remembered. Just how common were these time ripples?

"Your...dating adventures are responsible for the time ripples in this sector. To put it mildly, you undid things that shouldn't have been undone. And time is making us all pay the consequences. So here's what we'll do, kid. You're gonna return that to me. That's Overseer property."

She grabbed his wrist, undoing the clasp on the watch without letting him object. "Next, you're gonna fix the mess you created."

"How?"

"All those women you turned down. You have to go back and date them. In *real* time."

Daniel froze. That had to be a joke. "But... But I know the future. That'd just be a waste of time."

"Would it?"

"I spent like two years with one of them! I know how it ends!"

"Do you?"

"Can you stop asking me questions?!"

She shot him a glare. "Something that was supposed to happen never happened. That's the cause of this. To fix it, you have to *make* those events happen. Everyone you were supposed to date. You have to *date* them. That's the only way this works."

Daniel could sense the judgment in her tone. He tried to think of another way to get out of this. "I'd be wasting years of my life!" he argued.

"You'd be saving life as we know it. Sounds dramatic, I know, but I'm not wrong. If we don't stop the ripples, all of us are eventually gonna disappear. Like that coffee cup. Which you're gonna forget, by the way, after we're done with this conversation. So you can either do this and make it right or I have to do something drastic."

"Like what?"

She tapped on her gun. "Like go back to when you got the watch and erase you from this timeline." Daniel blinked, speechless. "Not up for that? Didn't think so," she said.

And with that, the Overseer set the dials on her own watch, then grabbed his hand.

Their surroundings snapped into place in an instant. They were back at his room as it had been months ago. "Here we are," she said.

Daniel looked outside. It had gone from day to night. Two dogs were in the middle of a barking match with each other while their owners were trying to restrain them. "So wait, where am I? Like, where's the old me?"

"You've set up a date with Ann and now you've gone forward in time to see if you two have a future. But instead of you coming back to cancel on her, we're just gonna branch off into a new timeline from here. One where you actually date Ann. You know, like a normal person."

The Overseer clicked her watch. The barking outside stopped. Daniel peeked out. The dogs and their owners were completely frozen.

"If it doesn't work with her, then we go onto Kristine. And then Steph. Until you experience everything you were supposed to experience. Text Ann to reconfirm you're still going out. Time will resume and the new timeline will begin."

"But I'm undoing what I actually lived through. Doesn't that create, like, another paradox? If I didn't live through turning down these women, how would I still exist to do this?"

"Doesn't work that way," said the Overseer. "As long as these *new* paradoxes fulfill what was supposed to happen, time will fix itself. You know how a string gets tangled and knotted?"

"Yeah?"

"There's always that grace period where you can still untangle it. Before it gets too much. That's where we're at, kid. Right before the point of no return. The point where we can still untangle the string."

The Overseer took his phone and pulled up Ann's number, then handed it back to him.

"So do it," she said. "Untangle it."

●

Daniel stood by the front door of the bookstore, waiting on his first date, his *real* first date, with Ann. It occurred to him that he might have watched this date before, but it wasn't actually him who had gone through it.

What if he said something stupid and he never got into a relationship with her in the first place? He remembered seeing his heartbroken self back on the couch, feeling the way he had felt after Chloe left. Yes, maybe he'd actually prefer to just screw it all up now. It'd be a quicker way to get to the next person. Finish the mission for the Overseer. Correct his mistake. Get out of this mess.

Then Ann walked in and the plan went out the window.

For Ann, it had just been a few days ago since she met Daniel, but for him, it had been *months*.

He forgot how much he had liked looking in her eyes at the party and the way she had made him feel the first time that he met her.

Their first date, time-wise, lasted about twelve hours.

But neither he nor Ann really felt time go by. She spent the night at his place, which was something he hadn't predicted, since he hadn't stuck around long enough to find out the first time he watched. Other than the embarrassment of not having a clean coffee cup for her in the morning (and feeling like it was weird that he had so few in the first place), it was the perfect first date.

After she left his place, he got to thinking. Yes, he knew the future. Yes, he had seen that in a year from now, it wouldn't work out. But...couldn't he just enjoy being around her for now? Couldn't he just enjoy not being lonely and broken up over Chloe again?

So he kept seeing her. A couple dates in and she was all he could think about. Whenever she texted, he'd always smile and text back as soon as he could. Eventually, she was *constantly* texting him. Maybe she was getting clingy, but since he liked her already, he didn't mind. He *wanted* to text her all day. It was refreshing to not have to fight for someone's attention, the way he always had to with Chloe.

A few months in, he asked her to be his girlfriend. A month after that, they took their first trip together. But as the relationship grew, so did the fear.

Because he knew the future. He knew this relationship was doomed. That she was going to hurt him in the end. He tried to brush it aside and convince himself he was too in love right now to care.

But that love was starting to deteriorate. Whenever they'd argue, even over something small like what type of onions to buy at the grocery store, it was another nail in the coffin. *Is this why she's gonna leave?* he thought.

And yet whenever she said something nice or gave him a surprise gift or comforted him when he had a bad day, he couldn't really believe her either, even though he wanted to. She'd say, "I love you," and he'd wonder, *Do you really? You won't in a couple of months.*

Soon their one-year anniversary was approaching and the anxiety was taking over him. Ann would be leaving any day now. She'd drop him just like Chloe had. He'd go back to crying himself to sleep, waking up next to an empty space in the bed, and sleepwalking from day to day.

He knew what he had to do. And he didn't like it.

When he came over to her place the next night, he told her that it was over. That he felt like he didn't see a future anymore with her. He said it very matter-of-fact. After all, he thought, she was on the same page "You've probably been feeling this too anyway," he said.

But when he looked in her eyes, all he saw was hurt and confusion. She stammered, "No, I...I haven't been feeling that way at all." Daniel stared back with the same confusion. "But I thought...I saw..."

"You saw what, Daniel?"

What could he possibly tell her? That he had time traveled? He'd sound insane. And yet somehow, in knowing how it was going to end, he had acted so differently that he had changed the outcome and the timeline itself. Worse, after all these months of hating Chloe, now he felt like he *was* Chloe. He felt a sense of *loathing* towards himself for putting someone through what he had experienced. Chloe had left him out of fear of getting hurt and ended up hurting him instead. And now he was about to do the same thing to a sweet girl he loved who didn't deserve it.

"Okay, look, I'm sorry, I didn't mean what I said. I've just been confused." He reached out for her hand. He had to fix this.

But she turned away. "You don't know what you want, Daniel. That's the problem."

"No, that's not true."

"It *is* true. You say you want to be with me, but half the time, your mind's somewhere else. Whatever I try, it's not enough. So maybe you're right. Maybe we should just end this."

"I'm sorry, I — I didn't mean for it to be like this."

"Just go." She kept herself turned away and waited. Daniel couldn't think of anything else to do but comply. She hadn't shown much emotion, but when he walked out, he could hear her crying on the other side of the door.

He wasn't anything special. Just part of a vicious cycle. Hearts were broken. Heartbroken people went off to break other hearts. And it would continue over and over and over again. He had to stop it. He gave Ann a couple days of space before calling her.

Except when he called, the voice of an old man picked up on the other end. "Johnson Residence."

No. Daniel immediately hung up. He searched for Ann on social media. All her accounts were gone. He had hoped that she had just blocked him, but why would she have changed her number?

Then he visited her apartment building to check the register. There was a different name in her unit. She couldn't have moved out in just *two days* just because of him. He hoped she did because the alternative was much worse. At work, he approached Simon to see if he was right. "Ann and I broke up."

"Ann?"

"Yeah. You know, my girlfriend. The one you introduced me to at a party..."

"You had a girlfriend?"

Daniel ran off. He needed answers. Sure enough, when he was alone, the Overseer appeared.

"I warned you," she said. "The world's population just dropped by 1 million and nobody noticed except you."

"But how do I still remember?"

"You're a time traveler. Your memories linger longer than others. But you'll still forget eventually. Like that coffee cup."

"What coffee cup?"

"Exactly. Or your pasta maker."

"What pasta — never mind. If I keep going with the plan, do these people come back?"

"It's still possible, but you can't waste any more time. You still have to date the other two women."

"Wait," said Daniel. But the Overseer had already taken his phone. "On to Kristine."

"How? I only met her because I never went out with Ann."

"Not a problem," said the Overseer.

"She might not even exist now!"

But the Overseer went into the dating apps and started randomly swiping on the women. After a few matches, she handed the phone over to him.

"That should do it. Scroll through. One of them's her." She said with confidence.

Daniel looked through his matches. Sure enough, Kristine's profile was in the queue.

"How did you — ?"

"Like I said, your relationships were events that *had* to happen. No matter what, Kristine would still end up matching with you on these apps."

Daniel set the phone down, shaking his head. "I just had a breakup."

"Sorry," said the Overseer. "But you don't have time. None of us do."

So Daniel reluctantly started talking to Kristine. This time, *he* started the conversation. He didn't remember exactly what he had said to her when they first talked, but he had the gist of it. He thought about the future with her he had seen. How they had almost gotten married, if he hadn't screwed it all up.

He remembered the words that she had told him. 'You don't put in any effort with me.' Maybe he would just do the opposite of what he'd seen. Maybe that would give him a different result. Put in effort.

In a way, he'd be making up for what he had just done to Ann.

So this time Daniel was the one to ask Kristine for drinks next week.

Soon enough, they were dating and he had her over for cooking dinner, so he could show off this new pasta maker he had bought, though he had no idea how to use it. (And he couldn't help shake the nagging feeling that he was *supposed* to know how to use it).

Kristine was already different from Ann. For one thing, she wasn't as quick to open up. In fact, for some time, it still felt as if he hardly knew her at all. He knew what she did for a living, of course. Her general interests. How many siblings she had. What she liked in bed.

Maybe he just needed to give it time. So he did everything he could to be a great boyfriend. He went all out on her birthday. Made sure to befriend all her friends. Gave her all his attention when she was with him.

So why was it that every time he did something nice for her, she'd always seem to run away? She'd thank him in the moment, sure, but then, she'd retreat into work and barely talk to him for a week. Naturally, this just made him push harder. He'd text her more to ask how her day went. He'd offer to cook for her more often. *Anything* to avoid being accused of not 'putting in the effort'.

Which was why it shocked him, four months into the relationship, when she said, "I don't think this is working for me."

No. No, this isn't right, he thought. *We aren't even close to the time that we broke up.*

Daniel wondered if maybe he had missed an initial breakup from his travels and the two of them would get together again after this.

But he knew that was just wishful thinking. It was the way she had said, 'I don't think this is working for me'. It was the same tone he had heard when she called off the wedding.

All he could muster in response was one word: "Why?" As in, why was this over, out of nowhere, *again*? Why couldn't he just make something work? Why was nothing he did good enough for her (or for Chloe for that matter)? *Why?*

And Kristine simply responded, "I just feel like you're too...clingy for me."

The first time, he hadn't made enough effort with Kristine. Now he had made *too* much. Maybe Kristine had just never really wanted him. Maybe she was destined to make an excuse to leave.

Maybe it wasn't even Kristine. Maybe it was just his luck in general with love. Maybe he'd always be disappointed and never find the right person.

And the Overseer returned again. This time, Daniel had nothing to share. He simply asked, "Those ripples still happening?" She nodded. Before she could elaborate, Daniel cut her off. He didn't care anymore. "Let's just get this over with."

There was one woman left: Steph.

"Lucky for you, she hasn't been rippled out of existence yet. I checked. You still have a shot at fixing this," said the Overseer. She looked like she was about to leave, but she stopped. Perhaps there was sympathy in her step. "Good luck." And with that, she was gone. It occurred to Daniel that if he pulled this off, he might never see the Overseer again.

With Ann and Kristine, he had tried to go against what he had seen. Now, what would his strategy be?

This time, there'd be no strategy. And maybe that, in itself, was a strategy. Maybe he just needed to act as if he *didn't* know the future. A part of him hoped that meant this would work out. Another part of him told him to stop being an idiot in getting his hopes up.

If the Overseer had been right about these relationships being destined to happen, then Steph would still be working at the shop now.

So he drove over and walked in. Sure enough, there she was at the cash register. He almost didn't recognize her at first without the big glasses. She must've been wearing contacts today. She wore her hair tied back and her outfit was different from what he remembered, but he figured he could have the same conversation. That was going to be the easy part.

As expected, she agreed to get coffee with him. Like before, he asked when she was off work. And like before, he scheduled it for her day off. So he arrived on that Tuesday. 5PM. The coffee shop next to the place that she worked at. And the two of them talked.

They talked for six *hours*, to the point that the place closed before they were done.

Daniel was surprised by Steph at first. It had been maybe even a year at this point since he had *actually* met her for the first time. She seemed *funnier* than he had remembered. Was she actually funnier? Or did he just *get* her humor better? And did he also find her more attractive now than before because of it?

"You know, it seems weird," she said, "But the other day when you came into the shop, I felt like I almost knew you from before."

Daniel laughed. "Really?"

"Yeah, I don't know. You just seemed so...familiar. Or I seemed familiar to you. Like did we go to school together or something?"

"I'm a SoCal boy and you're from the East Coast. I doubt it."

"I know, but still! I don't know, you just seemed like... someone I've already known for awhile. Like, you *knew* I'd say yes to coffee. Like you expected it."

Daniel just shrugged. She wasn't completely wrong. "Well I didn't know for sure. But I figured I didn't have anything to lose."

"See, a lot of people say that. But most of them don't actually act like it," she said, "What's your secret?"

He shrugged. "I'd say, learn not to expect anything."

"That's it? So you just expect to be disappointed and let yourself be surprised."

"No, expecting to be disappointed is different from not expecting anything. Because if you expect to be disappointed, you're still expecting. Which is the problem." Daniel hardly recognized what was coming out of his mouth. It felt like he was making shit up as he went along and it just happened to sound profound.

But Steph smiled and said, "I like that."

Hell, maybe it was *profound, then.* He continued, "I mean, it's basically what they say. Hope for the best, prepare for the worst..."

He'd have to put that mentality to the test soon. Because later that night, Steph agreed to go on a second date.

And in another life, it was the second date that was also their last date.

Daniel had figured that the outcome would be different from before. But whether that would be better or worse, he'd have to see.

He went into the date half excited and half feeling like a prisoner due for execution. About thirty minutes into it, she said. "I have something to confess."

Uh oh, he thought. A part of him wondered if this would be when she'd end it. Which would be really awkward, since the food hadn't even come yet.

What she actually said, however, was very different: "I just got out of a relationship like a month ago."

"Wow," he said. Then without thinking, "Me too."

"Really?! Oh my God, I totally thought I'd scare you off."

Daniel laughed. *On the contrary...*

Questions then swirled in his brain. "So that day I asked you out to coffee...what made you say 'yes' then? I mean you could've just said that you were still recovering from the last relationship. I would've gotten it..."

"Yeah, well, breakups suck. But there's no use punishing the next guy about it, is there?"

Jesus, where were you three relationships ago? Daniel thought as he took a second to collect his response. "No... no, definitely not."

He was starting to feel something for the first time. Was it comfort? No, that wasn't it. Maybe it was *desire*, but not in the sexual sense of desiring her (though he wasn't opposed to that either). It was almost a desire to open up. To share again. To just be vulnerable.

He continued talking, "You know, if I'm being frank, there's a part of me that almost didn't ask you out. Not because of you, I mean, but because I guess I was just getting jaded from the whole experience."

"Yeah, I get you. It's hard not to get hurt doing all this."

Daniel leaned forward with interest. "What helps you just put yourself out there then?"

Steph let out a breath and thought about it. "Knowing it's worse if I don't."

"And you're not afraid of getting hurt again?"

"Oh, all the time," she said, "But if I let that stop me, I'm never gonna find it, am I?"

"I guess you're right."

"How about you? What keeps you going?"

Daniel thought about how he should phrase it. Then said, "Same as you, I guess. Faith."

Steph raised a glass. "To faith, then."

They toasted and kept talking through the rest of their dinner, but Steph's attitude stuck out in his mind. Here he had been, using a stolen time traveler's watch to avoid getting hurt, while Steph had done the complete opposite. No time travel, no peeks or knowledge of how things would turn out. Just complete faith that at some point, someone was going to make all the heartache worth it.

He paid the bill, of course, and as they walked out, Daniel could feel his heart pounding.

Here it is. The moment she turns me down.

He had *really* started to like her already. He hoped things would turn out differently this time, but he felt an odd sense of calmness as he walked next to her.

He had seen this play out from the outside. The hesitation. The potential preamble on how he *seemed* like a great guy *but...*

But nothing. He had been wrong before. Maybe he'd be wrong again. He wouldn't know unless he went for it.

"So...want a ride back?" he asked. The same question he had heard himself ask in the other timeline. He noticed it came out differently from what he remembered. When he had heard himself say it originally, it felt very tentative, as if he weren't really sure if she would say yes. Here, it seemed casual. Indifferent. Almost as if he had asked her to pass the salt.

It wasn't that he needed her to say 'yes' anymore.

It was that he'd be fine if she said 'no'. That no matter what answer she gave him...he'd be okay.

He stopped, waiting for her answer. She smiled.

"A ride? Sure."

Somewhere, in a kitchen across town, a coffee cup and a pasta maker reappeared, as if they had been there all along.

A girl named Ann was back in her apartment, pouring over a book.

And Daniel was walking Steph back to his car for a ride home.

He smiled. For once, he had no idea what was going to happen next.

Ben Wan's story "Shortcut to Happily Ever After" was originally published in Metaphorosis on Friday, 7 April 2023. See magazine.metaphorosis.com

About the author

Ben Wan is a cancer survivor who's been making the most out of his second chance at life. Aside from writing, he's a former musician who's performed in Carnegie Hall, a first degree black belt in Kung Fu San Soo, and a coach for Become Sharp in helping introverted clients succeed with dating, confidence, and social skills. He's currently the co-host and "Man Who Knows Too Much About Batman" for the podcast *Superhero Stuff You Should Know*, where his cat Alfie makes cameo appearances.

www.benwanwriter.com, @SuperHousePod

Copyright

Title information

Inner Workings

ISBN: 978-1-64076-304-3 (e-book)
ISBN: 978-1-64076-305-0 (paperback)
ISBN: 978-1-64076-306-7 (hardcover)

Copyright

Works of fiction

Publisher

Metaphorosis
a magazine of speculative fiction

Metaphorosis Magazine is an imprint of
Metaphorosis Publishing
Neskowin, OR, USA

www.metaphorosis.com

"Metaphorosis" is a registered trademark.

Discounts available

Substantial discounts are available for educational institutions, including writing workshops. Discounts are also available for quantity purchases. For details, contact Metaphorosis at metaphorosis.com/about

Metaphorosis Publishing

Metaphorosis offers beautifully written science fiction and fantasy. Our imprints include:

Metaphorosis Magazine

Plant Based Press

Verdage

Vestige

Joyful Heave

You can also find us:
@metaphorosis.bsky.social (Bluesky)
@Metaphorosis@writing.exchange (Mastodon)
www.facebook.com/metaphorosis

Help keep Metaphorosis running at
Patreon.com/metaphorosis

See more about some of our books on the following pages.

Metaphorosis
a magazine of speculative fiction

Metaphorosis is an online speculative fiction magazine dedicated to quality writing. We publish an original story every week (2016-2023) or month (2024), along with author bios, interviews, and notes on story origins.

We also publish monthly print and e-book issues, as well as yearly Best of and Complete anthologies.

Come and see us online at magazine.Metaphorosis.com.

The Metaphorosis Library Collection

Plant Based Press

Vegan-friendly science fiction and fantasy, including anthologies of the year's best SFF stories, from 2016-2020.

Chambers of the Heart
speculative stories
by
B. Morris Allen

A heart that's a building, a dog that's a program, a woman sinking irretrievably — stories about love, loss, and movement.

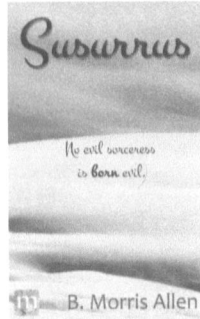

Susurrus

A darkly romantic story of magic, love, and suffering.

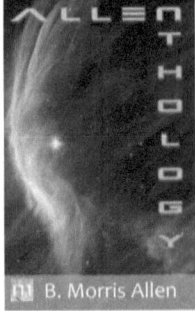

Allenthology: Volume I

Including three full collections of SFF stories.

Verdage

Science fiction and fantasy books for writers — full of great stories, often with an additional focus on the craft of speculative fiction writing.

Reading 5X5 x3

Changes

How do stories move from 'maybe' to published?

Here are 15 case studies of stories published in *Metaphorosis* magazine.

Reading 5X5 x2

Duets

How do authors' voices change when they collaborate?

A round-robin of five talented science fiction and fantasy authors collaborating with each other and writing solo.

Including stories by Evan Marcroft, David Gallay, J. Tynan Burke, L'Erin Ogle, and Douglas Anstruther.

Score

an SFF symphony

An anthology with an emotional score from the heights of joy to the depths of despair — but always with a little hope shining through.

Reading 5X5

Five stories, five times

See how different writers take on the same material.

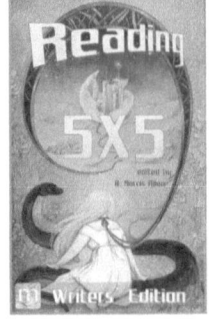

Reading 5X5

Writers' Edition

Two extra stories, the story seed, and authors' notes on writing.

Vestige

Novelettes, novellas, and novels by Metaphorosis authors.

The Nocturnals
Mariah Montoya

Night is Dangerous. Day is deadly.
Where day and night last thirty years, humans move constantly stay ahead of the night and cruel Nocturnals that call it home. But a boy is lost out there.

Science fiction and fantasy anthologies with innovative and unusual themes.

Museum Piece
an unusual collection

A gallery of the strange and outrageous

Step right up and enter a world of wonder and oddities! These museums are not your typical tourist traps. From the Museum of Lost Dreams to the Museum of Fine Regrets, each exhibit will take you on a journey you won't soon forget.